UTHRAITH

TAURISTAR: BOOK TWO OF THE DARK STELLAR LEGACY

JESSE M HARVEY

ISBN: 978-1-956344-08-0 (Paperback)

ISBN: 978-1-956344-07-3 (e-book)

Cover design and formatting by: Books by E M Garner

Publishing House: Mighty Mama Mouse

Pen Name: Jesse M. Harvey

"There's as many atoms in a single molecule of your DNA as there are stars in the typical galaxy. We are, each of us, a little universe."

    - Neil deGrasse Tyson

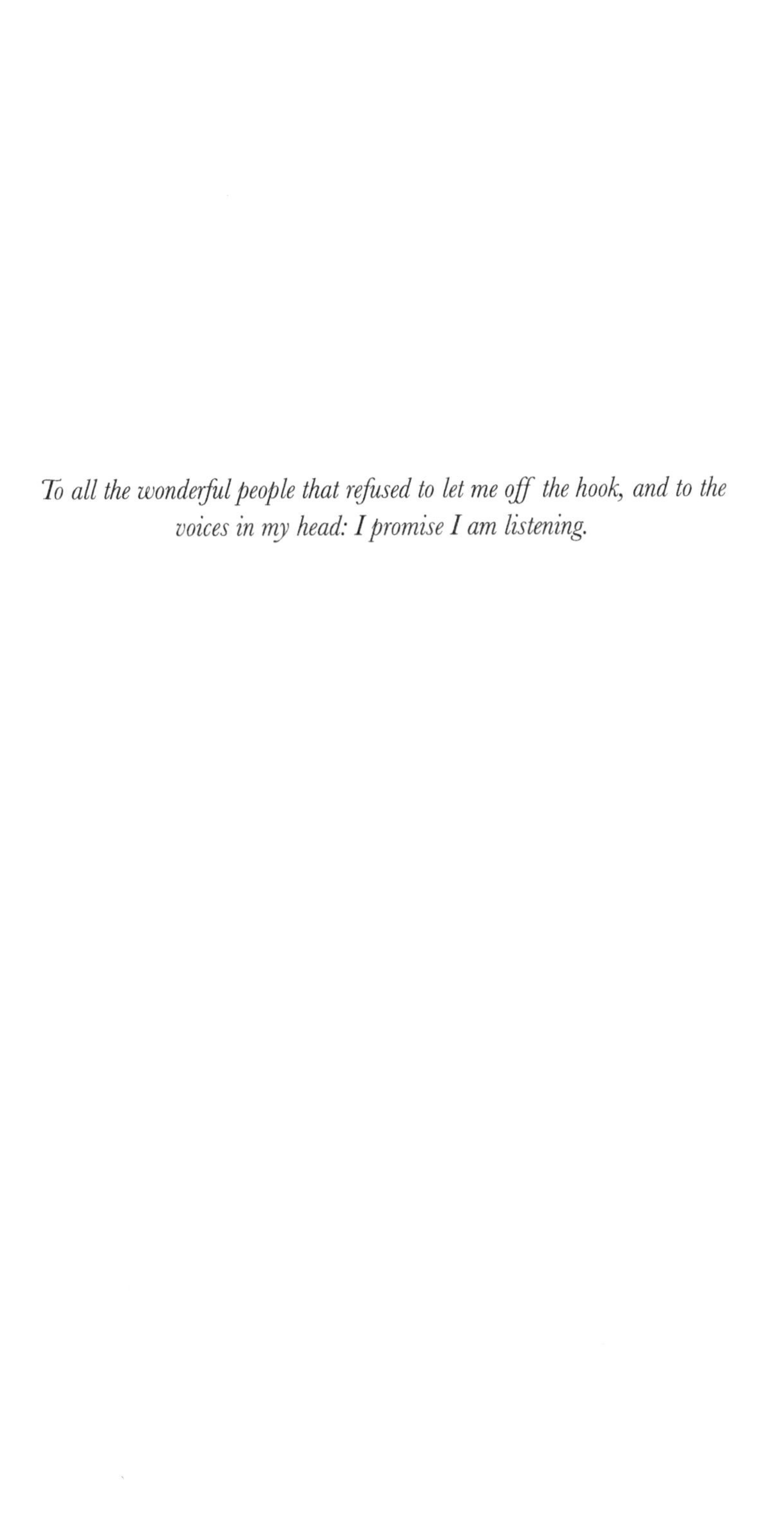

To all the wonderful people that refused to let me off the hook, and to the voices in my head: I promise I am listening.

CONTENTS

Content Warning   ix

Returning to The Citadel on Planet Arcem   1

Not Chapter One: Preliminary Review Panel   7

1. Before Preliminary Meeting   11

Not Chapter Two, Still Preliminary Meeting   22

2. Day before Preliminary Meeting   26

Not Chapter Three: Preliminary Meeting, Continued   34

3. A Cannibal and a Psychic Go Shopping. What Could Go Wrong?   36

Not Chapter Four: Still Preliminary Meeting   47

4. Scythia's Easy Guide to Making Friends/Enemies   52

Not Chapter Five: Preliminary Meeting—still Going   62

5. Struggles of the Stickman   66

Not Chapter Six: Are We Done with the Preliminary Meeting Yet?   74

6. Paradise behind Glass   78

Not Chapter Seven: Couldn't this Preliminary Meeting have been an Email?   87

7. Do Galactic Empire Bases Have Cafeteria Lunches? Yes, They Do   91

Not Chapter Eight: The Review Begins   98

8. Teamwork Makes the Dream Work!   101

Not Chapter Nine: Really Guys, This Is Serious   112

9. What a Night . . . Uthraith Should Have Stayed Home   117

Not Chapter 10: The Galactic Empire Enforces Body Autonomy. Any Citizen under Review May Choose Execution at Any Time   127

10. Actually, Can I Have My Dinner to Go?   130
    Not Chapter 11: Illegal Biomass Exportation
    Is Punishable by Loss of Citizenship   138
11. Self-care is the Best Care   142
    Not Chapter 12: Honestly, It Was Just a Little
    Riot . . . We Didn't Kill Everybody!   151
12. Cue Scythia's Training Montage   155
    Not Chapter 13: Never Trust Pastries from
    the Authorities   165
13. And That My Friend Is Called 'Stalking' and
    'Murder.'   169
    Not Chapter 14: Don't Ever Let Them Know
    That You Know . . . Ya Know?   177
14. Cue Djaem Montage   181
    Not Chapter 15: Nobody Puts Little Blue in a
    Corner   187
15. So Does This Mean We Are Friends Now?   191
    Not Chapter 16: Nothing Is as It Seems   202
16. The Cannibal and the Creampuff   205
    Not Chapter 17: Review Panel . . . 0/10,
    Would Not Recommend   215
17. Nah Ah! I Don't Have Feelings . . . You Have
    Feelings   219
18. Stranger Danger!   229
19. You Had One Job! . . . One!   236
20. The Power of Friendship . . . Mimosas and
    Mani-pedis   247

About the Author   251
Also by Jesse M. Harvey   253

CONTENT WARNING

- Profanity (specifically the C-word)
- Cannibalism
- Gore
- Violence
- Polygamy

RETURNING TO THE CITADEL ON PLANET ARCEM

BLOOD RUSHED IN HEAVY, pulsing waves.

Adrenaline surged and brought the world into sharp focus.

Time stretched and slowed as the lights from the ship's terminal flickered in a painful brightness. The blast shields were closed. This prevented the blinding light of the Terminus Star from burning Uthraith's eyes. The incessant beeps and chimes of the automated systems stabbed at his ears.

His skin tightened and shivered as he was blasted by cold air from the artificial atmosphere vents above. The faint chemical smell of the sterile air filled his nostrils. He hated it, but it would help battle the increase in temperatures as they passed through the planet's outer atmosphere.

A metallic copper taste bit the back of his throat while burning pressure pulled his lungs taunt as they demanded oxygen. Every time they came back planet-side, he could barely contain his excitement.

The voice of the ship began its countdown as it took position.

Uthraith's muscles tightened and coiled. On instinct, he flexed his hands to loosen the tendons. His mouth watered as his breathing increased, causing him to swallow hard. He felt the pull of the skin on his neck and cheeks as he worked his jaw left and right. He yawned, stretching his mouth open to its full length till his ears popped in the shifting pressure of the ship. His breath exhaled in a fast puff as he prepared his body for the shift.

The gentle thrumming of the ship's engine changed, escalating and oscillating till it was a bone-deep vibration. He slipped in his mouth guard, sinking his teeth into it to prevent them cracking as they jarred against each other.

His heart thudded heavily in his chest as the ship's shaking became more violent, and the re-entry alarms sounded. Flesh, bones, blood, and organs compressed and trembled, forced into the high-impact cushions of the seats as the ship collided with the planet's outer layer. Uthraith closed his eyes in pleasure and relief as gravity crushed down on him.

His joints popped and cracked as his own density pressed inward. The heavy downward drag became an even weight distributed over his frame. Uthraith gave a growl of satisfaction as he felt the heft of himself again.

He knew the instant they finished passing through the atmosphere. He could feel the moment they stopped falling and instead began flying.

The ship finished its re-entry into the atmosphere of Arcem. Once in free fall, its engines blazed to life as they slipped into a flight path to the Citadel landing pad.

He let out a deep breath as the ship leveled out. Excitement built inside Uthraith's chest as the ship passed through the spires of black steel and glass. They coiled up like twisted thorns to guard massive gates below. Their design left no illusion of their purpose. They were to bring death to invaders.

Uthraith reached out and quickly unhooked his harness, a grin stretching taut across his face. The flex and tension of his body as it moved against the drag of gravity helped give him definition, substance. Joy filled him as he pushed against the resistance of the world. The weight of his muscles as they pulled at his bones made him feel himself again. *Oh, how I missed this.*

The Citadel didn't have the gravity of his home world. Here, he moved as if he were only half of himself. Space was so much worse. He moved as if floating, bobbing along in the air like hollow seed pods on the water, unable to find purchase or momentum.

Uthraith preferred the heavy pressure atmospheres. They reminded him of the jungles of home. The atmosphere controls on the ship were always set to cold.

The others aboard the craft groaned and complained as they acclimated to the gravity. Uthraith felt the skin on his hands and feet itch, eager to touch solid ground. With swift steps, he headed to the cargo bay, going over his mental checklist of chores he would need to complete before he could leave.

He closed his eyes as his mind floated back to the bright suns of his world. The large canopy of vegetation and the thick, humid air. Uthraith could taste the heavy vapors on his tongue. He imagined the bay door opening, and the heat flooding his senses, warming him to his bones.

The automatic landing system eased the craft into the docking cradle with a soft hissing kiss. The machines beeped and spoke, but Uthraith was not listening. He smashed the heel of his palm against the button that controlled the door. He was out before the ramp had finished lowering, ducking around hydraulics, and squeezing through the narrow opening.

The air was clogged with the stench of machines and

people, the sky was the wrong color, and the sun barely warmed his skin. Still, Uthraith stood in full sunlight, tilting his head back to drink in the tepid world, grateful. He stood impossibly still for three heartbeats before he burst into action. Any that had the misfortune to be in his path scrambled out of his way.

His first stop was a terminal just outside of their designated docking area. After swiping his card, he impatiently watched the display. Scrolling through his long line of information, he found what he was looking for. A massive grin spread out across his face as he looked at his messages.

I will need to make arrangements. He checked his money balance and smiled.

"Good," he whispered as he considered what to do. "I will have to buy Ebil a gift and prepare for the birthing celebration. I will take Little Blue with me. She will enjoy it." He spoke in his own language. No one could speak it here, but he found the sound comforting.

The rest of the team had disembarked by the time he had returned. Raza gave Uthraith a nod, resigned to his behavior. Uthraith still enjoyed the annoyed look on her face.

"Unload first and then you can go," Raza snapped at his grin.

Uthraith knew the routine and headed to the cargo area. He had arranged it hours ago so that it would only take him a few minutes to have it offloaded. With a wide smile and a bit of unnecessary flexing, he played the beast of burden. Scythia laughed as he played up the role, showing her how strong he was. On his home world, no one ever looked to him for his strength.

After loading the last case on the hovering cargo skiff, Uthraith stepped over to where Little Blue sat watching the cargo bay. "You come. We go."

He smiled and took her hand. She returned his smile and

added an enthusiastic nod. Djaem frowned and opened his mouth to say something but was too late. Uthraith had already moved away. As he left, he ignored the number of people that tried to speak to them and several that were physically in his path. People moved like startled birds fluttering out of the way.

"Uthraith, what are we doing?" Little Blue asked, looking around eagerly. She smiled up at him, just happy to be included in the activity.

"You will help pick gifts for daughters." He straightened his spine and squared his shoulders in pride as he thought of them. All his children filled him with happiness. Little Blue looked nothing like the women of his world, but she had the same fire inside that they did. His daughters would like her.

Little Blue made a happy sound and nodded. "I didn't know you had daughters."

"Yes. Many daughters and sons. Wives gave me many children." He beamed with pride. "I was paid. I wish to send them some gifts."

Scythia's voice was full of excitement. It was a happy sound against Uthraith's ear. "I want to help pick out things for your daughters. How many do you have?"

Uthraith nodded. "Seven daughters and six sons. My wife will birth soon. My sons hope for a male to even numbers," he whispered as if it were a secret. "They think even numbers mean they win against daughters. It does not. My daughters are more vicious than my sons."

Scythia blinked as the sum filled her mind. "That is thirteen children . . . How many wives do you have?" Uthraith smiled as warmth spread across his face. "I have four wives. They are glorious. I am very lucky man."

Scythia considered this seriously as she followed him through the markets. "Can I have four wives?"

Uthraith grinned. "Have the number you can care for.

You must care for each. I return from mission, I send message to family, and I send gifts home. Set up interstellar communication with them for later. I will bring you. They will want to see you, Little Blue."

Scythia gave him a beaming smile. Others didn't feel it, but Uthraith could feel the heat of her inner flame brighten. It warmed him like a tiny sun. It made his day a little better.

NOT CHAPTER ONE: PRELIMINARY REVIEW PANEL

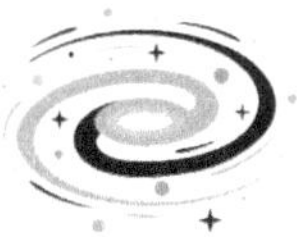

During the great war, reviews were rare. They were reserved for those accused of failure of duty or of an act just shy of treason. The reviews were held in public view, with all the great ceremony such a grave affair entailed. As the Empire expanded and the war ended, things changed. The list of offenses deserving of review grew. Now it was bloated beyond any recognition of its once-somber roots.

Instead of being a process of considering guilt, it was more of proving innocence. With the increase in volume, the process was streamlined for efficiency. The ceremonies were replaced with procedures. The respectability and decorum gave way to the cold brutality of dehumanizing bureaucracy.

In the western tower of the Citadel, three full floors were dedicated to review rooms for these panels. Each was an exact replica of all the others. The room itself was designed for the purposes of intimidation and diminishing of those being reviewed. Every angle, plane, and surface had been carefully crafted to serve this end. The pale glow from the walls was just enough to give vague impressions of the dimensions and occupants. It created an unnaturally backlit, cavernous room, filled with silhouettes and living shadows.

At the presumed center was a rectangular booth with six wooden chairs sitting side by side. This booth was encircled by a powerful ring of striated light glaring down at the empty chairs. This harsh, unrelenting blaze prevented those in the chair from seeing anything beyond the rectangle and completely exposed them to those hidden in the gloom.

Raza was the first to step into the chamber, her eyes on the glowing blue line on the floor. Her smooth stride played a confident tempo on the bare concrete floor. She had played this game before, and though she kept her gaze down, her shoulders remained square. Raza knew from experience it was important to keep up with the glowing light. She didn't feel like dealing with the pain and hassle if she came off the blue path. When the glowing line reached the edge of the 'accused' booth, it climbed the three short stairs, leading her to the platform and then directing her to the plain wooden chair farthest in. It never illuminated anything more than intended.

Raza stepped over the stairs in one barely extended step. They were tiny, each climbing only four inches and barely six inches deep. She didn't bother trying to see the people watching her, keeping her eyes lowered to protect them from bright lights. As she waited for the others, her fingers gripped the end of the armrest. Raza let her fingertips explore the edge of the hardwood until they found what she was looking for. It was a small series of half-moon indents, left from her nails years ago. She counted them silently in her head. *Room six.* She had left a mark on every chair she had occupied during her reviews. Her invisible act of defiance. They didn't want her to know which room she was in, but she made sure she knew every time.

The annoying buzz sounding over and over forced a

smothered laugh out of Raza. She didn't need to see to know who came next.

Uthraith kept outpacing the blue glow line. Every time he overstepped and outpaced the artificial guide, his footsteps flashed in a bright red outline. With every red footfall, there was a loud, scolding buzz. The blue line chased after Uthraith, trying to adjust to his course and pace. Over the buzzing, his deep voice filled the dark room.

"Ba'esh tot! I know where I go. I do not need stupid machine to tell me again."

A monotoned, rhythmic voice buzzed in, "Please remain within the nanobot circle. Any attempts to deviate will result in lethal applications from the in-place security system."

"She does not hear," Uthraith growled with a chuckle. "I know where I go." Even as the electric arcs crawled up his legs, he didn't change his pace or direction one bit.

"Please remain within the nanobot circle. Any attempts to deviate will result in lethal applications from the in-place security system."

The repeated warning was enough to bring Uthraith to the point of annoyance. Spinning, he looked towards the door. His eyes met with those of the tall woman standing to its right.

"I have heard you. Any other words to me will be your last. I will walk to you and let the nanothings do the rest." Uthraith's words were spoken with deliberate care, so nothing was lost in translation.

The woman's eyes went wide. "Please remain," she started, much of the monotone being replaced with fear. "Please, don't. He . . . he knows where he must go."

1

BEFORE PRELIMINARY MEETING

THE AIR WAS full of tension. The guards from the Nationalist Enforcement Bureau (N.E.B.) stood flanking the room. They were fearsome figures in full battle gear and still as statues, —all but the two holding their positions by the door. Their movements were subtle and small, unnoticed by the occupants in the room. They hadn't forgotten their previous encounter with the blue Star-born psychic. She had left a lasting impression one them. They both gripped their weapons tight, shared a prayer to the old gods, and stayed close to the door to ensure they were the first ones out.

Fallrick was only vaguely aware of the guard's odd behavior. He was otherwise occupied by the group in front of him.

Fallrick stood between the leather topped chair and his all-metal desk. His eye twitched as he felt the pressure inside his skull grow. A dull ache was beginning to form behind his eyes as he looked at four people on the other side of the desk. His team had been disarmed almost immediately when they entered the Citadel. He would soon be meeting with his superiors, and it would soon be his turn on the other side of the desk. He took a deep breath, trying to calm his nerves so that the headache didn't grow.

It didn't help. Through gritted teeth, he managed, "This was a zero-priority mission, a little test mission that would clear some backlog. You were supposed to show up, look around, find nothing, file a report, and come home." His voice was tight as he gripped the edge of the table. "Did anyone look over their briefings? Look at their roles on the team?"

Uthraith's cheerful voice boomed before anyone else could respond, barely allowing Fallrick's words to finish passing his lips.

"I kill things." He nodded and leaned forward to grin at Raza. She looked almost as annoyed as Fallrick felt. She elbowed his side sharply and hissed, "This wasn't a killing mission. That's why we are in trouble."

Scythia raised her free hand as she answered around a mouthful of cookies. "I did read the briefing. I am to provide protection from Ether threats. I give support and any intel I may collect from the Ether." After her answer, she stuffed her hand back into the bag that contained the small, round baked goods.

Fallrick didn't know where she gotten the cookies from, but he tried hard to not shout at her.

Raza let out a slow breath, trying to curb her irritation. "You even said we weren't supposed to find anything. A solid team adjusts and adapts as the mission changes. The parameters changed; we had to change with them. So, we improvised."

"Improvised?!" Fallrick's voice cracked out over the room, making the guards by the door flinch. The vein at his temple pulsed as his face flushed and darkened. Fallrick felt his anger boiling beneath his skin. His jaw twitched as he took a deep breath. A sound of pure frustration escaped as he waved his hands in the air as if the words he needed were floating around, waiting to be grabbed. It must have worked because he looked at Raza with wide eyes and slammed his palms down on the desk as he leaned forward.

"Destroying an imperial colony is . . . anything but improvising!"

"Twenty-seven," Uthraith interrupted. He leaned forward, drawing attention away from Raza. Fallrick blinked, and a puzzled expression replaced the rage.

"Twenty-seven what?" Fallrick asked, bringing his voice to more reasonable levels, if still filled with frustration.

"Twenty-seven people I killed. Scythia destroyed the Tyrling. Djaem . . . Woah, Djaem. I did not know little man had the stuff!" Uthraith smiled with pride at his team.

"Now is not the time for praise and bragging," Fallrick snapped. "You!" His glare fell on Raza. "In the field, it's your team. You have the experience . . . You should know better. This is how people get sent to reclamation!"

Raza simply nodded, slowly turning her face away from him. She knew exactly what he meant. This had gone sideways real fast, and in the end, it was her team.

Fallrick turned to Uthraith. "And you need to stop encouraging the newcomers to be so . . . so . . ."

"Destructive?" Uthraith finished for him with a smile. "Yes. This will do."

Fallrick finally turned his glare to Djaem. "There is so much wrong with your report. You had one job: to keep her under control! Not kill colony guards, lie to officials, start riots, and burn the station down yourself!"

"Now, in my defense," Djaem replied in a calm, even tone, "Scythia didn't destroy anything we weren't authorized to. As for the warehouse, we act as both N.E.B. and U.L.A. We had to investigate the smuggling. Once they started shooting, we had no choice but to defend ourselves." He gave a small flick of his hand and a casual shrug as he continued. "We took out a fully manifested Tyrling and stopped an illegal smuggling ring. I'd say the mission was a success."

Fallrick's mouth fell a gape. The disbelief of what he just heard overwhelmed his thoughts. For three full heartbeats he just stood there looking at the relaxed and casual posture of the hiver scum lord sitting in his office. "A success? You crashed a refueling ship into the hangar!"

Djaem's expression, posture, and tone didn't change one bit. "I had to stop his shuttle from escaping. That was both a rogue psychic and at least half a ton of unregistered Ether-crystals. If he had managed to leave the hive, there would have been no way to track him."

Fallrick's eyes went so wide they bulged, and he had to rub at the pulsing vein at his temple. The frustration filled his face but stole his words. With an exaggerated gesture that spoke volumes of 'that's what she is for,' he pointed both hands, palms up, towards Scythia.

Djaem looked at Fallrick and then at Scythia. "I'm sorry? Oh! She may be powerful, but that ship was shielded, and there's no telling what the crystals would have done with her flames." Djaem's confidence diminished for a moment as he cleared his throat and returned to his poised calm.

Fallrick saw the moment of uncertainty and realized the team was afraid. They understood they had screwed up and were trying not to show it. His eyes flickered to Scythia.

She had stopped eating and was looking between Fallrick and the team. Her hand was still in the bag of cookies. He took a breath and calmed his voice.

"You've seen it before. She can stop machines, anything technological, even shielded. She could have stopped the ship without any need for explosions. Know your damn asset and use it properly," he said in a calmer but stern voice. "Speaking of you, where are your suppressors?"

Raza shifted forward to answer, drawing in Fallrick's attention. "We just made planetfall and he doesn't take space travel well. We'll pick some up directly after this."

"N-no," Djaem said , the reminder of being in space causing his insides to quiver a little. "They should be ready tomorrow. The normal suppressors won't help her, but I haven't had time to contact a craftsman. I have the supplies so I will make contact directly and get them expedited."

"The . . . supplies?" Fallrick blanched at Djaem's words. "You have supplies? You have unforged Ether-crystals and enough psi-steal to interweave them?"

Djaem grinned. "I was already reprogramming the autonomous refueler. How hard do you think it was to redirect the last of the loaders to our ship? Yes, we have plenty."

Fallrick let out his breath in a long, slow sigh as he lowered himself onto his chair. He passed his eyes along the guardsmen and back to Djaem. "Bring that to my office at once so we can get it registered." He rubbed his face hard, and after a moment, he looked serious and grim at all of them.

"Understand this, you are all up for review! It is not a debriefing like this. Raza, you know. Get them ready. And please, for the love of the ancient ones, Djaem . . . don't confess to any more high felonies. Fucking hell."

DJAEM PACED SLOWLY in Fallrick's office. His mind spun and twirled in brilliant colors. Scythia watched the display as she nibbled on small round disks of heated sugar, flour, and animal fat. Raza called them cookies. They were soft and sweet with little crunchy bits. Scythia liked how they felt in her mouth. She reached into the bag and to her dismay, found that it was empty. She frowned down at the crumbs in the bottom of her little snack pack. Her mouth was very dry now, and she realized she didn't have anything to drink.

Scythia looked over at Raza. She was sitting with her feet up on another chair, drinking something from a small flask she pulled out of a pocket.

"Raza, can I have a sip? My mouth is dry," Scythia said in a little voice, trying not to disturb Djaem's thoughts.

Raza looked over the rim and shook her head. "Not a chance, Blue. The last thing I want is you drinking." She motioned to a small cupboard along one wall. "There are water cubes in there."

Scythia nodded and touched the panel. It slid open easily. Vapor drifted from the opening as she reached in and pulled out a chilled gelatinous cube. The water gave it a hefty vibration in her hand as she closed the panel. Sitting back down, she nipped on the corner of the square and sucked the water out. She sighed and looked back at Djaem, who was still pacing.

Fallrick had left to go deal with his own superior, who would yell at him, and he would have to explain the same way the team had. Then that superior would go be yelled at by his superior, each taking a turn. Scythia wasn't sure why this was necessary, but then many of the rules she had reviewed didn't make much sense to her. The data crystals didn't really explain why these systems and rules were in place.

Scythia had found only a small bit of information on official reviews. She understood that they were what preceded someone being sanctioned. Those sanctions could include but were not limited to additional service time, fines, prison, re-education, and reclamation. Those definitions were vague at best.

Scythia knew they were in trouble because they hadn't

followed proper procedures on the mining colony. Though she wasn't sure what the proper procedures would have been.

Raza said they could eat Kandaril shit and die.

Uthraith was so excited to be back, all he did was talk about his call home and what he would send to his family.

Djaem's mind had been a spinning top for a while. Scythia didn't think he was worried about the review. Something else was bothering him. He hadn't been sleeping well. He kept saying it was just bad dreams. Scythia finished her water as she continued to watch, worry creasing her blue brow.

Scythia let her mind drift. There was something, a whisper underneath the music of the Ether. She couldn't pinpoint it. Just when she thought she could hear it clearly it would stop. *It is evading me.* She blinked herself back into the present. *My team needs me here; I will catch it later.*

FALLRICK RETURNED and looked as if he were ready to have a drink and take a nap. Djaem understood the feeling. Uthraith followed close behind, shimmying into his seat. Djaem remained standing as Fallrick reclaimed his seat. He took a moment to fix his desk as if putting his thoughts into order. Djaem's fingers twitched. He wanted to realign the shelves behind him, just to give his hands something to do.

Uthraith smiled and looked around the room. "Debrief is done; we eat now."

Raza gave a snort of disdain and rolled her eyes so hard Djaem could hear the rattle. "You wouldn't be so at ease if it was your head on the block."

Djaem's eyes narrowed in confusion as he looked at Raza. "What do you mean? Why would Uthraith be exempt?"

Raza looked surprised. "Seriously? I guess Fallrick was right." She let out a huff as her feet hit the floor, and she reached forward to grab the data pad off the desk. After a few taps and a swipe, she handed it over to Djaem. "You need to do your research. Look at his designation and the footnote."

Tapping on the screen, Djaem followed the tabs to a small icon with the words 'active ambassador' in underlined and highlighted colors. Djaem looked between Raza and Uthraith and the data pad. After two full cycles, he finally whispered, "this says he is an ambassador. A real diplomatic-protection, special-privileges, imperial-exemptions ambassador."

Raza savored Djaem's surprise with a little laugh. Djaem suspected her day-drinking might have contributed to her outward expression. "Yes, allow me to introduce the only ambassador of Kravanc 4, Uthraith of the Danthmaw. He can't be disciplined by the review board. The worst they can do is send him home."

Djaem looked at the grinning Murder Mountain, who smacked a fist over his heart. "You?"

Uthraith nodded. "I am smallest of my tribe. Fast and good at words. I show everyone how strong and powerful my people are."

Djaem suddenly understood why Fallrick always had a headache. "Why don't you use a translator?"

Uthraith scoffed and waved a hand. "Stupid squawk box. Gets words wrong. I do it myself, no waiting. People think I dumb this way. It's better for me." He grinned wickedly. "Always they surprised when I think fast too."

Raza nodded and shrugged. "He isn't wrong: it's been working for him so far. The personal communicators have long delays because many of the words from his planet don't translate. His responsibilities are low because his planet is considered feral, and uncivilized trade is minimal."

Djaem smiled softly to himself as he considered this information. *This will help.*

Scythia joined in the conversation happily. "I know how smart you are, Uthraith."

Uthraith reached out and petted the top of her carefully braided hair. "Good Little Blue, you are very clever."

She beamed with pride and nodded, sitting up straighter.

Fallrick looked up from his desk, having finished his communication, and rubbed his face. "It looks like we are set up for the preliminary review, and then the official board inquiry will begin."

Scythia frowned and looked at everyone. "Preliminary? You mean there will be more?"

Raza nodded. "Oh yeah, these blowhards love sitting up there passing judgment. They will drag this out as long as possible."

Fallrick raised an eyebrow but didn't bother correcting her.

Djaem frowned as he considered the situation. "What are we looking at?"

Fallrick considered his answer carefully. "We need to make sure it doesn't escalate. There is always the backdoor politics to consider, but beyond that, we must show that your actions were better than the alternative. The damage to the space station caused massive shipping delays, and they still have yet to suppress the rebellion you started there."

Raza snorted. "Other teams have caused more damage than that, and rebellions happen all the time. Why are they in a twist about this?"

Fallrick leaned forward, his eyes narrowed. "I don't know, maybe it has something to do with the resurgence of the worship of the goddess Myurd!"

Uthraith frowned and shrugged. "I don't understand. There have always been secret followers of the old gods."

Fallrick moved his hand across the data screen and images of hive colony IX47326 appeared. The food stations had been overrun. The logos of the Empire were covered in graffiti, images painted with quick bare hands, one after another depicting a blue woman with orange hair. Some had her dancing in fire with arms outstretched; some had children figures all around her.

Scythia gasped in surprise and delight. "It's me! They painted pictures of me!" She clapped her hands excitedly.

Raza coughed and choked before she gave Scythia a sharp look. "Shh."

Djaem rubbed at his chin as he considered the images of the hive. "It's not hard to see why they are making the jump." He shook his head slightly. "The hive mothers used to whisper stories when I was a child. Myurd was a deity of extremes, full of passion and contradictions. To pray to her was to risk everything. She could be deliverance or destruction. In most of the old stories, she was both at the same time. She was often depicted as a protector of women and children, or a destroyer of men and civilization."

Djaem looked at Scythia. *That's not all that far off the mark.* He shook off that thought and looked back at Fallrick.

Raza glared at Djaem, her words a hiss. "Enough. Those stories are considered heresy, punishable by re-education, execution, or reclamation."

Fallrick's face gave very little away. Djaem met his gaze easily. *He isn't upset about Scythia developing a cult following. So, if not that then what is it?*

"What does this mean?" Djaem relaxed back into his chair.

Fallrick sighed and straightened. "We need to get her suppressors as soon as possible. We must show that she is under control. If they decide she is a threat, it won't matter who did what on the hive. She will take the blame. I will do everything I can, but it is imperative that she not use her powers until the review is over."

Djaem frowned and gave a nod. "I understand. I will get her suppressors immediately."

NOT CHAPTER TWO, STILL PRELIMINARY MEETING

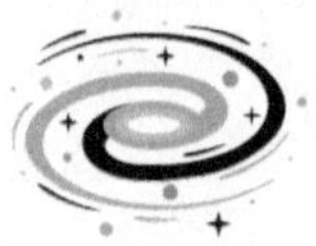

The woman stationed by the door to provide entrance protocols was frozen, pinned by Uthraith's intense stare. Her eyes dropped to the angry swarm around his feet and the arcs climbing up his legs. Any normal person would have been racked with pain, and if they remained noncompliant this long, incinerated. On this giant, it seemed to be little more than a discomfort.

The blue floor tint finally caught up when he reached the small stairs. Barely able to fit his toes and the ball of his foot on each stair, Uthraith made certain to step on every single one. The wood initially groaned under his massive weight, but the blue glow changed to green, and the structure seemed to become more durable. The reinforcing glow spread up one of the chairs. There was a buzz of angry protest when Uthraith moved that chair aside. He easily slid a new chair beside Raza. She shook her head and smirked at his petty acts of defiance, even lifting her hand to threaten a slap. When he flinched away, she just patted his cheek instead.

Uthraith chuckled. "Here we are again. Fallrick has this,

yes? No worries to give." The replacement chair creaked and popped as Uthraith shimmied into it.

Raza shook her head at his comment. "This one's a little more serious, I'm afraid."

The green tint moved itself to Uthraith's new chair, fortifying it, but was unable to re-extend the now-bowed legs. He shook his big head, unfazed; he had complete confidence in his companions.

Both Raza and Uthraith hissed in pain as a new, brighter light filled the room. They heard startled cries from those hidden from view. Several unlit lanterns scattered along the ceiling suddenly flared to life. They burned with an angry, searing light. The metal frames hummed as the rapid heat threatened to warp them. Raza whispered more to herself than anyone else, "Shit, girl . . . Just when I think I have an idea how strong you are."

Scythia tapped the thin metal pieces that Djaem had attached to the bottom of her shoes against the floor, smiling at the bright metallic noise it made on impact. The blue tinting turned green around where she had connected. After extending her foot, she brought it down with the metal tab under the heel touching first. Again, the glowing tint changed. With a delighted giggle, she continued this odd motion as she moved forward. She made a little game of watching the glowing tint trying to adjust and react to her steps.

With the sound of a crystalline wind chime in a gentle breeze, the pys-crystals of her suppressors glittered and glowed in a scintillating pattern. As the sparkling suppressors went to work, the humming lanterns began to quiet. The hot metal continued to glow even as the light dimmed. Too wrapped up in watching the tiny glowing outline of her feet left in her wake, Scythia didn't notice.

The kicking motion of her steps caused the long fabric of

her skirt to sweep and swish. She was fully inside her musical moment, tapping and dancing with the glowing tint and buzzing sound . . . Click-click-swish. Buzz, click-click-swish. Buzz.

Raza and Uthraith watched in amazed bemusement.

The distraction, however, led to peril. When the tint had guided her to the stairs, Scythia didn't notice the lift of the first small step. Her kicking foot caught the edge of the base, snagging her dress as well. A startled noise escaped as she toppled forward, and the crystals she wore flashed in a sudden bright surge. Her yelp was joined by one from Raza and several grumblings around the room.

Uthraith chuckled. "The anti-dazzle on the eyes is not needed, huh? Kyr'na? That was almost bad. Like blinder grenade."

Raza answered with no more than an annoyed growl.

Scythia looked around the room in a confused panic. Her eyes were wide, and she sat slightly hunched, as if expecting to be yelled at. Tears glistened in her eyes, but her face didn't show any physical pain, just fright.

What happened? I didn't use my powers, why did it flash? Her eyes pleaded with Uthraith, who was closest. It took a long moment before the words finally came out. "What . . . What happened?"

Uthraith's chuckle subsided almost instantly as he shifted in his distressed seat. "This is what happens to most of us when we trip," he explained as he leaned his massive form over the chairs. "We cannot reorient ourselves in the universe by twisting Ether, so we fall." His enormous hand reached out towards her. "Are you hurt?"

The way the chairs and booth had been arranged was such that the physics for any person of reasonable proportions to help another person who fell on the stairs to get to their feet would have required standing and taking at least two steps. However, Uthraith's all-around immense size and Scythia's stretched, and elongated form allowed for this to happen with Uthraith still in his seat. Her delicate blue hand was engulfed by his large rough one as he pulled her up with a gentleness that, again, ignored the rules of perception and physics.

Smiling once again, Scythia shook her head. "I'm okay," she answered with a cheerful tone. *As long as I am not in trouble.* She took the chair that the blue glowing tint on the floor now encircled.

2

DAY BEFORE PRELIMINARY MEETING

DJAEM SWALLOWED HARD against the uncomfortable lump in his throat.

It's fine. She is eager to please: this is your greatest tool as her handler. The rational voice in his head chastised his hesitation. His hands gripped tighter to the heavy container. He sat at the small, low table in the common area of the team's quarters. *You are supposed to cultivate the relationship so you can control her. That is how you can protect her from herself.*

Djaem frowned because a different voice whispered; *She trusts you. You should be protecting her. She may not appreciate the chains you put on her.*

It had been so long since he had heard that voice that he barely recognized it. However, he was having to ignore it more and more often. It was coloring his plans, adding details that weren't logical. Not enough to disrupt them, but enough to notice.

If I don't get her to wear these, it could mean reclamation or re-education. Hell, they may just end her. Not to mention me.

Scythia's hand reached out to touch his shoulder, startling him out of his thoughts. She moved to sit next to him.

She wore soft lounge pants and no shoes. *That's why I didn't notice her.*

"I heard what Fallrick said." Her voice was soft and calm. "Raza helped explain. They fear me. They fear my power. They want me controlled…chained." She looked down at her hands. "Do you fear me?"

Djaem slowly gathered her hand in his. Her fingers were so long and delicate. He was again surprised at their warmth and softness. *Can Star-born even get callouses?*

His mind began cataloging the differences between her blue silky hands and his rough, scarred brown ones. He shook off that train of thought. *Best to be honest; she may be able to read my thoughts anyway.*

"I did at first. Sometimes I realize how dangerous you can be, and I get scared. Not of you . . . but of what you can do. I know you don't like hurting people. I have learned that you would never hurt me. So, I am not scared anymore."

Scythia considered that and nodded. "That is fair. I am glad you know I wouldn't hurt you. You are my precious Gem."

Djaem tried hard to ignore the warmth those words caused. It spread outward from his chest. It was not easy when someone so extraordinary said that to him. *You are the handler, Djaem. handle it!* Logic shouted into his mind, trying to cool the heat in his chest.

"Your suppressors were delivered. I am going to need you to put them on and keep them on."

Scythia's face shifted to more of a grumpy pout. Her shoulder hunched slightly as she curled inward. She did the same when he refused to give her candy until she finished her vitae-paste.

"I knew you weren't going to like it so I decided to do something special."

Her pout lessened as she looked intrigued. "What?"

Djaem smiled and tapped the case. He pushed it to her. "Look for yourself."

Scythia gave him a suspicious smile and opened the lid.

Inside the metal container, resting on a soft, cushioned bed of black, winked a glittering array of delicate black crystals. They were embedded and fixed into a set of earrings, a necklace, two delicate anklets, matching bracelets, and a belt. The psi-weave metal gleamed like polished silver.

Scythia stared in stunned silence. "They are beautiful." She breathed as she reached to touch one softly.

Djaem watched her face carefully. "You must wear suppressors right now. I can't change that. But I can make sure they are the best. These are custom made. They don't have a feedback system like most suppression collars. They will sparkle and match your dresses and I had them add these dangly bits so they will make a little noise when you walk." He gave a smile. "I hope you will forgive me for making you wear them."

Scythia touched one carefully, and it glowed, shimmering with no sparks. "They won't hurt me?"

Djaem frowned. "They are supposed to minimize any discomfort, but I can't promise anything. You are more powerful than I really understand. But if you wear them, I can keep you safe."

She considered that for a long moment and then smiled. "Yes, Djaem. I will wear them. I will do this for you. So, you don't have to worry. This means if I am wearing them, I am free?"

Djaem nodded. "Yes, it keeps you from being locked up or worse."

Scythia smiled and nodded. "Good. Help me put them on."

Djaem smiled softly. "Thank you, Scythia."

One by one, he helped put on her shimmering, sparkling

shackles. *That was easier than I thought it would be.* The little voice decided to have the last word. *But much harder than you want to admit.*

THE NEXT MORNING, Djaem stepped through the sliding doors into the main room of the living space. He frowned as he looked at the large wall screen. It was terribly bright. *Scythia must have been playing with the settings.* He sighed inwardly. On the ship, he had to reset all the data screens almost every waking cycle. She would sit and cycle through the shades for hours.

The light emanating from the screen was almost painful. It was so intense that he felt heat coming off the screen. *That can't be good for the sensors.* He tapped the screen to bring up the settings.

Nothing happened.

His brow twitched as he tried again. *Damn it! Don't tell me she broke another one.* He swiped and double tapped on the screen. Nothing. He looked for the reset button but couldn't find one.

The image of the blue background with buildings and pedestrians remained. It was a motion image of the city. A bird flew by and landed on the edge of the image, startling Djaem. The graphic was set to peck at the screen, giving it the illusion of being on the other side. He looked at the detail on the bird's wings and became concerned. "This could be really expensive to fix."

He stepped away from the screen, giving it a hard look. "I really hope she didn't ruin it. I am not sure how she even managed to get it stuck." He looked for the power source. When he didn't spot it initially, he knelt to look under the screen. He swore under his breath when he realized the screen was embedded in the wall. "Shit, this is the dumbest design I have ever seen."

Raza had stepped out of the kitchen and leaned against the couch to watch Djaem on the floor.

"Whatever you are doing, I am sure you are doing it wrong," she snarked over the rim of her steaming mug.

"Scythia broke the data screen. I can't get the settings to adjust," Djaem said as he got back to his feet.

Raza frowned. "Wait . . . what?"

Djaem motioned to the large rectangular panel in front of him. "The data screen. It is stuck on this image display. I can't get it to adjust the light setting. It's so bright I can feel the heat, and it hurts my eyes."

For three whole heartbeats Raza just stared at him, her eyes wide and her mouth slightly open. When she finally blinked, she snickered into her mug. Her eyes danced off to the side as if looking for someone to share the joke with.

Fuck, I have missed something, and she is laughing at me. He resigned himself to incoming insults. Whatever it was he had missed must have been obvious. *Well, it will help with keeping her underestimating me. It will be good for team building. If she would just hurry up and tell me what I missed.*

He crossed his arms and gave her an irritated look. It was important for the one being teased to play along. Raza looked at his face and burst out laughing. Djaem did his part and played the wounded and annoyed party.

After a minute or so, Raza slowly eased down enough to take a deep breath. She wiped at her eye and took a deep drink from her mug.

"That's a window."

Djaem just continued looking at Raza, waiting. He didn't know that word. When she didn't explain further, he raised his eyebrows in an expectant look.

She smirked and shook her head. "Fucking hivers. It is a

pane of pressurized polycarbonate. It is clear so we can see outside and will allow UV light in. It's like those fancy ships that have observation ports."

Djaem looked at the 'window' in surprise. "What the fuck would you want that for? People can see in. Don't you lose insulation with that? Why would you not just use a data screen?"

Raza sighed and shook her head. "Boki, because humans need light. Because the sky is beautiful and not everyone likes living inside a dark, cramped box."

Djaem felt a wave of vertigo as he looked out and realized the only thing between him and the big, wide outside was a thin sheet of glass. He reached out for balance, his hand flat against the window, and felt the warmth from the sun against his palm.

Raza smirked inwardly and shook her head. *Sometimes Djaem and Scythia are so much alike.* She doubted that Djaem would see it. She realized she was smiling fondly and shook it off. Clearing her throat, she headed to her room after calling him stupid one more time.

DJAEM WATCHED THE WORLD OUTSIDE. He saw people walk by and then a fluffy-looking creature. *I wonder if that is what they call a dog.* He had never seen one in person. He turned to point it out to Scythia. *Oh, that's right. She isn't here.* He quickly headed to her sleeping quarters and opened the door. *She won't want to miss this.* He didn't bother knocking. His voice was loud and excited as he stepped into her room.

"Good morning, Scythia . . . Get up, I have something to . . ." His smile vanished with his voice.

Scythia's bed was empty and made. He frowned as he did a quick scan of her room. Her shoes were gone from next to her bed. Dread filled him. He checked the rooms one after another, and panic grew with each empty room.

She is gone.

He fought to keep the fear at bay. He knocked on Raza's quarter's door. No response. He knocked again. And again. His tapping turned into rapid pounding.

Raza yanked open the door, her expression an angry glare.

Djaem took a step back in surprise. She had completely transformed.

"What do you want?" Her voice was tired and irritated. Djaem had never seen her in such a state. Her hair was a frizzy, droopy mess. She wore no makeup. Her clothes were ragged, oversized, stained, and worn thin. She wore strange soft, fuzzy slippers and a fluffy robe that was dropping open. Only her murderous glare was the same.

Djaem tried not to let any of his surprise show on his face.

"Scythia isn't in the living quarters," he blurted, trying to express the urgency of the problem. Raza continued to glare at him. "She is gone. I don't know where she is."

Raza narrowed her eyes at him. "So?"

Djaem couldn't keep the dread from boiling over. "She is out there. Without any supervision! We need to find her immediately before something happens."

Raza sighed in irritation. "Not my department. That sounds like a you problem." She tried to close the door. Djaem grabbed the edge.

"Wait, you are the team lead. You need to help me find her," he said, holding tight to the doorframe. Raza glared at his hand like she might cut it off.

"Firstly, it is my day off. I don't need to do anything. Secondly, we are currently under review, and therefore there is no team. Ergo, no missions and no team lead. Lastly—and this really is the most important one—you are her handler. So go handle it!" She knocked his hand off the door, shut it, and locked it.

Djaem stood there stunned for a long moment. His mind whirled as he tried to figure out a way to avoid what he knew would come next.

He went to check inside the metal case. It was empty. Relief poured through him. *She kept her promise and wore the suppressors. And more importantly, I can track her.* He finished getting dressed and retrieved his portable data pad. He activated the tracking protocols and watched the location of the suppressors appear on the screen. He sighed. *There is no way to avoid it. I will have to go outside.*

He put on his specialized new coat and lifted the custom hood. The weighted, compression coat helped him feel less isolated. It was designed for hivers, the weights and pressure helped replicate the sensation of a crowd pressed in. It wasn't quite the same, but it helped with the panic. The hood and mask also kept his vision from seeing all the wide space around him.

NOT CHAPTER THREE: PRELIMINARY MEETING, CONTINUED

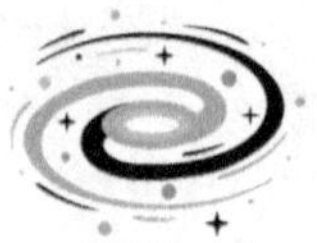

As Scythia wriggled in her seat, trying to make it more comfortable, the blue glowing path again appeared along the floor. A few moments later, the angry buzz sounded, and Djaem hastened his step to catch up for the third time. His eyes scanned around the poorly lit room. *Lighting to help hide. Not just their identity, but there's probably also riflemen hidden in here.*

The buzz sound repeated as he fell behind the blue path. The area around his feet now glowed red. The intensity of the red grew as he remained distracted. Raza leaned to look around Uthraith's form, a huge grin on her face. She gave no warning but watched with anticipation.

Without further delay, the red glow at Djaem's feet released an electrical arc that shot up and into his legs. A high-pitched yelp accompanied his sudden lift into the air. As his jump ended and his feet returned to a part of the floor not approved by the blue tint, a second shock commenced. Djaem scrambled forward, panting from the pain and surprise, entering the safety of the blue. Raza's laughter cut the stillness of the room.

"I told you to stay in the path," she gasped between

chuckles. "If you get too far, that can kill ya."

"The hell, Raza," Djaem yelled, letting his frustration show. "'It's 'important' is a little different from 'it will electrocute you!'"

The rest of his walk to his seat, Djaem grumbled and growled, but stayed perfectly at the center of the blue path. *And with these lights glaring on us*, he complained to himself, *I can forget about trying to get any visual cues.*

His thoughts were interrupted by a shrill warble coming from by the door. A figure had entered and turned right instead of following the blue path. As the lanterns lit up again, Fallrick's surprised face could be made out for a few seconds.

Running on instinct, Fallrick had followed his feet to his regular destination. He stopped short at the alarm and made haste to correct his mistake. He gave a quick hop back into the blue path and made his way to the booth.

"What is this?" hissed an electronically modulated voice from beyond the lights. "There are only supposed to be four here."

A second modulated voice answered, "It is a team of five."

"One was to be sequestered," a third digitized voice added. "Fallrick, when you get to your seat, explain."

Fallrick nodded, keeping his eyes on the blue tint. He had already triggered the nanobots to set an alarm; he had no intention of making it worse by speaking in transit. Silence and compliance were key to entering, and he had accidently moved towards the panel. If the nanobots saw him as a threat, they would stop shielding him from the arc cannons on the floor. Being in this room without the approval of the microscopic machines was a death sentence. He pushed back the memory of the time a team had failed at review, and their protection swarm was dismissed.

3

A CANNIBAL AND A PSYCHIC GO SHOPPING. WHAT COULD GO WRONG?

THE INNER CITY was a maze of narrow walkways and alleys created by the squat, square buildings. The streets didn't flow in even lines or were organized on a grid. They were an afterthought, haphazard pathways around the true purpose of the Citadel. This was a military base positioned to defend the outer ring of the Empire. Anything of vital importance was beneath the thick armored plating of the street. The under city was the beating heart of the Citadel.

Uthraith and Scythia had no trouble leaving the towering fortress of the Citadel and passed unnoticed through the relatively empty streets of the inner city. They moved through the security of the main gates with little more than a wave and a nod.

Once they went through the metal sliding blast door, they were hit full force by the sun from above. The walls and force shields of the city blocked much of the UV rays of the harsh sun. Uthraith smiled as he felt the warmth touch his face. The outer city was a sprawling and bustling metropolis. The streets were wide and flowed neatly one into the next. The mono structures of the inner city were gone. The outer city reflected the people that lived there: colorful, diverse, and inventive.

Uthraith smiled as he led the way into the bustling streets; Scythia hurried to catch up. The other pedestrians of the city gave them a wide berth.

Yes, it is wise to step aside and watch. Behold our glory. Admire our strength and be thankful of our passing.

AS THE EXOTIC monsters passed the security gates, most averted their gaze, stepping away from the danger. Most, but not all. A set of brown eyes filled with the bravery of the very young watched the scene with interest. From her perch in a second-story balcony, the young girl watched as the crowd parted. Their fear created a bubble in the flow of traffic around a feral headhunter and a jewel-clad Star-born. Ripples of awe and fear spread out around them as they passed.

The headhunters were the stuff of many bedtime stories used to frighten children into good behavior. Later in life, they would hear the tales again, but this time as warnings: 'Stay away from the outer ring; that's where the feral live. They will eat you and drink your blood from your own skull.'

This particular Murder Mountain lived up to all the nightmare-inspiring stories her brothers told. His skin was so heavily tattooed in black tones it was impossible to be certain of his natural hue. The marks emphasized his musculature and increased the visual effect of his bulk even as he moved with feline grace. He wore the skins of monsters she had no names for, and the decorative skulls he wore on his belt were proof enough she didn't want to give a name to such nightmares.

In equal measure to the fear created by the feral was the curiosity inspired by the sparkling woman next to him.

Star-born were rarely seen planet-side. Her figure was stretched almost a head and shoulders above those around her.

From the girl's vantage, it was impossible to tell their true height. The crowd around him barely reached his lower chest, and the Star-born managed to reach just above his shoulder. Their height was where their similarities ended.

He was a study of earthen tones, ready to blend and disappear into any landscape. She was a burst of color and glitter. Her hair was strands of orange, red, and white fire braided back from her face. It fell from her temples and her crown, a stark contrast to her bright-blue skin. The rest of her hair was loose, falling around her shoulders and back.

Her brilliant coloring drew attention to the black-and-white style of her noble dress. It was sleeveless with a high back and a square-cut neckline. The skirt was full but cut angularly, so the front was at her knees and the back at her ankles. It swished around her tall knee boots. Its vertical pattern of black-and-white edged with silver emphasized her height. Gems sparkled at her throat, waist, wrists, and ankles, shimmering with every move. The girl was certain she was a Star-born princess walking with her feral bodyguard. Using her data screen, she recorded their passing to prove what she had seen.

She watched them with wonder and awe until they had moved past the open market. Once out of view, she ran back inside to show her family.

PRIDE SWELLED in Uthraith's chest. *How very fine my Little Blue looks*. She looked much better than any of those rich ladies at the diplomat meetings. Scythia reminded him of his eldest daughter at her first fire dance; although, they didn't look anything alike. Beau was over seven feet tall and a lean tower of muscle. She could outrun and outjump most of her siblings. She was going to be a great hunter. Her skin was a beautiful mix of reds and golds, speckled and mottled with black spots. All had watched her dancing. *It is a very good thing she looks like her mother.*

Uthraith did nothing to conceal his grin as he continued towards his destination. He was eager to be about his business. It always took some time when he returned planet-side to set up the communication relays. *They are going to love Little Blue.*

DJAEM DID his best to follow the tracking signal from Scythia. The problem wasn't the signal. It was the city. The streets were a confusing, twisting mess. There was no pattern or grid layout. It was completely unlike the flowing and curving mines or carefully constructed hive worlds.

It should have been a simple thing to follow her signal, but the bustling walkable paths intersected and interchanged. They didn't flow in straight lines or even with a logical flow of construction. After finding yet another dead end, Djaem turned and retraced his steps to find another way to follow the little blinking light. She wasn't far away; it was simply about finding a way to reach that location.

I am going to install a guidance system in the suppressors, not just a tracker.

Once he was well into the crowded shopping district, Djaem was able to pull back his hood. The sun felt good on his skin. In the crowded market with the tall buildings around, the enormous sky seemed more manageable.

People of different sizes and shapes passed by him in the crowded streets. He worried if Scythia had felt overwhelmed by the crowd. *No, she will be fine. Those suppressors will have made this a much easier place. It wasn't as crowded as the hive. If she keeps them on like she promised, she will be fine.*

It did little to abate the worry floating around in his mind. That may have been why he missed the woman at first. He didn't notice her in the background noise of the city. His attention was focused on finding a tall blue figure.

You would think a person as different as Scythia would stand out more.

He didn't notice her until she had grabbed his arm and yanked hard. Djaem let out a startled yelp and was spun around by an angry-looking redhead.

She was slightly shorter than Djaem, looking up with bright-blue eyes. She was pretty in an approachable sort of way, with a cute dusting of freckles across her nose and pinchable, rounded cheeks. Djaem managed to hide the knife he had pulled and slipped it away in a smooth gesture. If she noticed the motion, she gave no indication.

"There you are, Sleakia! You two-timing son-of-a-bitch!" she shouted, poking Djaem in the chest. "You think you can just change your hair a little and I won't recognize you!"

Djaem groaned inwardly. *Not this again.* This was not the first time he had been mistaken for someone else. The drawback of having features that look like everyone else was that you look like everyone else. Anyone else . . . Apparently, he looked like Sleakia.

"I am sorry . . .," he tried to explain. She slapped him hard across the face.

"How could you just leave me there? You think you can just duck out in the morning as you please. I even had to pay for the room, you bastard. You said you loved me!" Big tears started to form in her eyes, and people were starting to take notice. Djaem winced at the sting in his cheek as he looked back at her.

"I am not who you think I am." Djaem tried again to explain. His data pad beeped, telling him that Scythia had started to move again. *I do not have time for this.* Djaem sighed in irritation as he considered his options.

"I was never the man you thought I was. It was all a lie. I work for the Visaderous. Everything I ever said to you was a lie. I was told to seduce you so that I was in the right place at the right time." He let his tone turn cold. She would be better off without whoever this Sleakia was, anyway. She was cute and she would find someone better.

The girl gasped in surprise. Her eyes were wide. "What? That doesn't even make any sense. You expect me to believe that bullshit!"

Djaem shrugged. "It's true. Whatever you thought you knew about me wasn't true, and you should forget about it."

She glared angrily at him. "You son of a dracisi whore!" She slapped him hard across the other side of his face. "If I ever see your face again, I am going to scratch your lying eyes out."

She turned and stormed away. Djaem hoped Sleakia made himself scarce. With a heavy sigh, Djaem rubbed his face as he looked back at the data pad. He was just glad not to be mistaken for a husband again. That had been so awkward to get out of last time.

Djaem picked up his pace and followed the little dot that was on the move again.

I need to get her a damn communicator.

SCYTHIA WAS SMILING. The sun felt warm on her skin, the sounds of the market bustled around her, and her shoes clicked loudly against the stone street. The air was full of scents she didn't recognize, some pleasant and some sour. She could almost taste them. It was so different from the sanitized air of the transports or even the environmentally controlled air inside the Citadel.

She was fully in the Here and now. Her suppressors kept the Ethers music playing far in the distance if she needed it, but it didn't touch her. Djaem had said she could go out if she wore them. They didn't hurt but were more like wearing the wrong shoes or clothes that were cut to the wrong size. She had quickly gotten used to them and soon completely forgot about the discomfort in her excitement of the world around her. She walked with Uthraith, enjoying the bubble of space he created. It allowed them to shop in comfort and ease through the crowded market.

She helped pick out toys, clothes, practical and impractical novelty items. Soon he was carrying several bulging bundles on his back as they left the market district. Scythia carried her own purchase with great care. Her long arms wrapped protectively around the heavy rectangular box. It was about twelve inches tall and eight inches wide. The strong metal case protected a beautifully decorated biosphere. *I don't know why they call it a sphere. It's a cylinder. Maybe it's because the top is dome shaped.* The cylinder was glass and decorated with fine silver edging and the base was made from endurium.

As lovely as the container was, that was not what had caught her attention. Inside the glass grew a miniature tree. It was called a Flerimond. Its bark was a deep purple, the leaves were a bright shimmering blue, with spiky edges in red. Uthraith had said they looked like bloody weapons. Some internal process of the plant caused it to glow brilliantly when out of direct UV light. According to the very enthusiastic seller, the high ladies liked to hang them as living lanterns, though that wasn't the primary function of the Flerimond which meant world's bloom. If properly tended, it would produce enough oxygen to supply an adult human's daily basic intake indefinitely. It would also produce a sweet candy-like fruit. These fruits were the size of a cherry but gave a full-grown human all the nutriment they needed for a day.

Scythia didn't know or care if that was true. Even with the suppressors on, she could see the lovely golds and pinks swirling in the Ether around the plant. *It glows like the moon. And it sings the most beautiful song, full of melodies and harmonies.* The singing was what had drawn her to it in the first place.

Scythia looked down at the case in her arms, clutching it tighter. A memory flashed painfully through her mind, making her wince at the charred and burned edges of it. With effort, she was able to hold onto it this time.

A child Scythia was sitting in the cool light created by a mess of glowing roots. The fruits were the size of her childhood fist. Juice dripped down her chin and stained her white dress as she greedily ate the delicious treat. Scythia winced again as the memory slipped away. *I am sure it's the same kind of tree. Maybe someone can tell me where the big ones grow.*

She smiled again and hummed the tune of the Flerimond.

They left the bustling noisy crowds of the market district. The streets widened; the buildings grew tall, and their shape and architecture changed. They became works of art made of metal and glass. Flags and symbols decorated many of the structures. Soldiers in different styles and types of uniforms stood guard or walked around.

The people changed too. Clothes from thousands of worlds swirled by her in every variation of color and construction. A woman walked past them and sneered at

Scythia as her guards circled her, their eyes following Uthraith's every move.

Scythia frowned and looked at Uthraith. He shrugged. "Diplomats." He didn't expand on it as he led them to a large building with all the different flags attached to the outside. "What is this place?"

Uthraith smiled as he held open the door for Scythia. "The Hubb. Diplomats work here. I make calls home here. Only a small delay."

Scythia nodded and walked through the massive doors. Her heeled boots clicked loudly on the real stone floor. The black marble beneath her feet was filled with flecks of gold and silver sparkle. Scythia grinned a little. *I am walking on a star-filled sky.* She was busy looking at the matching pillars that held up a golden ceiling. It took her a moment to realize it was just colored that way. The roof was made of an energy-conserving material. She wondered if it helped with the relays.

Uthraith tapped Scythia on the shoulder, and they headed to one of the many back corridors with a lobby area. It was much smaller than the previous grand entrance lobby. From there, Uthraith took her back to a small room where one end was just a large data screen.

They sat down, and Uthraith preened his clothes and hair. After a moment, the screen started coming to life, and a spinning circle told them it was connecting.

Then light filled the screen. Scythia had to blink many times before she could see. The image on the display was a world of dark-emerald foliage and golden sand. Shouts could be heard, and there seemed to be a mad scramble of shapes. Suddenly the view was filled with people. She realized they were looking from above at a large open area. There was a massive group of people, close to thirty, of varying ages and sizes.

It was Uthraith's family.

They were all big. But their range of bigness seemed to vary more on age than anything. It was hard to judge exactly their size since the trees also seemed to be enormous. The only reason Scythia even realized they were abnormally tall was that there was a woman standing there holding a small device. It was the remote control for the video relay. It seemed tiny in her hand.

Uthraith beamed. The translator couldn't keep up with the many voices all booming at once. Scythia watched in amazement as the faces all smiled and talked, and she could feel Uthraith's joy even through the suppressors.

He broke into common speech. "This is Scythia. I call her Little Blue. She is new to team." He turned slightly in his chair and scooted her forward so she could be seen. Scythia had a wall of faces staring at her intensely. They were all tan and tattooed. Some young, some old. She could see bits of Uthraith in almost all of them. She found herself feeling a little shy but also happy to be included.

She smiled and gave a little wave. "Hello. I am Scythia. It's nice to see all of you."

A man made a strange noise in his throat and said a few words. The only one she recognized was 'Star-born.' Whatever he said had several of the women hitting him.

Uthraith laughed and shook his head. "I keep Little Blue. She is a great sister." Scythia beamed at that statement. It made her feel warm and light when he said it.

A few other women started talking quickly, though she didn't understand, and the translator could barely get the context of the questions.

"Uthraith, are these all your sisters?" Scythia said with another little wave.

Uthraith laughed and shook his head. "Oh no. My wives. Those in back are sisters." He leaned forward and started talking to the women, who all laughed and some blushed.

Scythia nodded and smiled. "Wow, they are all so pretty and strong."

Uthraith nodded. "Yes. My women. Some big, some small. All women good, but my women are best." A swarm of children filled the view. "Oh! My children!" He roared in delight.

Scythia decided to give him some privacy to speak to his family. She needed a moment to process the strange mix of delight and pain radiating in the center of her chest.

NOT CHAPTER FOUR: STILL PRELIMINARY MEETING

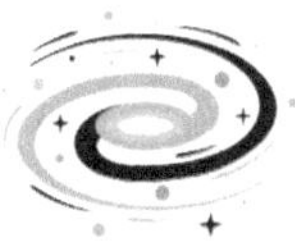

Fallrick took a moment to push back old memories and collect his thoughts. He could do nothing for the teams of his past. He needed to focus on preserving his current team.

"I advised for S.H.4911594 to remain sequestered," Fallrick explained. He managed to sound unaffected by the uncomfortable seat below the glaring lights. "But he declined."

Deep within the gloom, several of the large oval chairs spun to face the isolated figures in the wide-open room. Only two of those enduring the brightness of the light's glare could make out the movement. Even with light-shielded eyes like Uthraith's, there was little more than an impression of shapes.

"He disregarded your orders?" one of the shadows within shadows asked. The voice was unnaturally even and cold.

"Sirs and ladies, understand," Fallrick responded. "As I have been demoted, I no longer hold sufficient rank to give these people orders. The team will generally follow my instructions, but this is one of the rare occasions where a decision was made to simply take my words under advisement."

Muffled grumblings emanated from different points in the gloom. Echoes and shadows prevented any estimate of the number of people in the room.

One voice to the left brought forth words. "Are you saying this team has no director? No accountability?"

"I wouldn't say that," Fallrick called back, barely suppressing the laugh from his voice.

Djaem interrupted, his voice filling the room easily. "If we had an administrator, this counsel wouldn't have been gathered, and this review would never have happened. It would appear we have greater accountability than anyone else in service." Djaem crossed his arms with indignation.

"I still have rank," Uthraith bellowed, a broad grin overtaking his face. He nodded at his own idea. "Perhaps I should ad—" His words cut off as he tried to wrap his tongue around the alien word. Giving up after a moment, he resorted to a simplification. "Lead! Yes, I should lead!"

"N-no," Fallrick stammered out as quickly as he could. "Uthraith, you don't understand even half of what administering entails." Fallrick returned his eyes to the gloomy shadows of the panel. "S.H.4911594 does have a point. If I am granted an exception, this entire situation could be resolved right now. Give me administration over this team."

One by one, almost all of the glaring white lights changed to red. Two individual lights cast blue, indicating that the panel had rejected the request.

"So, Ess . . . Aiche-Four . . . Ninety-One One-Five . . . Nine Four, why did you decline the instructions? What makes you think you have that authority?" The voice of the shadow in the third chair growled before it snapped, "Can we please just use the subjects' names?"

The lights to the panel turned green as they voted to use names.

Djaem smiled and nodded as he answered with smooth confidence. "For a nationalist's inquiry, there is no declining a panel dictate. If a subject is instructed to remain sequestered, they must do so."

The green lights faded back to white as murmurs of agreement and understanding rose again, filling the gloom of the room.

"Yet you still refused," the third chair pushed.

"In a universal law inquiry, all subjects are to be present, with no exceptions, under penalty of death and disloyalty. Since this panel has both, I am obligated to follow both commands. The attendance requirement was written, but the sequestration was verbal. Written commands always take precedence. Is this not the Emperor's will?"

Fallrick's snickers joined several from the panel. Several shadowed heads moved in an up-and-down motion slowly. It looked suspiciously like nodding. Uthraith's face twisted into the broad smile of a proud father.

Raza, despite the creases of annoyance on her forehead, couldn't help but crack a grin of her own. *Perhaps this stupid hiver was as good as Fallrick had made him out to be.*

Scythia's joyful smile was followed by her voice. In a far too cheerful tone for such a grim statement, she added, "Besides, this is scary enough as it is. If I didn't know where my Gem was, I might get scared."

A voice speaking up from the gloom near the panel interjected. "Yes, we don't want her to be scared."

"May I make a file statement, for the record?" Fallrick leaned forward quickly as he spoke, now projecting his voice in a military manner, intentionally pulling attention away from Scythia.

"Several of the panelists, through reputation or direct

contact, have expressed discomfort with the presence of S.H.4911594, also known as Djaem. Sequestration was granted for security and to set panelist worries at ease. Having been a panelist, I can assure you there is no way he can manipulate you now that wouldn't be available to him if sequestered. The audio modifications, sight denial, and other security systems remove enough of your personal touches that his subtle cues and manipulations can't be employed. He is at his most powerless, aside from being in space." He looked across his team. "Does this satisfy the panel?"

The oval-backed chairs turned towards each other for a brief discussion. All murmuring cut out as the sound-dampening systems activated and allowed nothing but silence to reach the team. Despite this, Djaem sat silently, mouthing words, and gave a nod. Uthraith knew it wasn't possible for the little man to see in the dark. *There is no way he is able to actually see what they were saying.*

"What is this talking you do?" Uthraith asked Djaem.

Turning his gaze to the giant, the nearly featureless man whispered back, "If my calculations are correct, I know what they're going to say. It has to be one of three people. One will persuade others, one will back down, and one will stand alone."

As the chairs turned to face them again, green, and blue lights began to show, with only one red light in protest.

Djaem looked at the single red light. "I do understand, and even though it's a minority in the vote, I would advise accepting Kael Chad Tinren's position. You should listen to him. The Kael has seen me work and knows that I am too easily underestimated. He knows me from my home world. Back on the hive I stood security for two review panels he was on; he has good reason for this fear. If presented with the command in writing, I agree to remain sequestered for future sessions."

A shadowed figure erupted from the sixth oval chair. "You, see? We are not safe! He is dangerous, and nothing we do will make this panel secure. Not from him. Not from any of them! He's an abomination, a criminal. I'll have no part of this!"

As the figure stormed off, Djaem offered further assurance. "If anyone else is uncomfortable, just put it in writing so I don't get punished for following orders. That's all I ask."

4

SCYTHIA'S EASY GUIDE TO MAKING FRIENDS/ENEMIES

SCYTHIA LET the door close quietly behind her as she peered down the hallway, first one way and then the other. Everything looked the same. The sound of voices to her left made up her mind, and she moved towards the noise. The hallway curved slightly, opening into a large room.

She didn't recognize anything. There were large plush chairs and tables, where a mix of strange beings sat, chatting in a cacophony of languages. The crowd was dispersed around the large room. Scythia spotted a small empty table along the far wall. It was made of clear glass and overlooked a courtyard garden. *I wonder if that is really there or just a screen image.*

Scythia felt a strange invisible pressure building as she moved through the crowded room. *It cannot be caused by the Ether. Between my suppressors and the ones in the walls, I shouldn't feel anything.*

It took a moment for her to recognize the feeling. It came from the people in the room. Scythia could feel their eyes watching her as she slipped past them. The noise dimmed around her as voices lowered to whispers. Scythia considered the many examples of Raza and Uthraith. Her dark eyes focused on her destination, keeping her shoulders straight and her head high.

Long legs carried her gracefully to the empty table, and she slid into the provided chair. After a moment, the noise of the room returned, and the pressure dissipated as interest in her waned. Scythia studied the lovely garden scene, with flowers and trees of reds and oranges. A delicate petal drifted from one of the branches, swirling its way down to the cracked and dirty pathway. It joined a small company of petals that were fluttering with tiny scraps of trash before getting caught in the mud under a bush.

Oh, it's real! Isn't it funny how it's the dirty and discarded things that let you know the rest is reality? Scythia sighed in frustration. *I hate this. It's like missing one of my eyes.* She knew the Ether was still out there because she could hear the distant sound of its waves thrumming while she was trapped in the strange empty bubble, unable to reach out and touch it. Whenever Scythia tried to look at the world through the Ether, she saw nothing but blank walls.

I know they are all around me. The music, the lights. I should feel them. But it's just empty . . . silent . . . lonely. I miss watching Djaem's crystal palace. The hot tears stung her eyes, blurring her vision of the garden. Blinking rapidly, she turned her attention back to her new treasure. With delicate and deliberate care, she opened the sealed case.

Sunlight filtered through the window and the display case of her biosphere. A smile of delight and wonder took over Scythia's face. The glowing purple roots of the tree trembled and wiggled in delight. The glow dimmed, allowing her to see the fluorescent green veins that ran along its bark and up to the beautiful leaves. After the initial shiver, she watched as new leaves uncurled, lime green with pink tips.

Scythia leaned her nose down, practically touching the

glass of the display. She saw that the edges of the leaves were pulsing, transitioning between a golden orange and a scarlet red. Hidden among this colorful foliage hung the strange, spiky fruit. They were no bigger than her pinky finger and dangled from delicate vines. Most were the same shade of purple as the rest of the tree. However, there was one glowing and sparkling; it was a bright-green gem.

"You look the same!" a tiny voice said eagerly, startling Scythia. A blue hand pressed against the center of her chest as she tried to calm herself. *Everyone keeps sneaking up on me! I can't sense anything this way.* The voice belonged to what Scythia presumed was a child, though she had no way of knowing the age or gender of the being in front of her.

They were the same in stature to a child, with large, circular golden eyes, and irises of vertical slits. Their face was shaped to allow for a jaw designed for biting attacks. A set of gills were visible along the thick neck. Their skin seemed a mix of scales and leather, mottled with greens and browns, and they wore a strange suit obviously designed to allow for movement through alien environments, which included a spherical helmet filled with clear but thick liquid. The helmet's visor was open; otherwise, Scythia wouldn't be able to see its features.

"I look the same?" Scythia repeated, trying to keep her mind on the conversation.

They stepped forward, barely tall enough to see over her table. They rested gloved appendages against the edge to peer up at her Flerimond.

"Yes. Look like the tree. Both glow, sparkle, full of energy. Beautiful. Dangerous," the being spoke, its words strange and ill fitting.

Scythia realized the mouth wasn't moving. The childlike voice was coming from a universal translator. *Uthraith is right;*

those translators aren't very good. She smiled and felt a blush fill her cheeks as she looked back at the tree.

"Thank you. That is very flattering."

They both sat in silence for a moment as tiny flowers of white began to bloom. The glowing-green gem fruit shifted and shuddered then dropped. It bounced and rolled across the ground inside the biosphere before falling down a specially designed collection apparatus. The biosphere buzzed and whirled before giving a strange little sigh, and a light blinked at the bottom of the base.

"Push button," the little golden-eyed stranger said, eager. A mitten-like hand waved. Scythia reached over and gently pressed the glowing button. A vapor rose out of the little drawer that slowly slid open to reveal the spiky fruit. It was about an inch in diameter. The nearly translucent skin was a bright green that shifted to a brilliant emerald color at the points. The stem and a single leaf were still attached at the top. Bits of dirt and moss clung to the spikes.

They both leaned forward and gazed into the tiny gem. Inside swirled sparkles and shimmers like a miniaturized galaxy.

"That is called the Bacavita. It is highly prized. One tiny berry will completely replenish a living being for a whole day. Some believe it will heal the sick," a deep baritone voice spoke from over their shoulder.

Scythia looked up, and up. *He is almost as tall as me, but he isn't all stretched.* The new arrival stood with relaxed confidence over her. The armored uniform he wore accented his lean, muscular build, enhancing his catlike silhouette. The delicate tattoos on his face and neck stood out in bright contrast to the chalklike color of his skin. This drew attention to the fact that his hair was a slightly different shade of cream. All of this framed his lovely red eyes and angular features. His full, slightly pink lips curled into a smile as he watched Scythia study him.

He is very pretty. I wonder what he looks like in the Ether.

"Not long ago, wars were fought in the Reaches over these plants. Today, in the inner ring, they are decoration," the pretty man said, giving Scythia a little smirk as he leaned forward. Scythia looked at the golden-eyed one, who was staring at the green jewel. Without the sight of the Ether, there was no way to see the thoughts and feelings of her new golden-eyed friend. So, Scythia was more than a little surprised when she realized she could feel his sense of longing, sadness, and desperation. She felt them in a way she never had before, as empathy.

Long blue fingers reached out and delicately plucked the glowing fruit from the drawer. The tiny compartment closed as soon as the fruit was removed. *It's so heavy for such a little thing.*

Scythia took hold of the gloved flipper-like hand of the being with the golden eyes. Those eyes looked at her, their double eyelids blinking rapidly from both top-to-bottom and side-to-side. The face lacked a nose as Scythia understood it, though it was possible that they wore a mask. There was no real way for her to know what the being was and what was their environmental suit. A strange sound that the translator couldn't communicate escaped the strange little person as she held their 'hand.' She smiled and carefully set the precious fruit in the curve of their appendage.

Several things happened in that heartbeat. The pale man moved too fast for her to see. In one blink, he was relaxed on the other side of the little golden-eyed being the next, he was so close she could feel his breath against her skin, a cold blade pressed against her throat.

Scythia was only vaguely aware of the others in the room as she looked up into those deep red eyes. They were cold and intense. *There are little gold flecks in the red of his eyes. Oh, he is wearing eye makeup.* She watched the surprise and confusion fill his expression.

"Nexdare, release her!" the childlike voice commanded.

The man moved away as if he were burned. The weapon had vanished. He bowed deeply to them both. The being was looking at where she still held his 'hand.'

"Are you giving this to me, Star-born?" Even through the translator, the voice seemed to tremble.

Scythia turned her attention back to those golden eyes. "Yes."

"What do you want in return?"

"To know I gave it to you."

"Why?"

"Because it makes me feel full when I help others."

"Do you understand the value of this fruit?"

"Only that it has a high value to you, and a small value to me."

"And you will still give it to me and ask for nothing in return?"

"I wouldn't know what to ask for. I don't need anything."

There was a long moment of silence as they continued to look at each other. Neither had moved their hand. They were a strange living portrait, neither perfectly still nor moving.

"What is your name, Star-born?"

"I am called Scythia."

"Scythia Star-born. I will not forget. The waters run deep." The appendages moved and the fruit disappeared into a suit compartment. The translator turned into a different language Scythia didn't know, and the golden eyes bowed and joined a small group of similar looking beings. All different patterns and shades, but it was impossible for her to tell one from the next.

The man named Nexdare looked from the little being to Scythia.

"I had no idea the Constellation Confederation was getting involved. I must admit, that was impressive. Very subtle." He moved and sat down across from Scythia.

Scythia watched him. *Maybe his translator is malfunctioning.*

"I don't know what the endgame is, but the fallout is going to be epic." He smiled charmingly as he leaned his elbow against the table. An overhead voice chimed, and several people started raising from the seats. "Just in time for the show." He winked and stood up. "I can't wait to see your handiwork." He followed along with the group of small beings. Scythia watched the beings of a variety of shapes and sizes flow out of the room through a set of large double doors. A woman in an imperial uniform stopped in front of Scythia, looking concerned.

"All the Constellation delegates need to be in attendance. Please come with me." She seemed a little flustered.

Scythia nodded and closed her case with care. Picking it up, she stood and followed behind the woman. The Hubb attendant seemed to fuss and flutter around people. They didn't follow the crowd but instead went into a smaller, separate room. Scythia was very confused by what she saw there.

Three tables were set to form a U-shape. Each table seemed to have a theme, and the people at each table seemed to follow those themes. Their uniforms were accented and designed with matching colors and symbols. It took her a moment to realize they were Star-born. The decorative belts and bracers they wore were antigrav systems to protect their bodies from the pressure of the planet's gravity. They were all tall, though only a handful had the strange elongation similar to Scythia, fewer had her unusual coloring. Hers was bright and even. The others came in more of an ombre gradient. One was a soft, pastel shade of green with deep blue hair, and the other was shades of pink. The most interesting thing was that across their faces and necks were patterns of scarification. Raised pearlescent scars of ridges and swirls, symbols and lines covered all their exposed skin. Though the symbols were similar, each person's marks were unique. *I wonder if it's like Uthraith's tattoos.*

The room went silent as she was brought in. A figure sitting in the middle of the farthest table was the first to speak. Scythia studied their faces and markings. The blue hair and pale-green skin were very pretty. The cut of the uniforms was almost interchangeable. The differences came in the colors and symbols. The group on the left was made of blue, whites, and silvers. The middle table was made up of black, red, and gold. And the last table on the right was orange, green, and black. The symbols made no sense to Scythia.

"What is the meaning of this interruption?" The voice was deep and low.

The young woman that had brought Scythia looked at the group.

"I was told to bring all the Constellation delegates to the conference room." She looked calm, but there was a flutter of irritation in her voice.

A softer, higher pitched voice from one of the side tables spoke up. "She is not one of our delegates. I have never seen this woman before."

The frustrated escort frowned and looked accusingly at Scythia. "You didn't tell me you weren't with the delegation," she hissed.

"You didn't ask me. I was following instructions. You said I should go with you," Scythia said, trying to be reasonable. Djaem and Raza had been very clear she was to follow instruction from those in authority when neither of them were present.

The woman's frustration seemed to increase. "You could have said," she hissed before turning to the room. "I am so sorry for the interruption." She gave a bow and turned towards the door.

"One moment, please." A rough, scratchy voice spoke from the corner of a table. The voice came from what appeared to be an elderly man. Scythia was only guessing that since they had a gray beard covering their chin. "What is your name?"

Scythia gave a small smile. "I am called Scythia."

The old man nodded and motioned her to come closer. Scythia obliged and stepped into the middle of the three tables. There was a general hush in the room.

"What clan are you from?" the old man asked.

"She is of no clan; she bears no marks," a male voice to her left said.

Across from that voice, a female spoke up. "Perhaps she is one of the lost ones."

A different male voice broke in, "Where is her AG?"

The room fell silent again. Scythia could feel the pressure of their gazes. Scythia didn't bother trying to figure out who was speaking; she was looking into the pale-green eyes of the old man.

"She doesn't seem to need one. Her psychic powers are strong enough that she can compensate for the gravitational pressure." The old man smiled as he spoke, his gaze traveling to the leader at the middle of the table.

The male voice seemed incredulous. "That is ridiculous. It must be hidden in her clothes or something."

The female voice spoke again. "Just because you aren't strong enough to do it doesn't mean it can't be done."

They soon fell into a squabble. Scythia wasn't listening to them; she was looking at the old man. He nodded slowly, as if he were coming to a decision. "Thank you. It was a pleasure to meet you, Scythia. You should go now, or we will spend the next hour arguing about you."

Scythia gave a little smile and nodded. "Yes. I should go. Uthraith is waiting for me. Thank you." She turned and walked out of the door, a flustered assistant following in her wake.

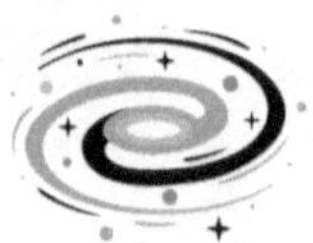

"I couldn't even say where the review board should begin," a slightly modulated voice intoned from one of the egg-shaped shadows to the right. "Topical, individual, chronological—this is an absolute mess!"

"Individual," Uthraith called out. "Then, you be done with me and I go."

Fallrick shushed him with his hand. "We need to be serious right now."

A smirk crossing her face, Raza murmured to Fallrick, "I think he is. I could go second. Get on with my inter-mission vacation."

Fallrick gave a side-eye glance but kept his face expressionless.

"This was supposed to be a training mission," one of the shadowed figures barked. "How? How did you manage . . . this! Look at the size of this list! It was a training mission."

"Yes," Fallrick answered calmly, with no emotion in his voice. "It was selected from the N.E.B. training missions list. Fully authorized and funded. This one already had the start of a follow-up mission being written prior to completion."

"Exactly," the voice snapped back.

"The outcome of the investigation was predetermined with such confidence that rooting out the cult was the next assignment. However, this cult had a fully manifested, bound Tyrling. An officer of the N.E.B. involved with them. I don't think the other investigation really has any bearing at this point."

The voice from the panel growled, "Because they ruined it! They messed up the whole investigation."

"I am a little confused. It's starting to sound like you're unhappy that we found the sleeper agent," Djaem responded with feigned confusion. His voice was just loud enough to carry a hint of dramatic flair. "Not that there was one . . . but that we found him out."

Fallrick lifted his hand, silencing Djaem. "If Artos's input was considered while making these assignments, that would explain why the subcults always lead to minor parent cults. As it turns out, the subcult was the master's own home. It was a blessing from the God-king that the monster wasn't fully developed. You all know what a Tyrling can do on a hive world?"

Those words hung in the air like a poisonous cloud. Everyone held their breath a little. Djaem blanched and leaned forward as he tried to focus on his breathing. Scythia reached and soothingly rubbed his back as Raza softly spoke to Fallrick, "Djaem is a Balial III incident survivor." No one questioned Djaem's reaction. Everyone knew the horror of that incident.

Fallrick stopped speaking and nodded pensively.

The brief quiet of the panel ended with a modulated voice that was slightly more delicate coming from amongst the raised chairs.

"If process and protocol had been followed, it might be easier to understand what happened. Their investigation largely bypassed the town. It was almost as if they knew to search primarily in the mines. The outcome is wonderful. It's such a blessing that every member survived. This much danger on a training mission is not ideal. They are not facing charges about coming to a conclusion, Fallrick; they are being charged for the several violations of standards and protocol. They don't even seem able or willing to compose themselves properly in this review. What can the Empire expect of their future?"

From the wooden chairs, four sets of eyes looked to Fall-rick, who sat silently, deep in thought. It took nearly thirty seconds for him to answer. In the quiet gloom, that seemed like forever.

"There were two senior members of the team present. Both are quite experienced. I was available through relay as back up. They were being shown process and protocol during the mission. When the environment became too dangerous for the instructions to continue, the training was put on hold until team safety and survival could be assured." His voice was calm and steady as he spoke.

"Yes," a different voice growled from amongst the panelists, "but that doesn't answer how they knew. It doesn't answer why they avoided all the usual channels or any of the things that led to them being in so much danger to begin with."

"We had a hard time," Scythia mumbled, "both getting there and being there. The trip was tough and being in the hive hurt. We had to take what we knew and just go with it."

"It was easy to tell there was danger—" Djaem started, but Raza finished his sentence for him "—from the minute we stepped into the inspector's office. Things weren't right. Something was off. None of us could put our finger on it yet, but it was there."

"Dah," Uthraith barked. "I wanted to plasma him."

"And when the team put their exceptional talents to work," Fallrick wrapped up, "they knew they needed to look in some more . . . hidden places."

"Hidden places?" The voice from the panel projected more disgust than the requested information.

"I could feel it," Scythia said. "Before we landed on the planet, I could feel something very wrong. There were too many people. I couldn't feel where it was . . . so we needed to get a better look."

"And that brought us past all the checking in with guardsmen and what-not that you'd normally see," Raza added.

"Well," Djaem corrected, "most of the checking. It was clear right away that the guardsmen were fearful of our presence and that they knew nothing about the Ether anomalies. Even their psychic seemed to have no idea."

5

STRUGGLES OF THE STICKMAN

DJAEM MOVED PURPOSEFULLY DOWN the hall, actively ignoring the feeling of sweat trickling down his back. The extra padding, he had to wear under the oversized armored uniform was turning it into an oven. Even with the additional layers he had tucked inside, it still shifted awkwardly around him. He made a mental note to steal from a smaller person next time.

The extravagant design of the Hubb building made his search a long, arduous process. He had searched several rooms in this wing and still had found no clues as to where Scythia might be. The last person he had spoken to said they had seen Scythia come this way. The data pad he had collected from the front lobby desk said all the Star-born were being sent to a meeting in this western wing. However, the layout of the hub was circles within circles. *They have made getting turned around the goal.*

His mind whirled as he went through the possible locations she might have been taken. The tracker was impossible to use in this building. All electronic communications were suspended inside the diplomat's square. The data pad from the front desk blinked an alert. 'Unauthorized personnel.' He tapped on it, and a small image of Scythia popped on the display. He groaned and picked up his pace. This would not look good at the review.

It didn't take him long to come onto the scene. Scythia was standing stubbornly by a wall.

"I told you, Uthraith said for me to wait for him here. He brought me. He will come and retrieve me when he is done. I will wait for him." Her face was calm and collected.

There was a woman with a data pad looking more than a little frustrated. "What delegation are you with?"

Scythia shook her head and shrugged. "I am not with a delegation. I am with N.E.B.U.L.A."

There was a collective gasp and the woman stepped away as the guards stepped closer. "You are not authorized to be here."

Djaem winced and quickly inserted himself into the crowd, moving with ease till he was standing next to Scythia.

"Scythia, I have been sent to collect you," he said in a calm, even tone. He was surprised when her demeanor didn't change. *She doesn't recognize me.* There was a strange sensation in his chest. *Am I disappointed?* Up until now, she never failed to notice it was him. *That's good, right? It means I can hide from her.* He continued to play the part of security, explaining that she was in his custody. *It means that she is vulnerable. She can't 'see' the way she is used to . . .*

Yeah, because we made her wear those pretty chains. He shoved away the offending sentence and guilt that came with it.

A Dolmarvol approached, and Djaem felt fear coil around him. *Why is he here?* He swallowed and saluted with the rest of the diplomatic guards.

"Still causing a ruckus?" He gave Scythia a flirtatious smile.

Djaem slid his thumb out of the cuff of his sleeve to

where he kept his curved dagger. Alarmed that his hand had moved on its own, touching his blade, Djaem took a calming breath. *What the hell was that hand; are you trying to get us killed? That's a Dolmarvol! He wasn't threatening her, calm down. Besides, if he is flirting with her, he is the one that's in danger.* Djaem tried to force the tension out of his body.

If the dangerous warrior noticed, he gave no indication. "It's ok. I will take her wherever she wants to go."

Scythia smiled up at the Dolmarvol as he slid next to her. "Hello again, Nexdare. Did things go well with your friend?"

He blinked and gave her a little surprised smile. "Oh, yes . . . my friend is very happy. Many people are not as happy, but he is very pleased."

Most of the guards backed away. Djaem wasn't surprised. The bright-colored tattoos were the signature of the order of Dolmarvol, and their armor was designed to stand out. The bright colors served as a warning. It was a way for everyone to know it was them and act with caution. The order was small in comparison to many of its kind, but they had fearsome reputations.

He was still flirting with Scythia, trying to convince her to go with him for drinks. *Wow, he really is fearless if he wants to go spend time with a drunk Scythia.* A quiver went through Djaem as his mind played through the possible scenarios. He didn't like any of them.

Scythia giggled at something he said, and Djaem felt heat spread across his neck. He clenched his jaw to concentrate on keeping still and calm. He needed to make sure she didn't go anywhere.

Scythia shook her head. "That sounds fun, but Uthraith is going to be finished soon. I need to stay where he can find me."

The Dolmarvol smiled and nodded. "Alright, I will find you another time. You're hard to miss."

Scythia's cheeks turned purple as she smiled at him. Djaem was grateful for the faceplate on the helmet. Without it, someone might have spotted the angry glare that appeared too quickly on his face to keep hidden. *Keep it together, you idiot.* He stepped forward again.

"Scythia, I will escort you back to Uthraith. Then back to the Citadel." Something must have finally clicked because her face lit up with recognition.

"Oh!" She smiled and nodded. "Yes, of course." She turned to Nexdare, still full of bright happiness. "I have to go now. It was nice to meet you. I hope you find me later."

Nexdare's expression shifted as she looked at him. He seemed surprised and nodded, watching her as if he had never seen her before.

Djaem understood the feeling. There was something about that excited smile that still left him feeling as if the world was shifting under his feet. *She* was *terrible for anyone's mental equilibrium.*

He turned her down the hall and back towards the communications center. Once they reached the hall with Uthraith's room, he stopped and opened his visor.

She giggled as she stared at his face. "You look so different. You snuck up on me!" She looked him over. "You are so good at that."

Djaem tried to keep his voice calm. "What are you doing here?"

"Uthraith wanted me to talk to his family and help him buy gifts. It was so much fun; I got to see so many new things."

He meant to scold her for leaving, but he found he was too relieved to do more than listen as she expounded on her adventure in the market.

Uthraith left his little room, and a fierce scowl took over

his face as he stalked towards them. "Is this little man bothering you, Blue?"

Scythia laughed and shook her head. "Djaem came to find me."

Uthraith leaned down to study Djaem's face, and it took several long moments before he started laughing.

"I will need to get you a special pin so I will know it is you." He patted Djaem on the shoulder, who tried not to wince at the heavy hand.

"Come on. Let's get out of here before anyone notices she is here," Djaem said, lowering his visor again.

Uthraith didn't move. "Interesting. The Hubb is hard to enter, hard to navigate, and no trackers work here. That is a guard uniform. Getting here, finding her . . . That is a big risk just to find Little Blue." His grin turned mischievous as he leaned forward, putting his face level with Djaem. "So eager."

Djaem kept his face relaxed and his tone neutral. *Am I really the only one that can see how dangerous she is? Doesn't matter. Let him think what he wants.* He put a hand on Scythia's elbow and said quietly, "It was very difficult. So, let's go before all my effort is wasted."

Uthraith laughed and nodded. "Yes . . . it is time for training!"

THE CITY under the Citadel was where those assigned to the N.E.B. squads trained. There were separate and common areas. Uthraith thought it best to keep them in the private rooms for now. Once there, he knew he was right.

"It will not bite," Uthraith said firmly as he watched the little Stickman. Djaem's face shifted once again, looking like he was sucking on a zengabi berry. Uthraith crossed his arms and relaxed his shoulders. The picking of the weapon was an important step for any young warrior.

Uthraith understood that Djaem had been deprived of his youthful training. He pitied the little man. Weapon choosing was a sacred rite in his world. These inner worlds raised their young so soft and fragile. *It is as if they want them to be slaughtered by their enemies.* A frown creased Uthraith's brow. *Perhaps that is the point of keeping them soft and untrained, so when the beast comes, they fill up on the weak and helpless while the powerful and wealthy escape.* His expression turned thunderous for a moment as he looked at Djaem. "Choose to protect your life."

Djaem jumped, his brown skin going a little pale as he turned back to the weapons. Uthraith smiled softly. *They will not feast on my friends. I will make them strong.* He crossed his massive arms and waited.

Djaem snatched up the largest of the handguns. He frowned as he tested its weight before setting it down again. He repeated this with every handheld firearm that was neatly lain out in a row on the table.

Little Blue waited patiently at the loading station at the end of the firing range. It had taken her less than a heartbeat to choose a rustic, antiquated projectile weapon. It was a simple chemical-based slug thrower. Uthraith preferred energy weapons or plasma rifles because there was no bulky ammunition to carry. They also had better accuracy and distance.

Little Blue was clever and reminded Uthraith that energy weapons were not a good choice for her. He recalled the way the energy machines responded to her power. For her, simple weapons were better. *I will teach her to use a spear. With her height and long limbs, it will be very good.*

Uthraith was doing his best to be patient. Raza had explained why Djaem had never used a gun. On hive worlds no one ever wanted to use a gun. Because it was impossible to fire a gun without hitting bystanders. Only the N.E.B. or the U.L.A. used guns on hive worlds. Uthraith smiled as Djaem finally settled on a small energy pistol. *Yes, my little Stick is very clever.*

"Excellent. Good choice. It suits you." Uthraith snatched up a large energy pistol that dwarfed the weapon in Djaem's hand, yet somehow seemed a little too small for Uthraith.

"Remember, size of gun does not matter. If you do not hit, power does not matter. Learn to hit with small gun. Over and over, it always hit. Then no need for a big gun." Uthraith's smile stretched out across his face.

Uthraith helped them take their positions at the shooting line. He knew his teammates were capable, but they lacked the fighting skills they would need to survive missions. N.E.B. teams were modular in design. Each role from death-bringer, hunter-killer, inter-face, psychic-support, combat-medic, and even tactical-planning were interchangeable positions. If one died or was inoperable, a replacement would be selected and assigned. Uthraith never paid it much thought. Raza and he were partners and worked together to stay alive. They had been assigned to many teams. Many teams that had either been killed or reassigned.

Blue and Stick are different. He could feel it in his bones; it was skjebne. He would make them stronger by training and fighting with them. They had power, but Scythia didn't know enough to dodge when things came at her. She didn't even know how to throw a punch. Djaem couldn't hit a target if it was three feet in front of him. He had seen proof of that.

"On the line." Uthraith gently placed noise protection over Scythia's ears. "Very loud, strong recoil." He showed her how to take her stance so that she was braced.

Djaem watched them closely and tried to mimic the stance. Uthraith stepped over and looked at his form. "Good to learn from others. Your gun is very strong." With a grunt, he stepped back and crossed his arms as he watched them.

Djaem's forehead was all scrunched up as he stared down the range at the target.

"Fire," Uthraith's voice commanded.

Scythia's weapon boomed. The muzzle flashed as the tiny explosion inside hurtled the small deadly projectile downrange at her target. Her eyes were wide, and she sucked in a deep breath as she held onto her pistol.

Djaem managed to fire the pistol without dropping it. Any sound from the weapon discharge was lost in the echo of Scythia's gunshot. Djaem's gaze flashed to Uthraith with heated annoyance. The giant man laughed. No attempt was made to mask Uthraith's amusement at Djaem's expense.

"Energy weapons very quiet. Plasma bolts have little recoil. Easy to use, easy to transport."

Djaem shook off his irritation and nodded. "I see." His gaze traveled from the small weapon in his hand to the target down range.

Scythia blinked and smiled as she looked at the pistol in her hands. "So much power in such a little thing." The sound dampening caused her to shout.

Uthraith patted her on the head. "Well done, Blue. Your eye travels down the barrel. Follow eyeline to target. Breath out as you fire. Always squeeze gentle. Never jerk."

He turned to Djaem. "For you is the same. You fire much faster. No readjustment. Don't think. Just look and squeeze."

He smiled and stepped back. "Again!"

NOT CHAPTER SIX: ARE WE DONE WITH THE PRELIMINARY MEETING YET?

A voice booming from the panel seating drowned them all out. "Even basic protocol sets up more of an investigation trail! An enforcement team can't just go and do as they please, then hope that they're doing the right thing. They should have known that from training!"

Uthraith boomed back at the voice. "Yes, slow down the smart ones. That man says, 'Stop them from doing what I cannot because the person we do not trust anymore will not know what we are doing if we do it their way.' This! This is great wisdom!"

"Ahem," Fallrick glared at Uthraith as he interrupted. "The two newest members of the team had no training prior to the mission. None whatsoever. Our funding for the virts and data crystals was repurposed, and someone moved our mission completion time up by five hundred hours."

A brief murmur went through the panel. "You mean to tell me that the missing score for the psychic handler isn't just a typo?"

"Well"—Fallrick almost faltered—"it's missing because it was never assessed, but it's also pretty accurate."

There was a confused grumbling.

"The psychic's score is missing too," the female voice on the panel added.

"Yes, it is. They weren't able to get a score. She . . . she broke the pain inducer before they could narrow in on a rating." Fallrick looked over to Scythia, catching the brief surprised look on her face. Shame seeped into her expression as she looked down at her hands. Djaem gently touched her arm and gave her a reassuring smile.

"How can his score be both missing and accurate?" a different voice on the panel challenged.

Djaem looked deep into the surrounding gloom. *I guess I better explain this as simply as possible.* He took a deep breath to fortify himself. "I am not psychic."

"Ha!" Raza snorted with a roll of her eyes as she nudged Uthraith. "We saw what you did to the psychic guardsman."

Scythia forgot her guilt, and a smile of joyful pride spread across her face.

Djaem answered Raza, trying to explain. "He wanted to look at my thoughts. I repeated my self-hypnosis mantra that I use to stay calm. Once he was drawn in, I did a quick read of everything there. Posture, expression, inflection. The amount of perspiration and where it was. He had a simple mind. I just gave him what he was after, and it was too much for him."

"He still hasn't recovered!" a voice barked from the panel. "His treatment will be extensive, and his expenses should come from this team!"

A different voice cleared their throat and attempted to bring the questions back to their origin. "That explains the mental attack, but records show telepathy, mind control, mind reading, and clairvoyance."

Fallrick answered now. He made no attempt to hide his pride. "I have made it very clear in our team's charter statement. They are the best. He is just that good at what he does. None of it is metaphysical in any way. He simply reads the signs and cues he is presented with."

"Even you said he doesn't have access to those cues here, but he identified a member of the panel." The softer, more feminine voice responded. There was a gentle question there but no challenge to the statement.

"Two," Djaem said evenly. He smirked and wiggled two fingers at Scythia. "And narrowing in on a third."

Fallrick made no attempt to hide his swat across Djaem's thigh. "I did say that . . . and as you can easily see, he's better than I anticipated."

"Even you underestimate them! This team is a danger." The angry voice was followed by several suppressed voices in agreement.

"Then," Fallrick hesitantly questioned, "should I assume that this team is under review for being too good? The panel has only presented issues with their positive capabilities. It has seemed displeased at a mission outcome far beyond what was expected. It expresses fear at their talents and displeasure at their exceptional performance despite a lack of training. If this team is simply too talented to exist, let me know. That brings the charter into question."

The control lights turned back on, indicating that the panel was reclaiming control of the conversation. The panel murmured amongst themselves for a few moments and the lights turned red. As one of the egg-shaped chairs turned to face the five gathered in the small booth, a grumble could be heard as the audio suppressors stopped muffling the sound from that chair.

"If the charter of this team is why they are so arrogant and unwilling to follow rules and procedures, perhaps it needs to be challenged."

The team all looked to Fallrick as he understood the meaning of the lights better than all the others combined.

"Perhaps," he answered, his indifference so unmasked it seemed intentionally emphasized. "Simply bring that up with the Voice of the Emperor. I had specific permission to establish and deploy a T5 team."

"Is T-5 supposed to be impressive?" The second chair gained focus. "Even I'm rated T-5. It's good for the general public, but just being in the top five percent is nothing to dismiss this type of conduct over."

6

PARADISE BEHIND GLASS

SCYTHIA DIDN'T BOTHER HIDING her smile as she clicked and swished alongside Djaem. Her shoes echoed faintly down the long corridors as they walked.

She enjoyed learning to fall so she didn't hurt herself. It was fun to throw a punch or kick. Raza had promised to get the heels of Scythia's shoes modified so she could kick better. She missed the Ether, but every day she was learning all the fascinating things her physical body was capable of. How it felt to run, to sweat, to stretch, and to bend. *There is so much excitement in being in the Here and now.*

Uthraith had promised to get her a special pistol that would be easier for her to fire. Even though her fingers were long, the pistol had been very heavy.

Djaem seemed in better spirits now that they had left the training area. Raza and Uthraith had been called away to a meeting and would join them later. Scythia hummed happily as she gazed at the walls around her, following along behind Djaem.

The layout of the Citadel was an elaborate maze. There were no lifts from one floor to the next. There were long winding halls and sharp stairways leading to the higher levels. The communal eatery for those working for N.E.B. was a few levels higher, closer to the surface and the work-stations.

The path made long spirals around as they led up, and each hallway became more and more grand in design till eventually huge archways of intricate carved stone rose over long marble floors trimmed with metal pillars. The trim of the walls and floor were decorated with dramatic figures in motion, or detailed geometric shapes forming complicated patterns. The metal and stone were either the deep gray of wet slate or a mirrored obsidian black.

Scythia watched a blurry shadowed reflection of herself in the stone wall. She smiled as she looked at Djaem's counterpart as he walked away. The undefined blue face of the woman in the reflection stared back at her. Scythia grinned as she lifted her arms and swayed in a dancing motion. Her fuzzy duplicate moved in time with her, and the flashes of sparkle from the jewels seemed to be the only thing bright in the mirrored world.

Djaem's shadow counterpart kept moving through the murky depth of the stone's reflection. Scythia swayed and danced down the hall before giving a flourishing bow to her dance partner. Her heels clicked out a rapid tempo as she hurried to catch up to Djaem.

The trims of the floor and walls were metallic gold and silver. The high polish of the metals curled and swooped in intricate, delicate patterns. Scythia thought it looked as if the gold and silver were a living thing growing out of the stone, like tendrils of shine spreading out like thorny vines.

They passed through a set of carved double doors and into the inner halls. The reflective wall of black ended and changed into a massive walled atrium. On the inside grew a majestic forest. It was a window to another world. Scythia slowed as she stared into the strange, beautiful world beyond the glass.

Rich, dark dirt was thick with moss and undergrowth, and trees and plants grew so large and dense it was impossible to see the other side. She stepped closer and looked up but could not see the top through the canopy. When she touched the glass, it was smooth and cool to the touch, but the artificial sunlight warmed her skin.

Djaem took her hand and led her to the narrow door at the edge of the clear wall. The door opened with a hiss as they stepped into the completely different atmosphere created by the large green space.

Warm sunlight filtered down through the thick leaves, and the heat and humidity gave the air a heavy, sultry feel against her skin. She took a deep breath, and while there were none of the pollutants from outside, this was not the sterile perfection of a cycled atmosphere. The air was full of scents, the sweetness of pollen, the musk of dirt, and she could taste it all in the moisture of the air.

It's like my little biosphere. This is what it would be like to step inside of it. Scythia was mesmerized.

"DJAEM, LOOK!" Scythia grasped his arm and pointed towards the tree branches above them. "Look . . . I have seen those in the data crystals. The ones with feathers are Avaes, and those other ones are called Rhopalocera. They are so colorful!"

Djaem looked up and watched the feathered creatures hop from branch to branch. He had only seen a few birds in his lifetime, and none of them had ever looked like this. He felt a smile tug at his lip as he watched them. Their delicate, graceful but excited movements reminded him of Scythia.

"That bird looks like you. It's blue and has bright orange feathers." He smirked a little as he reached out to tug on the edge of her orange braid. She smiled at him before turning her gaze back up to the delicate creature above. As she followed the path to get a look at the fluttering creatures, she and Djaem moved farther into the atrium and into a small circular opening among the trees.

Djaem could see out into the hallway as they moved along the path. His vision moved past the trees to the figures walking by the glass wall. His brain captured the image of these people in painful detail. *Their floor-length black robes barely move as they walk. They must be armored.* The mark of the Emperor was stitched with real gold thread against the heavy black of the robes. They moved in silent formation down the long corridor, their faces covered with blank masks. Djaem knew who they were in an instant. Dread sent icy fingers dancing down his spine in the humid air.

The Faithful. Everyone who lived within imperial rule knew of the Faithful. In some systems it was considered a crime to not recognize them on sight. They were both the saviors and bogeymen of the imperial world. Zealots from the inner core, they served as the hand of the Emperor. They follow his order and his alone. *Why are they in the Citadel?*

Once when he was a boy, Djaem had once seen an envoy ship from a distance. He could recall the fear of those around him. *Nothing good had followed its arrival.* Fear was gripping him tight as his mind whirled and spun with the possible outcomes. Those thoughts collided, shattered, and scattered into the air as he looked back at Scythia.

She stood in the center of the atrium, reaching up towards the artificial sky. Her head was back, face raised towards the light as she reached for the singing birds. Djaem felt his heart pound rapid-fire against his ribs. A heavy pressure squeezed his lungs, making it hard to draw in a breath. His mouth was dry even as a bead of sweat tickled his neck.

With her arms raised above her head, it appeared as if she were making an offering to the heavens. Her skin was made of stolen sky, and her hair became strands of woven flame. Her suppressors only added to her magnificence. They sparkled, not from the light of the sun, but from within. Scintillating with her power, the jewels shimmered and flashed a prism of colors around her.

I can understand why so many think of her as otherworldly, a goddess walking among mortals, coming to torment and entice men.

The birds and butterflies followed the pull of her gravity just like everything else.

One bird after another hopped down into her hand. Each one made her laugh in delight as she held them gently. She whispered softly to them as they sang and popped about her arms and shoulders. Butterflies alighted upon her hair, resting easily on her still form. Their wings shifted back and forth as if breathing her in.

Djaem remained frozen, unable to move or think. The lights and colors etched themselves in the synapses of his soul. This moment would remain in his mind long after all others had faded to gray blurs. Some tiny voice in the back of his skull whispered, *Now . . . Now, I am truly doomed.*

SCYTHIA WAS unaware of Djaem's dismayed thoughts as she looked at the tiny creature singing in her hands. It was a relief that even through her suppressors she could sense the Ether here. It was muffled through the thick wall, but it was there. It sang to the Ether that existed inside of herself.

"This place is so strange. They don't belong here. The air is different from outside. Even the energy is different. Like the Ether came from somewhere else," she said in a delighted whisper towards Djaem when he finally approached. He looked a little flushed and sweaty. *Maybe the environment doesn't agree with him.*

Djaem gave her a little smile. "376 years ago, the war raged with the Illidari. This world was a barren landscape barely capable of supporting life. The Emperor ordered the Citadel to be built. It was to stand against the enemies of the Empire." Djaem moved closer to Scythia, reaching forward with slow, careful movements. He scooped a butterfly from her shoulder, his hands cupped with delicate grace. He studied the colorful wings as they moved in front of his eyes.

Scythia watched him take the butterfly off her shoulder. He was so careful not to touch its wings. He kept his hand open, allowing it the option of leaving anytime. The wings opened and closed slowly, relaxed.

"Organic material was collected from hundreds of worlds, brought to Arcem, and used to help cultivate a sustainable habitat here. As the war raged on, the other worlds died, but life here flourished under the protection of the Emperor's troops." His voice was low and soothing, as if trying to keep the delicate insect peaceful.

"The atriums of the Citadel are each distinct and complete. Memorials of the dead worlds that brought life to this one, there are over thirty-four unique atriums in the Citadel, each one containing a perfect recreation of the world lost during the war."

Scythia was drawn into Djaem's words. His voice was patient and gentle against her ear. She couldn't see his sparkling palace, but she felt it and could almost hear his music. The warmth from the sun above filled her and let her mind get lost in the slow rhythm of those beautiful wings.

"I am always amazed at how much you know," she said with wonder.

Djaem laughed, and a warm and full sound brushed like velvet against her ear. "How would I know any of that? I am a hiver; we barely know anything about our own planet, much less the Citadel."

Scythia looked up at his face in confusion. He was grinning mischievously at her. "It is written on that stone plaque over there." He motioned off to her left. She hadn't seen it because she was distracted by the birds. She grinned at him, and he gave her a little wink. "Sounded like I knew what I was talking about though, didn't I?"

She nodded, giving a little laugh back at him. "You are very clever." Scythia felt a strange pull at her chest. She stared deep into the warm brown of his eyes. She found the tiny flecks of green and gold hidden there. She liked his eyes. There in his iris, she could find little patterns distinct to only him. His face was serious and the air between them became heavy. She felt her heart kick up a bit as he stared back at her. *What is this feeling?*

THE MOMENT ENDED in the abrupt fluttering of butterfly wings. The birds took to flapping and twittering their displeasure, then scattered into the air. Djaem felt the hairs on the back of his neck stand on end. Scythia must have felt it too. Her eyes narrowed as she looked past him. He knew without looking. He could tell by her face. Dread crawled up Djaem's chest and tried to strangle him. He turned slowly to follow her gaze.

The robe figures had stopped. One of them had stepped forward to press a hand against the glass. The hand was a soft shade of purple with long and slender fingers. It was impossible to tell if they were male or female. There could be no doubt they were Star-born.

Scythia shifted to stand closer to Djaem. He knew her uncertainty matched his own. The moment stretched uncomfortably long before the hand withdrew back into the robes and the figures moved back from the glass and farther down the hall.

Djaem finally remembered how to draw a breath. *Get yourself together, man. That's a fast dig to a shallow grave.* He had learned from a very early age never to let anyone see his fear. His mentor had always been very clear. Never let them see you sweat, cry, or bleed. If they think you're invincible, they won't want to test it.

"The Emperor gains and gives life as other things die." A voice low and heavy came from their right. A man stood there as if materializing out of Djaem's nightmares. Scythia flinched back and shifted a little. *She hadn't seen him either. She should never play bluff cards.*

The stranger wore the black-and-gold embroidered robes of the other Faithful, but his hood was down. It revealed an older man with a shaven face and a bald head covered in black tattoos, the same as on his robes.

The most distinct feature was his eyes . . . or more accurately, his lack of them. His eyes had been replaced with almond-shaped chrome filler. Delicate black designs were etched into the shiny metal. They did not blink. The wrinkles at the corners of his mouth and brow were the only thing that gave testament to his age. It was impossible to tell with the long robes, but he seemed fit and stood tall with square shoulders.

"That is what the atriums are meant to remind us of. That as one thing dies, the energy isn't lost, just transferred to a new vessel. It is good that the young can appreciate them. As time goes on, some forget the meaning behind such beauty. That is why it is carved in stone. Excuse me, my team waits for me."

He gave a soft smile to them both. Neither spoke, still frozen in place. Djaem nodded and gave a smile.

"Oh, yes, focus. Thank you for the wisdom." He managed to keep the tremble from his voice and pulled Scythia out of the man's way. Djaem made sure they both bowed at his passing.

The zealot nodded to them and lifted his hood back over his head and face, moving to the glass door. Stepping through the threshold, he joined the others, and they continued down the hall.

The air came back into Djaem's lungs in a rush. He praised his stars that he hadn't said anything treasonous at that moment. He had several practically blasphemous ones pass through his thoughts today. Or worse, Scythia doing anything with her ability would have been disastrous. If the zealots decided you were a traitor, it was considered treason to argue with them. It was said that the Emperor spoke to them and through them at all times. Djaem had no interest in finding out if any of the stories were true.

Scythia was gripping his arm so tight it was starting to hurt. Djaem turned and smiled, trying to reassure her. "It's alright. Don't worry. It's time for lunch, come on."

She sighed and took a breath. "Yes . . . food. Food sounds good." They quietly left the atrium and headed to the cafeteria.

NOT CHAPTER SEVEN: COULDN'T THIS PRELIMINARY MEETING HAVE BEEN AN EMAIL?

Fallrick brought his hand to his mouth, trying in vain to suppress the huff. His huff turned into a snicker and then progressed to outright laughter.

Raza looked at him, genuine concern on her face. "Shit, Fallrick! Are you trying to get us—" Her words cut off as the buzzing from beneath her chair climbed into the audible range. She looked down to see the blue, having gone to yellow, starting to slowly return to its nice, safe, original hue.

"Sir"—Fallrick pushed through his laughter—"you don't understand the actual citizen ranking system. You are T minus 5 rated. And that's good, in a quaint and pathetic sense. I am a T2 rated administrator. In this specific field of competency, I was identified in the top one percent. Within that top one percent, I was rated within the top one percent of it. Only one in ten-thousand citizens can match my year-to-year score in public administration. As an overall citizen, I am in the T minus 0 rating, with a global assessment of utility competency within the top one percent of all persons."

"I see," the female voice from the panel answered. "It's a different scale, then? It isn't T minus, but T factor?"

Fallrick nodded. "Yes. However, it focuses on a specific field. The global competency rating doesn't go beyond T minus 0."

"Then explain," she continued, "what this means for the members of your team, exactly."

With a deep sigh, Fallrick glanced across the four seated around him. "To start, I am the only member of this team who is under-rated for it. I am the weak link and should be replaced as soon as a T5 administrator is found. You have all seen Djaem show off what makes him so unique. His ability to read people based on subtle cues . . . it reaches a point at which he can easily be mistaken for an active psychic. That, believe it or not, was only a T4 ranking. It's his ability to go without notice that makes him T5. Not to hide, but to stand in front of you and have you never even registered that he, specifically, was there."

"I understand it took several years to retrieve him," a voice from the panel remarked.

"Next, and equally unquestionably, is Scythia. While under suppression, she was able to overcome the distraction caused by the pain inducer and then fry its circuits. She was able to channel Ether flame intense enough to melt the deck plates in a spaceport without immolating herself. She is rated T4, but only because the population of psychics throughout the Empire is too low for a T5 rating to be granted. This puts her potentially in the same category as the Emperor himself."

"You dare blaspheme at a review?" The words shouted from the back of the panel chairs were loud enough to be heard over the audio suppression. All the lights flashed red.

Fallrick gave a moment for the lights to return to a pale white before he spoke again. "It isn't disloyalty. She is in the same class as he is. I never said she was as strong as him, and his competencies and experience go far beyond hers. But looking at only raw strength, she falls within the same category as the Emperor and five others. One in one-hundred million psychics are thus rated."

Fallrick paused for a moment to allow the panel to process or ask questions before he continued. "Moving on, we have the one who offers the purest physical danger through combat or—"

"Yes," a voice on the panel interrupted. "Uthraith and all of his people are deadly warriors. And what about Raza?"

Fallrick cleared his throat in annoyance. "Ahem. I was talking about Raza. Uthraith's threat capabilities make him T3. He could hand-select the hundred best warriors of his home world and still be no match for how dangerous she is." Fallrick managed to control his irritation as he waited for the rumblings on the panel to conclude.

Uthraith gave a large goofy grin as he leaned towards Raza. He curled a massive arm around her and tugged her into a side-hug. She eyed him, annoyed, and gave him a practiced jab in the ribs.

"If given a name, Raza will find the target and she will end them. Given a location, she will eliminate every hostile in it. You're all familiar with the Thryxian Pirates situation, right?"

"Oh, right," the female voice on the panel answered. "She led the team that took out their flagship."

Fallrick chuckled but managed to keep his face serious. "She was operating alone. The rest of the team was eliminated before they ever reached the ship." It took a long moment for those words to sink in and the panel to settle. Fallrick again tried to keep his frustration hidden as he waited for the murmuring to die down.

"Uthraith is an interesting one because his specialized

competencies never pass T3. He can survive a direct hit from a pylon rifle. We have vehicles that can't do that. He can hit a human-sized target at two miles with his own **PR**. He is a master of stealth and intrusion. He is very well versed in traps, small units, and theatre-wide tactics. He's actually an expert at negotiations, though some find his methods inappropriate. With all these T2 and T3 ratings, he is rated T5 in his ability to fill team gaps. To do whatever they need him to."

"Except medical," Uthraith added. "I take blood out, not put it back in."

"He's on this team more for his mind than for what people assume of him . . . but please, feel free to underestimate him more," Fallrick concluded with a touch of biting sarcasm.

"So," the female voice asked with an uncertain pace, "what does T5 look like? Why would this team deserve special exception?"

"One in a hundred get a T rating. One in ten-thousand people get a T1. Then million, then hundred million. We can't rate beyond the one in ten billion of T5 because there are too many minute considerations. Besides, the T6 community would be small, only three people. The term 'the best of the best' often refers to T1. To this team, T1 are as much an obstacle as a novice is to T1. The Will of the Emperor wanted four teams that would never fail, and so far, there is this team and one other."

The female voice spoke as the lights turned red again. "While this is impressive, it doesn't excuse what was done. Unfortunately, we can't proceed with an incomplete panel. We need to reconvene when we can fill all the seats again. For day one orders, get the new members of your team some training. This mockery will not be tolerated tomorrow."

7

DO GALACTIC EMPIRE BASES HAVE CAFETERIA LUNCHES? YES, THEY DO

THE EATING AREA was large and looked as if it could hold several hundred people at a time. It was rather empty at the moment, with a low din of noise filling the air.

Scythia sat at the table, gripping the edge as she waited for Djaem to return. He had left with trays to go collect their food from the line. He had asked her to hold the table and make sure no one else took it. She didn't really understand why anyone would try and steal the table, but she did as he asked.

Within the N.E.B. headquarters there were a number of these cafeterias and dining halls. Djaem was excited to try the different food items. Several were things he had only ever read about.

Scythia was glad he seemed to be happy. She couldn't see his crystals, so she was trying to learn to read his body language. It was much harder to do than she had originally thought it would be. Raza said it was more important to look at body language than faces. She said people lied with their faces; truth was in the body.

He returned with two large trays. Scythia's mouth

watered at the smells wafting up in the steam. Djaem grinned mischievously at her. "If anyone asks, this was for the diplomat from Kravanc 4."

She nodded and leaned forward to look at the colorful dishes. "What is it?"

Djaem shook his head. "I am not sure. I grew up on vitae-paste and occasional cloned fruits. Some of this is organic, like grown in the dirt. I didn't even know they still did that."

Scythia looked at it with wide eyes. "How do we eat it?"

Djaem smiled and straightened. "Oh, that is the easy part." He brought out the data pad and flipped through some tutorials. Huddled together, they watch the people in fine clothes and elegant styles carefully go through the instructions of the different utensils and proper manners while eating. They took turns attempting these maneuvers and encouraging each other to try again when they didn't work as advertised.

Scythia was attempting to position the delicate prongs of the eating apparatus into a chunk of tender birdlike meat when Uthraith arrived. Raza followed, and they sat in the additional seats. They shared a look and a smirk.

"What are you doing, Little Blue?" he asked in amused confusion.

Scythia looked up; her face scrunched with frustration. She huffed slightly, trying to remain calm. "I am trying to eat this. But these stupid things are hard to use."

Uthraith grinned as he shook his head. He did his best to not laugh. "Don't bother, just use a fork. Why are you having her use those ridiculous things?"

Djaem managed to use the pronged device like he was born to use it. "It's good practice to know how to use all the different etiquettes," he said, his hands moving delicately as if he had been eating at a royal table all his life.

Raza laughed and shook her head. "You look silly. Eat your food."

Djaem gave a sigh and set down the device. With a resigned look, he picked up his fork but couldn't hide how eagerly he started eating his food.

Uthraith gave no shits and just used his hands. Scythia relaxed and enjoyed her meal, trying a bite of all the different food presented. Some were sweet, some savory, others tart and bitter. She enjoyed all of them. The food crunched between her teeth or felt soft or mushy. She laughed at the things that felt gross or slippery. She enjoyed it all, even the ones she didn't like. She was just delighted by all the different textures and tastes. All the new sensations and reactions to it. Some of it seemed familiar but most was completely new.

She was so engrossed in her meal she didn't notice the grim faces of her comrades or the serious tones of the conversation. They made no effort to draw her into their doom and gloom. They silently agreed it was better for her to just enjoy her meal.

"YOU ARE NOT HEARING ME. The Faithful are here, in the Citadel."

Raza could hear the strain in Djaem's voice. She could tell he was doing his best to keep his tone even and low. *Doesn't want to upset Little Blue.*

Uthraith took another bite as he nodded. "I hear. I don't know why I should care."

Raza tried not to scoff. "Even if you did know who the Faithful were, you wouldn't care." Raza pulled her bread apart and put a piece in her mouth. She kept her face relaxed and slowly chewed her food. The soft warm bread became flavorless mush at the thought of the Faithful.

"Where did you see them?" she said as she tossed down her bread.

Djaem glanced around before he answered low to avoid being overheard. "We were in Atrium 27 at the time. One of them was there. He was older, and his eyes were full replacements. He spoke to us before he joined the four others in that hall."

Raza's lunch felt heavy as dread unfurled inside of her, taking up space in her stomach. "That's a full fist. They usually send one and his guards. But a full fist of the Faithful? I haven't ever seen one of those before."

Djaem nodded. "Do you think they are here for us?"

Raza scoffed. "For us? No, we may have fucked up but nowhere near enough to warrant the Faithful. Certainly not a full fist. They must be here for something else. But we should be careful."

Djaem nodded in agreement. "Either way, when the Faithful land, the cleansing fires are sure to follow." He took a long drink and looked down into the glass. Raza could see him replay an old memory. "Fires are dangerous on hive worlds. But when the Faithful called for the cleansing, it burned for days. No one would go to the sector after that." He shuddered and shook it off.

Raza nodded. "Don't worry, this isn't some little hive world in the Reaches. This is the Citadel. It is an intergalactic hub and the historical bastion. Even the Faithful will have to tread carefully. We just need to get through this review and not give anyone a reason to look at us twice."

Djaem looked frustrated as he leaned forward to whisper. "How can you be so calm? Even if the Faithful aren't here for the review, the review board could try to impress them and send us for cleansing or re-education."

Raza frowned and gave a sharp shake of her head. "No, that won't happen."

"How can you be so certain of that?" Djaem slowly set down his fork. Raza could feel his eyes. It felt as if he was looking into her mind. She instinctively pulled back, her face closing down.

"Raza knows. If she says so, it is so," Uthraith said with confidence.

Raza almost winced. *Sometimes your helping is anything but.* "Fallrick won't let us be sent anywhere."

Djaem raised a disbelieving eyebrow. "I am just supposed to trust him? He is the reason I am even here."

Raza felt heat rise in her chest. "No, you are here because someone in your precious hive sold you out. They turned you into the N.E.B. to save their own skin. You would have been sent to re-education or reclamation if Fallrick hadn't collected you."

Djaem continued to watch her. If he was surprised, nothing about his face gave it away. The moment stretched uncomfortably. Neither Uthraith nor Scythia seemed to notice.

"You trust him. That's unexpected coming from you. What could have he possibly done to warrant such confidence from you?" Djaem's voice was soothing and pleasant. Raza knew what he was trying to do.

"Yes, I trust him. He will take care of us because we are his team. He worked very hard to get us all together."

"Yes, did you know we are his only team? That is unusual. Normally they run four to five teams at a time. And those teams are almost never hand-picked. It made me curious, so I did a little digging. Did you know he was a cluster commander?"

Raza froze. She forced her body to remain relaxed. She

kept her face in a mask of nonchalant dismissiveness. "What's your point?"

Djaem didn't let it go. "He was a cluster commander of over half a million people. A demotion to squad leader is enormous. Why didn't they just execute him? What did he do? It must have been pretty bad."

Raza raised a brow. "You don't know what he did?"

Djaem's eyes narrowed slightly. Raza could practically hear his gears spin. "But none of this is a surprise to you. You already knew." He interlaced his fingers over his plate, resting his elbows on their side. He made a little stool for his chin as he watched Raza. "What happened?"

Raza shook her head. "You said you looked at the files."

Djaem's eyebrow twitched. "I see you don't know what happened, only that it did."

Raza felt a flash of heat in her cheeks as she leaned forward with a threatening fork. "Even if I knew what happened, I won't betray the only person in the whole damn system worth saving."

Djaem sat back in surprise. "Interesting."

Raza sneered and flipped him a rude gesture. "All you need to know about Fallrick is that we are important to him. He won't let the imperialists have us."

Djaem looked skeptical and went back to his food. Raza turned her attention back to the room. *I know Fallrick. He would do whatever he has too. Neither of us can afford to do any different.*

"Our real threat isn't the review. It's politics. At this level, the moves are petty and brutal. I have seen entire squads sent to reclamation because someone on the board was trying to hurt someone in acquisitions."

Djaem frowned. "You mean between the N.E.B and the U.L.A.?"

Raza laughed bitterly. "I thought that at first too. But

from what I have seen, the moves between those two must be strategic. They get monitored by the Capital. The Emperor doesn't like it when his organizations fight. It's bad for optics. However, infighting is encouraged. It keeps any group from growing too powerful and weeds out the weak."

Djaem considered that for a moment. If Raza had blinked, she would have missed the little smile that darted across his face. A shiver of worry danced across her skin. *Ancients save us. Fallrick, you better be right about this.*

"Well, if you want to protect him, we should find out what he is up against." Djaem said with a smile.

NOT CHAPTER EIGHT: THE REVIEW BEGINS

The tiny windowless gathering chamber in the corridor leading to the review room was simultaneously cramped and enormous. It achieved this through its dark narrow flooring and wide, vaulted ceiling. Fallrick paced as much as the limited space would allow in front of the team. His shoulders were tight, and his movements stiff. Fallrick's lips curled in, his teeth pressing sharply into their inner lining. He searched his mind for the words he needed to give to the team but was coming up short at every stop. *This isn't a preliminary meeting. They need to understand that. How do I make them listen?*

The tense silence was broken by a cheerful tone in Scythia's voice. "The training has gone wonderfully. My new instructors are so nice and I think they like me."

Fallrick froze in place, eyes going wide. His hands flexed in and out of fists as a stress line appeared on his forehead.

"Did they find Administrator Vokilsen yet? Remember, the one that was originally assigned to you?" Fallrick's voice was pinched and just a little high from trying to keep it pleasant.

Scythia blinked in confusion and looked at Djaem before she shrugged and shook her head.

"I am not sure who that is so I don't know. Did you want me to go ask someone?" She gave Fallrick a little smile, trying to be helpful.

Fallrick's head dropped into a hand, and Scythia let out a deep breath.

Uthraith and Raza shared a chuckle. Djaem had started to join in until the frustration-fueled glare of Fallrick stopped him. That look hadn't worked on the other two in years.

"Is this funny?" Fallrick's tone was razor sharp. It was clear that he was less than pleased. "Do you think the last time went well for us? Just in case you weren't aware, let me be sure there is no further confusion. It did not. They are eagerly awaiting a reason to rip this team apart, recycle what they can't use and repurpose what they can. And I can assure you, none of that is pleasant." He took a deep breath, trying to calm his speech and regain his decorum. "Alright, here is how this is going to work. You will all follow protocols. You stay within the nanobot barrier. You take the seat it assigns you. You talk to the panel with hostile respect. Most of the charges are pathetic, but some . . . some of them are rather severe!"

The four seemed to finally realize how serious he was, and they all fell silent, giving various nods of agreement. Fallrick was grateful to have their cooperation without their usual outbursts.

"When they talk, when they ask questions, you wait until they are done before you speak. No more interrupting. You contain your reactions. You let me speak whenever possible. You assume you know nothing about any of them, and you assume every last one on the panel has a personal vendetta against you. Most review panels have to be assigned because no one wants to do it. This is a completely voluntary panel, and that's never good." His voice calmed as he gave instructions. He smoothed his hair and straightened his uniform jacket.

"You heard him," Raza said, uncharacteristically free of sarcasm and defiance. "We had a good day, in so far as deflecting minor charges and getting a severely hostile member off the panel, but we set up a bad image. It's time to fix that. There are two people who aren't in a position in which seeing us fail automatically helps them; everyone else gains if this goes against us."

The harsh lighting of the waiting room shifted to a soft green shade, alerting them it was time. They exited the room and lined up single-file in front of the gray doors with the small green light above it. They waited an additional three minutes. As before, they were signaled one by one. Each entered quietly, walking within the glowing path and to the seats on a small, isolated stand. Again, Fallrick messed up, turning right after entering the chamber. Quick to correct his mistake, he joined them under the lights.

8

TEAMWORK MAKES THE DREAM WORK!

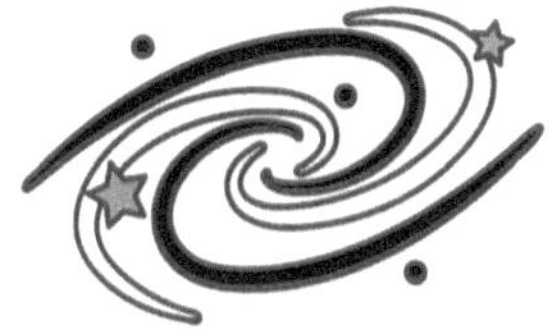

FALLRICK SIGNED his name at the bottom of the data page. He pressed his thumb on the seal square and set the glowing sheet onto the outgoing allocation pad on his desk. He took a moment to squeeze the arch of his nose and look out across his office. He rolled his neck and shoulders, trying to ease the ache that was starting to develop there. The inter-linked beep alerted him that the forms were sent. He picked up the sheet again and moved on to the month requisition reports with a sigh. *Every time.* Taking a deep breath, he reviewed the forms, searching for any discrepancies. Finding none, he resubmitted the forms for the third time. *At least the pettiness is consistent.* He knew why the resource department always hassled him with every bit of paperwork. All bureau-cracies were soulless grinds. Grudges were the gears, and favors were the only grease that kept anything moving. He had made his fair share of enemies and allies.

It had taken a considerable amount of work to get this team together. Carefully planned and timed favors so that he had the right amount of pull to get what he needed. *I finally have a team I can work with; I am not about to lose them.*

Finally finished with daily tasks, he started looking through the evidence brought forth by the review panel. He carefully sifted through the information, writing up key points that might sway the members as well as considering how he might reach them outside the review. A light flashed from his bookcase, giving warning of her approach. He carefully switched his screens to other paperwork but didn't move any other way as his door slid open.

She swooped into the room with the grace and poise suited to any noblewoman. Her imperial uniform was modified. The shoulders were decorated with her insignia and designed an inch too wide, which gave her the appearance of broad shoulders. Her dark hair was swept up in an intricate design of braids. Her hat was pinned into place. The rest of her uniform was tailored to fit her curves. She wasn't classically beautiful: her face a little too square, her lips too thin, her eyes a bit too close together. But she knew how to use everything she had. Her makeup was perfect, accenting the good and downplaying the bad. She was perfectly put together.

Her long fingers were tipped with metal claws. Augmented for weapons, they were razor sharp and according to reports, were able to secrete their own toxin. If rumors were true, they forced the victim to feel everything even as they were paralyzed.

"Good evening, Commander—oh forgive me, Squad Leader Fallrick." She smiled viciously as she sat down across from him, posing at the edge of her chair. Fallrick continued to study his paperwork, doing his best to suppress his bile.

"Good evening, Captain, and congratulations on that new rank. I put in several letters of recommendation." He kept his voice pleasant.

Her expression momentarily soured before she forced her smile back into place. It did little to improve the feel of her visit. "Thank you. Your support is appreciated, as always. I am sure you will be happy to know I intend to repay your kindness whenever possible."

Fallrick barely managed to suppress his reaction to the veiled threat. "I am sure you will be kept quite busy as a new trinary."

Her smile turned predatory as she leaned forward. "Oh, I will always find time for you, Fallrick. In fact, I will be departing soon for my new position, but I just had to stop by."

Fallrick finally set his work down and interlaced his fingers on his desk, meeting her gaze. "Oh? And to what do I owe such tremendous courtesy?"

"It's about your new little team. Just back from their first mission and already under review? That must be a new record, even for one of your teams. But it is a wonder how the panel got the information so quickly."

Fallrick smirked slightly and nodded. "Yes, that is interesting. That may seem scary for you, from what I recall of your service. However, they completed their mission and all of them returned. That is what matters."

Her lip twitched upward in a micro expression of contempt. Her eyes flashed, unable to contain her hate. She looked around the room. "I suppose it is very important for you to keep your team. As it is the only one you have."

Fallrick nodded and shrugged. "Waste not, want not. How many teams have you replaced this cycle exactly? It's so hard to keep track."

She waved a dismissive hand. "It doesn't matter; they are disposable for a reason. That was always a weakness of yours, Fallrick. You get too attached to things. I will soon command more systems than you have people."

May the old gods spare those people. "So why concern yourself with my little team?"

She looked pleased as she rose and moved to rest her hip against the edge of his desk. She leaned slightly so she was hovering over him. Her face seemed genuinely pleased, even eager, as she lowered her voice into a conspiring whisper.

"I just had to see your face when you found out," she said, dragging a metal claw across his desk. It left a tiny trail of venom in the scratch it created.

Fallrick braced himself. It was never good when Arlessa looked happy. He knew he would have to take the bait. He was ready for her, no matter what she threw at him.

"And what is that exactly?"

Arlessa's smile split her face as her malicious glee came to the surface. "The Faithful are in the Citadel."

Fuck, I am not prepared.

"WHERE DOES HE GET THIS STUFF?" Scythia said as she picked up the strange, glowing orange orb from the display shelf behind Fallrick's desk. She lifted it to her eye and looked into it. Strange little dots swirled and moved, never coming into focus. A grin broke across her face as she watched the distorted images of Raza and Djaem.

Djaem rifled through the desk, looking at files and putting them back.

Raza flicked her fingers across the data screen as she scanned them. Her voice was distant and distracted when she answered. "Most are souvenirs from the different worlds he was deployed to. Fallrick was an exceptional asset. He has been on many missions."

Uthraith was opening up little boxes and examining objects on the shelves across the room. "Yes. He was known even in the feral worlds. He was to be sent to the Capital."

Djaem paused and looked up at Uthraith. "I still want to

know how he ended up like this. A shitty squad leader in the Citadel at the ass-end of the Empire?"

Raza smirked a bit. "That depends on who you ask. There are different stories. Some say he slept with a nobleman's wife. Some say he arranged the murder of a rival. It's all shit; I think it was a political trap. It was his military record that saved him from being executed or sent to reclamation. I don't know why, or from whom."

Scythia frowned, confused by that. "Like a snare?"

Djaem smiled a bit as he continued his investigation. "No, she means a conspiracy. His enemies set him up to fail at something and then had him punished for it. Most likely, to seize his position or get him out of the way."

Scythia nodded like she understood and went back to the shelves. She placed the orb back on its stand. She moved along the shelf until her attention turned to a bizarre contraption. It had little gears and wheels inside. She searched until she found a tiny crank and lever. She carefully lifted the lever and turned the arm. A soft tinkling melody played as the gear pieces moved, making a small box open. Small figurines emerged from hidden compartments. With clockwork precision, they weaved an intricate and delicate dance.

Raza's head lifted, and she closed the data pad and went to sit down in her usual spot in front of the desk. She pulled a small stiletto knife and began to use it to clean her nails.

Djaem noticed. Scythia and Uthraith were too busy to care.

FALLRICK STEPPED INTO THE OFFICE. He stopped just inside the door, looking at the current occupants. Irritation rolled off him in a palpable wave.

"I believe I told you to not touch my things." His voice was low but surprisingly calm. Djaem looked up and closed the draw he was in. He took the file he was looking at and sat in the chair he had occupied earlier.

Uthraith remained by the display case. He had found a small puzzle game. It was made of metal with hoops and loops to detangle and reassemble. Scythia didn't seem to hear anyone. Her entire focus was on the music box.

Fallrick slid into his seat with a sigh. He quickly put his things back in order, gathering his patience and thoughts. *Can I trust them? How much should I tell them?* His thoughts were spinning. The tinkling of his music box felt soothing in the quiet office.

"The Faithful are here," Raza blurted out. Fallrick looked up in surprise. Raza was leaning forward, her elbows on her knees. Her skin was pale and her expression, tight.

"Don't worry, that means they aren't here for us. It seems they have been here for a day or so. If they were coming for us, they would have done so already." Fallrick kept his voice soothing and calm. Raza understood the dangers better than most. She had survived the Faithful's cleansings once before.

"How can you be so sure?" Raza said, her outer shell of calm holding up well.

Fallrick's smile didn't reach his eyes as he tried to ignore the horrific memories that fluttered to mind. "If we had been their target, we wouldn't have seen them before they were on us. For now, we are not their objective."

Djaem nodded. "What is their objective?"

Only the tinkling of the music box was heard for a few heart beats. Raza shook her head and started pacing the room. Djaem leaned back as he closed the file. "You don't know."

Fallrick kept his chin up as he looked at them. "No, but we will see soon. They sent a full fist. Which means whatever operation this is, it has the complete backing of the Capital and the Emperor."

"Is that supposed to make us feel better?" Raza snorted as she retrieved a water cube from the cooling unit.

"It means that whatever this is, it's massive and important. Trust me, none of us are that important," Fallrick said with a small smile. "We should focus on how their presence will affect the review. With the Faithful in house, the members of the panel are under more pressure. So, we won't be able to use our usual means of influencing the review. They may try to use our review as an example. To show that they are hard on those that step out of line."

Raza sat back down and shook her head. Djaem considered this. "If everyone is worried about sticking to the rules, what we need to do is use the rules to show we were in the right. If it was all in the name of the Emperor, there is no line they wouldn't cross. We just show that we were following U.L.A. law."

Fallrick sighed. "It would have to be very convincing, and we would need someone from the U.L.A. to back us. We are N.E.B., and you all were on a razor's edge out there with the lines."

Djaem smiled as he considered that. "Then let's make some friends."

A scoffing noise came from Raza. "That isn't going to be easy. This place runs on pure spite and pettiness. How exactly are we going to make 'friends' with someone on the other side of the aisle?"

"We find someone who has the same problem as us. We can't be the only group concerned about the watchful eye of the Faithful. We find out who else needs allies."

Fallrick nodded. "Yes. Excellent plan. I have to meet with some contacts and see if I can find out why they are here. This will give us a better idea of how to plan for it. For now, stay out of the way and out of sight. Go to your assigned training sessions and back to the living quarters. I will be in touch soon."

There was a consensus as they stood up from the chairs. As they made their way to the exit, Fallrick stopped and looked back to the display shelf. He fought to suppress a smile as he moved to stand next to Scythia. He reached past her and picked up the small music box. "Here, why don't you take that to your room? You can give it back later."

She beamed and nodded excitedly. He motioned her out of the room and watched her leave, clutching her new treasure.

He took a moment to shake off the feeling that lingered in her wake. *Focus. You won't be able to help any of them if you don't focus.*

FALLRICK SLIPPED SILENTLY DOWN the narrow corridor. He hunched his shoulders and walked tilted to fit through the space without brushing the walls. The maintenance tunnels were old and greasy. No one bothered with the meticulous cleaning that happened in the grand hallways. A distant clang gave him pause. He wasn't the only one who used these pathways. Besides the maintenance crews themselves, many of those that wished to pass unobserved walked these tunnels.

He did not pause again until he reached his destination. The heat from the pipes left a thick layer of sweat on his brow. He didn't bother wiping it away. He knew there was no point.

Stepping through the maintenance door, he was hit by the wall of hot, wet air. His hair sagged as beads of moisture collected on the strands. His skin flushed and his uniform fought to maintain its shape but was quickly losing the fight. None of this slowed Fallrick down.

The thick jungle filled the atrium, crowding out the view of the windows. He lifted the thick, flat leaves to reveal the slim path carefully cultivated in the dense flora. This time he had no choice but to squeeze past thick vines and massive root systems. The buzzing of unseen insects and other life-forms drowned out the sounds of Fallrick's heavy breathing. He knew he reached the center of the atrium when the thick roots curved sharply away, rising up overhead. They formed a kind of caged ceiling to the tree above.

As the vegetation grew upward, it created a pocket. It was a small naturally formed room with a floor made of rock and crystal formations, covered in a carpet of purple-and-emerald moss. Water dripped down from the vines and leaves above. It condensed on the root walls and flowed in tiny streams between the rocks to pull at the very center.

Fallrick would've liked this space if it weren't for the heat. He moved to sit on a moss-cushioned rock. He removed his outer coat and unbuttoned the neck of his shirt. It did little, but he felt he could breathe at least.

It took his appointment another ten minutes to arrive.

Governor Wissame Jageme finally pulled himself through the foliage. As always, he managed to look dignified and unflushed by the heat and humidity. *I bet he has one of those environmental protection systems.* The governor was quite Fallrick's senior. His hair was thinning and pure white. But despite his advanced years, he was fit and healthy. His movements might have been slow, but they lacked the stiffness or tightness that most men his age suffered from. *Those anti-age treatments really work. The rich really don't live like the rest of us.*

Wissame smiled as they shook hands. "Sorry to keep you waiting. I slipped away as soon as I could. We are all busy with this ambassador dinner. What is so urgent?" He eased down to a different rock clear of moss.

Fallrick frowned inwardly as his mind processed that response. *The governor must know the Faithful have arrived. Why isn't he worried . . . Unless he is trying to see if I know they are here. What game is he playing?* Fallrick decided to play along for the time being.

"The Faithful have arrived. I wanted to warn you. The timing is suspicious. Do you know why they are here?" Fallrick kept his tone as neutral as possible. Despite the heat, a chill of dread prickled his skin.

Wissame nodded and smiled. "I know they arrived. They say it's to oversee negotiations with the Pezsyk. It is important to the Emperor." He shook his head, but his smile never faltered as he dismissed it. "It's nothing new."

Everything is wrong with that statement. Fallrick forced a smile onto his face. "Of course. I am sorry for pulling you away from your celebration."

Wissame stood up and brushed off his outfit. "I know it's difficult for you, being cut off from the information you are used to. You were once involved in all the politics, and I know how much you enjoyed them. Someday, the Emperor will see your worth again. Be patient and do your duty." His smile was a perfect mask, completely unmovable. But his eyes were intense. They weren't full of fear. It chilled Fallrick to the bone. *I have seen these eyes before. Those are the eyes of an Immobilis.* Fallrick kept his face blank and bowed.

Wissame reached out and squeezed Fallrick's shoulder. "Don't worry so much. You are just a small fish now. You are not important enough for the Faithful to notice you."

Fallrick tried to push the fear creeping up his legs and into his torso away. "Of course, I didn't mean to overstep." He was careful to keep his tone formal.

"Don't forget what happened on Acies; I haven't." He

gave another squeeze before he released Fallrick's shoulder. It took all of Fallrick's willpower to not grab his friend and demand answers. He focused on his breathing as he looked at his friend.

"It is time for me to go, old friend." Wissame smiled one last time.

Fallrick watched as he disappeared back into the jungle. With dread dragging at his every move, he made his way back to the maintenance tunnel. *What have you done, Wissame?*

NOT CHAPTER NINE: REALLY GUYS, THIS IS SERIOUS

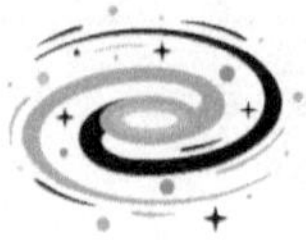

The room was the same as before. Shrouded and obscured, the large oval chairs were still circled and unlit. The panel was not yet ready to start the inquiry. It could have been that they simply wanted to force the reviewees to wait longer. It was also just as likely they were bringing the new member who replaced Kael Tinren up to speed. Djaem stared at the barely visible glints of light off the back of the chairs. His lips had moved slowly, silently forming words, when the second most excruciating pain he had ever experienced shot through his body.

It began on his right side, halfway down his ribcage, then radiated outward. It was somewhere between freezing and electrocution. His lungs refused to bring in air, his vision dimmed as his stomach clenched in agony. When the pain receded and the world returned, he made out Uthraith's voice, but he wasn't listening. His mind was trying to process what had just happened and how to stop it from ever happening again.

"Knock that shit off," Raza hissed at Djaem. "Remember? Best behavior?"

Uthraith's hand settled lightly onto the smaller man's back.

"Raza, not okay. He is not armored in his skin. Your nerve-strike hurts me." His deep tone was full of reproach. Moving his face in close beside Djaem's, he asked, "Are you alright?"

Djaem could barely manage to get air back into his lungs so he didn't bother trying to answer. His response was a simple nod. *Those simple pokes Raza uses to get Uthraith in line are very serious attacks.* As his mind cleared, it whirled with new scenarios and calculations. The gravity of his current company sank in heavily.

The lights on the lanterns flared to a blinding glare. Alarms sounded and the scent of ozone lifted into the air. Raza looked around frantically for the source. Fallrick knew instantly and gently took Scythia's shoulder.

"Scythia, Djaem's alright. Raza didn't mean to hurt him. It was an accident. Please stop what you're doing." He kept his voice soothing but firm.

Scythia's expression relaxed and her posture slouched forward. Fallrick barely managed to avoid flinching as slender blue fingers came to rest over his extended hand. Scythia smiled at Fallrick.

"I wasn't going to hurt Raza. The data crystal said that I can use my powers to help someone feel better. I just wanted to try." Her voice was bright, and her smile comforting.

"I can show you how to do that later," Fallrick replied, "but they don't want us touching the Ether right now. That's why the alarms sounded, and it didn't work."

Djaem shook his head, looking both impressed and a bit frightened. "Actually, I think it did. The numb spot . . . it turned warm." He had drawn a breath to say more, but a voice could be heard through the vocal suppression field of the panel area.

"It was bioequalization, just calm down. She couldn't—" The rest of the words were too suppressed to hear.

Fallrick shook his head, his fingertips trying to massage the frustration out of his temples. *This is not how today was supposed to start.* There was enough movement flickering from within the gloom to know that the discussion was becoming heated.

"I'm familiar with Magister Fallrick," a voice said from the panel chairs. "I've seen Raza's work. I've heard of the other two; we can begin."

The other chairs spun and moved forward. When they were settled, their movements became impossible to discern, but enough to know where their seats were. The row of indicator lights turned green. The official review had begun.

"Those words were in the record," the female voice said, "so for the record, former magister."

"Officially former," the new panelist acknowledged, "but some of us can see beyond bureaucratic nonsense and give a man of great service and sacrifice the respect he deserves."

Fallrick gave a subtle nod of his head. He used that movement to whisper to his team, "We have no allies on that panel."

"We will start with the violations of rights of citizenship," a disembodied voice began. "Any citizen of the Empire, human or otherwise, is bestowed with certain rights that none, not even the Emperor, may remove. Needless to say, these grave violations can make all other aspects of the review unimportant."

Fallrick returned a surprisingly relieved smile. "Wonderful."

"Will and determination; the team's psychic handler was identified employing mental insertion, not just suppression, on citizen targets."

Everyone stared at the elevated seats in silent disbelief. Raza finally spoke up, the confusion clear in her voice. "We established yesterday that he's not a psychic."

The audio suppressors surged for a few moments, leaving the team in an awkward silence. The team glanced between each other, waiting for the panel to regain itself. When the lights transitioned from yellow to green, Fallrick took the initiative.

"Scythia, the psychic, also attempted this act twice. With her lack of training, she didn't realize the implications. Further, the first did not have an impact on any prohibited pushes or consent violations. The victim gave over a piece of property that did not belong to them and then immediately had it returned. Upon seeing she didn't know, the team immediately counseled her."

"And the other?" the female voice from the panel asked. It was difficult to tell if the voice was modulated or if the strange tightness was from frustration.

"Scythia's other attempt wasn't a push. It was a suppression of impulse control to an extent beyond our current understanding, which caused it to have push-like qualities. While I understand the victim is still recovering in the hospital, the test results have concluded that they were given no outside thoughts. Their own thoughts became amplified to an overwhelming extent."

When Fallrick finished, Scythia added in a quiet, pouty tone, "I just wanted candies."

A different voice from the panel spoke up. "Is the handler willing to absorb the medical expenses and the expense of the sugar stolen and ingested?"

Djaem nodded, but before he could speak, Raza interrupted. "I am. Can I put some of it against her conditioning bonus?" The indicator lights went out for a moment, quickly lighting back up. One yellow, one red, four green. They blinked off and then back on, all green, indicating the request was granted.

9

WHAT A NIGHT ... UTHRAITH SHOULD HAVE STAYED HOME

THE IMPERIAL EMBASSY hall was located on the surface-city of the Citadel. It was an elaborate structure with wide entryways, curved archways, and high spires. Made of the same monochromatic material as the rest of the fortress, the design of the building turned the blocky, ridged material into flowing swoops and curved lines. Uthraith liked the wide doorways. He knew the inner structure of the rooms was as deceptive as everything that took place in them. It is a place built for lies. Hidden alcoves and curved halls were designed to allow spies to remain unseen and whispers to travel. It also allowed for the more adventurous to have privacy for more intimate meetings.

Uthraith smiled as he stepped out of the inner recess of a hidden alcove. The lovely woman catching her breath remained behind. He gave her a little wink as he finished reattaching his belt and made sure his display skulls were in place. He considered if he should leave early on his way back to the main gathering hall. Music drifted towards him from down the hallway. *Once dinner starts, I have to stay.*

He moved through the crowd. The elite throng were

dressed in their finest. Most wore the traditional clothes of their people. It was a riot of colors, textures, and designs. Some wore shear silks or heavy metals, others wore furs and feathers. Uthraith's leather battle gear was not out of place here among the many diplomats and negotiators. He was dressed as he would for the ceremonies on his own home world. His armor was fashioned from the skin of one of the most dangerous beasts of his world. He never bothered to explain that his people didn't really have a different outfit for ceremonies or the rituals. The number of weapons was the only way to discern which event was occurring.

He preferred to wear all of his gear here. He had learned quickly that the weak, pathetically soft, and spoiled diplomats were dangerous. Their words were poisoned fruit, sweet and deadly. Raza called it the viper's nest. *She is not wrong.* He had been bitten a time or two, but he had found his footing. They believed him a dumb brute, so he kept that image. He made no attempt to join in the polite conversations or use good manners. He didn't care about their threats, but his people did need him to do his duty here.

The diplomat's dinner was different: exclusive. Uthraith was the oddity there. Most nights Uthraith would not have hesitated to spend the time making the weak, squishy nobles uncomfortable. But Raza had asked him not to make the review more difficult. He moved towards the exit when a group of men slipped in front of him. A tingle of warning passed along his skin. Frustration left a bitter taste in his mouth. Lord Deculhut stood in his way. The man was fit, tall, and able. He had dark hair with a trio of scars that racked down his left cheek. Despite barely coming to Uthraith's chest, the man was a roadblock.

"Leaving so soon, Uthraith? Well, at least I will be able to enjoy my meal for a change." He sneered and the two men flanking him gave uneasy chuckles.

Uthraith's eyes narrowed. *He wishes to goad me. This is a trap. If I stay, I fall prey to whatever plot he has; if I leave, I look like I am fleeing. Fucking viper. I will kill you someday. But right now, the team needs me.* Uthraith straightened to his full height and smirked.

"Yes, you enjoy what I leave behind for you."

Lord Deculhut's expression turned sour as his eyes snapped to Uthraith. Whatever his response was going to be was cut off by a loud, perky sing-song voice.

"Yo-hello!" The cutesy cry cut through the tension of the moment as Lady Millianya Fraygar, or Milly as she insisted to be called, arrived at Uthraith's elbow. Lord Deculhut winced visibly and looked away. Milly gave Uthraith a bright smile and completely ignored Lord Deculhut's presence. *I wonder if she says it that way just to annoy him.*

Uthraith was unsure of how old Milly was. Her beige complexion had a dust of freckles and a rosy hue. Her pale pink hair had been braided into an intricate crown around her head. She wore a high-neck gown of gold and amber, trimmed with green, the colors of her clan. It fit her lush frame well, giving her an elegant but modest appearance. Her curvy frame only came up to Uthraith's elbow. Her lips were curled into a perfectly practiced smile. With her round-apple cheeks and dimples, it gave her a cute, youthful appearance. Uthraith knew she was far more dangerous than she appeared. *She is like a small fluffy creature with big eyes and floppy ears that could devour me whole at the first wrong move. I like her.* She had been an ally in these viper pits.

"Yo-hello, Lady Fraygar," Uthraith replied in a deep, respectful tone.

"I was looking for you. Would you take me into dinner tonight? My escort seems to have departed."

"As you command," Uthraith said with a slight bow, holding out his arm. She reached out and rested a hand on his forearm to walk with him towards the designated dining room for the diplomats. Her adorable smile remained in place as she looked around.

"Lord Deculhut is far too pleased with the arrival of the Faithful. He is up to something. He was downright magnanimous in a negotiation earlier today. I don't know what it is. Be careful."

Uthraith nodded as he leaned over to whisper into her ear, but the words never made it out of his mouth. As he leaned down, her scent reached him. It was a familiar scent, some plant from her home world. It was a mix of fruit and flower, both floral and sugary. She wore it often. Because he was used to the perfume, he smelt the change instantly. The bitter spice of fear hidden under the petals.

She is afraid. Deeply afraid.

Uthraith kept his own mouth shut as they took their seats at the table. He gave her shoulder a squeeze of reassurance as he pushed in her chair. His seat was farther down the table because their rank and station didn't match. The back of her hand brushed against his leg as he stepped away. He understood. *I will have to keep my wits about me. Damn . . . guess I won't be drinking the wine tonight.*

Clan Fraygar were one of the few alliances his people had. They fed most of the Empire, which included his world. Because of their shipments, his people hadn't had a starvation season since their alliance. Babies had survived and grown strong. Unlike other clans in the Empire, they had not tried to make his people dependent. Instead, they had helped his people learn to grow their own crops by bringing seeds from other worlds that could survive the harsh conditions.

Even the food eaten at the Citadel was in some way created or enhanced by the Clan Fraygar.

To keep their power and influence in the Empire limited, they were not allowed to have their own army. Uthraith didn't understand all the bizarre arrangements that kept the Fraygarian fields protected. All he knew was that every planet, kingdom, or clan they fed was obligated to help defend their fields. And everyone knew those fields were defended fanatically. Even his people sent warriors.

Uthraith had learned that the king of the system where planet Fraygar was located; had guards that were second to none. They were completely loyal to that system to the point of refusing to even serve the Emperor or the Faithful. The Kravanc people knew not to fight the Belacist. Pretty pink Milly had been trained by the only being Uthraith feared. Rosic had retired from protecting his king when he had been stabbed in the skull through the right eye. His fellow guards had perished, but Rosic had managed to use the dagger from his eye to kill the assassins. Afterwards, he went into service to Milly's family. Uthraith didn't want Rosic to think he had allowed Milly to be hurt. His planet might not survive such a thing.

Everyone settled into their seats. The diplomat next to Uthraith smiled up at him as she sat. She seemed to have recovered her composure from their encounter in the alcove. Her makeup was flawless and her hair back into place. He lifted his glass to hide the satisfied smile. He wondered if she had replaced the torn undergarments or was just sitting there without. He shook off the pleasant line of thought and looked around the room, searching for possible threats.

His eyes briefly met Milly's as she looked around the table. Her smile was still firmly in place, and he could even hear her giggle. He liked her laugh, and it sounded wrong, sharp and tight around the edges. It sent his nerves on edge. The delicate eating tong in his hand gave a sharp groan in protest as his fist clenched, bending it in the middle.

The woman next to him gasped slightly under her breath. He felt his blood rush through his body. He very much wanted to murder the people in the room. He swallowed the last of the liquid in his cup and took that moment to calm himself.

The dinner bell chimed, silencing the room as the governor and his wife claimed their seats at the head of the long table. There was a bit of ceremony at the start, and Uthraith used that moment to try and calm down. It wasn't working; his skin prickled in warning. His instincts told him danger was coming. He slipped his hand onto a weapon as he waited for the target to reveal themself.

"Good evening. I would like to thank you all for joining us tonight," the governor said in a calm, soothing tone after he claimed the room's attention.

The lovely woman to his right dipped in a bow. "It's wonderful to see you all. And looking as splendid as ever. We shall begin with—"

The loud bang of the dining hall doors slamming open interrupted the governor's wife. The table turned in unison, gasps and protests died with swift, stifled deaths. The Faithful had arrived.

The governor straightened in his seat, his expression stern while his wife, a brave woman, smiled pleasantly.

"Honored ones . . . we weren't expecting you. This is a special dinner reserved for the diplomats of the Hubb. Decorum dictates that only those with diplomatic status may attend." She gave a deep curtsy.

The five robed figures moved into the room. Uthraith had never seen the Faithful in person before. Their robes hid their weapons, but he knew they carried them. He could smell the ionized plasma. Three males and two females. Under it all, he smelled something rotten, as if they carried rotten flesh on their person. His instincts screamed to move, to run. He kept himself still, waiting. His eyes darted to Milly. Her face was slightly down, her hands folded. A pleasant but blank expression was firmly planted on her face. Her eyes darted to him from beneath her lashes. Her freckles stood out against her now ghostly pale face. Everyone was afraid. Even Lord Deculhut looked concerned.

The Faithful never altered their speed. They moved purposefully but not hurriedly. As they approached the governess, the leader lifted one hand and flicked his fingers. Two of the Faithful to his left broke the formation, moving swiftly, and took hold of the governess's arms. She let out a cry of protest, and many at the table flinched as she received a back hand for her trouble. She was quickly restrained and pulled to one side. The governor barely maintained his composure as he rose to his feet.

"What is the meaning of this?" His voice was steady and cold.

The front robed figure pulled back his dark hood, revealing a scarred face with metal-covered eyes. Even without pupils, it seemed clear he was looking back at the governor.

"The meaning behind events is never as relevant as the consequence of those events." The way the metal-eyed man spoke set Uthraith's teeth on edge. It had a pleasant and friendly timber; it was a voice that could lull its prey. Uthraith fought the urge to plug his ears. Something flashed in the corner of his vision. His eyes darted to the source. Milly shifted her simple flat bracelet again, casting a flash at him. Her face was still blank, but her eyes met his. She passed one hand palm down over the back of her other, just the tiniest of movement.

He felt something inside relax. She had more experience here, and though her skin was pale, she seemed confident. He needed to be calm, wait to see what prey this monster was after before making himself a target.

The Faithful came to a stop just at the head of the table.

The metal-eyed man smiled softly. "For example—" The blade was drawn swiftly and swung with deadly precision. A red spray crossed the table and onto the chair behind the governor. There was a heartbeat of silence before realization seemed to dawn on the governor. It didn't matter because in the same heartbeat, his head rolled from his shoulders and his body slumped back into the chair and a dark stain quickly spread around him.

Only a handful of people at the table were perceptive enough to see the strike as it occurred. Some were even able to respond. A woman fainted dead away. Several men were on their feet. Most fell back against their chairs.

These were the outliers, the inexperienced of those from the feral world. The rest of the diplomats didn't move. They had learned early to never flinch in front of the Faithful.

Uthraith realized he was gripping the edge of the table. The metal was dented beneath his fingers. He was growling low in his throat. He forced his breath to become even. Milly was looking at him. Her face was blank, but her eyes were intense. He focused on that. It helped. *How had she not even blinked?* Uthraith did his best not to look at the dead man.

The governor's wife was hauled away.

"The consequences for betraying the Empire are swift and irrefutable. The meaning behind it isn't really as important as the outcome." The metal-eyed man sighed and looked at the chair. With a second flick of his wrist, a rush of servants came from behind a wall.

There was a dizzying display as they rapidly removed the chair with the governor's body still in it. Machines were brought out, and the stain on the floor was removed and a new chair brought forth.

A voice translated from the clicks and whistles of a diplomat from the distant feral world said, "On our world, we know that we must question traitors before we execute them. The dead do not give the names of their conspirators."

The leader of the Faithful turned his metal eyes to the scaly figure. His lips curled upwards. No one would ever mistake that expression as a smile; it was a threat, a promise of cruelty eagerly anticipated. "Even death will not protect the governor from the wrath of the Faithful. He will answer our questions and reveal his allies to us."

His words settled heavily over the table as the realization dawned. Uthraith felt uneasiness pass through him. *They can question the dead. I have no doubt of it. Little Blue could do more than question.*

"Now, since the governor is no longer available to attend this meeting, I will be sitting in as interim governor. Just until a new governor of the Citadel has been appointed. I am lead arbiter of this fist. Please call me Loga." Loga smiled and sat down in the new chair.

"Something smells delicious." He lifted the blood-splattered lid of the food tray. With an excited expression, he passed the lid off to a servant. He looked down at the meal with a relaxed poise. "Oh wow, this is quite the meal. So decadent. What is the special occasion?"

There was a moment of silence as everyone at the table tried to calculate the risk of speaking, and the counter-risk of remaining silent. Lord Deculhut cleared his throat.

"The meal is usually this grand. It is how the governor liked his meetings. And Lady Fraygar was always willing to assist in providing the resources."

Uthraith narrowed his eyes as he stared hard at Lord Deculhut. *I wonder what noise he will make as I crush his limbs. He is too cowardly to bestow honor on. I would not wish to contaminate my body with his filth. I wonder how long he will last before his heart gives out.*

The thought of Lord Deculhut's dismemberment did

help improve his mood a great deal. Milly, however, was now under the direct scrutiny of the metal-eyed man.

"I see, so you provided this bounty," he asked as he picked up a fork. He took up a napkin and carefully wiped it clean.

Milly gave a small bob of her head as she looked down at her own tray. "Yes, my lord, it is our duty and privilege to feed the people of the Empire."

The man with chrome eyes smiled at her. "Well, it would be a shame to let such a feast go to waste." He nodded and all the tray lids were removed. The table was somber. "Eat up, everyone. There is plenty to go around." His voice was ominous as he cut into his meat and watched the table as people slowly ate their delicious meal. For most, it tasted of ashes.

NOT CHAPTER 10: THE GALACTIC EMPIRE ENFORCES BODY AUTONOMY. ANY CITIZEN UNDER REVIEW MAY CHOOSE EXECUTION AT ANY TIME

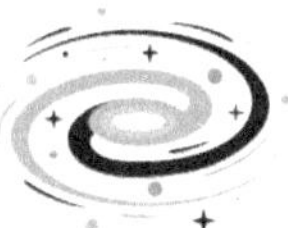

"Material deprivations, privacy intrusions . . . Why are these included? They shouldn't even be on the list," one of the voices on the panel stated.

"Actually," Djaem's voice was low and hesitant as he interrupted, "that wouldn't be an N.E.B. issue, but we are also U.L.A. I wouldn't contest them being risen. I would like to mention that all of them were brief and remediated as soon as possible. If there is a complaint from a citizen, not a collective agency or social body, I would rather answer for the charges than simply have them moved aside."

The seats of the panel members pivoted to face one another, and the audio suppression turned up. All the lights went yellow, indicating a vote was coming. One of the voices could still be heard but was too muffled to make out. Clearly, there was someone who was very angry about the little intrusions the team had done.

All the lights eventually turned green. The panel had voted unanimously.

As the chairs returned to facing the five in the tiny booth at the center of the massive room, the female panelist began to speak. "It would appear that the requisitions were all from nonindividuals and, as such, cannot be held against you. The record should note that some of the requisitions had been entrusted to individuals but were not private property. As to privacy violations, no private residence was involved in a complaint by its residents. The public location complaints appear to be little more than attempts to impede your investigation. These complaints shall not only be dropped, but purged as marks against each of you, and there may be a follow-up investigation into those who aired them."

"Next, we should discuss self-determination," an angry male voice from the panel added.

Fallrick looked at the panel, an exaggerated expression of confusion on his face. "We already established that no mind control was used. Haven't we covered this?"

Each member of the team scanned the faces of the others to see if anyone knew what was going on. It was Djaem who stopped the glancing first and started to nod. "We discussed free will. This is self-determination," he said in a hushed tone, eyes darting about as swiftly as his mind raced over the entire mission. "The only thing I can come up with is the kids. If any of those children were there willingly, we could be in some real trouble."

"Guardsman Richter Ohnsforth did not consent to being eaten," one of the panelists said after the team had their short time to prepare themselves. "As representatives of imperial enforcement, you have every right to take a life if doing so will help to advance your investigation. Each and every citizen has the right to decide permissible care of their remains. Unauthorized eating of an imperial citizen is a crime that even diplomatic immunity can't put aside. All citizens have the right to their own body and their own mind."

Every eye in the little booth turned to Uthraith, who had a broad and spreading grin on his face. The rest of the team had varied expressions. Both Fallrick and Djaem looked shocked, both searching for words. Raza was clearly annoyed but not truly worried. Scythia's face was full of a proud gratitude.

"They must understand," Uthraith said, projecting his voice to the panel, "it is the way of my people. He was given a great honor."

"An honor he didn't consent to," the female voice answered back.

Uthraith shook his head and waved his hand. "You do not understand. What are the words? He did consent."

"Your diplomatic protection will cover a great deal, Uthraith, but this may have gone too far," a different panel member added.

"Check data crystals," Uthraith said, "for both ritual and the video. You will see. He participated."

"How so?" Fallrick was too taken by his own curiosity to avoid asking a question that should have belonged to the panel.

"I drop my weapon and grab my knife. He lowers his head. I draw the patterns. He looks to my eyes. I lower my blade. He attacks. This is the ritual. Who wins fight gets to eat the other."

There was a long pause, with the panel and the team all silent. Djaem stared at the giant, wondering if the story he had just spun was made up. It wasn't like Uthraith to lie, and he gave no indications of deception, but it all seemed so far-fetched. As Djaem puzzled over it, assessing the look of pride and confidence Uthraith had, it became clear. *This psycho honestly believes that the poor guard did that on purpose.*

10

ACTUALLY, CAN I HAVE MY DINNER TO GO?

THE SILENCE STRETCHED slow and painful over dinner as everyone tried to maintain their calm in front of the Faithful. Arbiter Loga ate enthusiastically, sighing with satisfaction as he finished his plate.

"That was a fine meal. My compliments to the chef and the provider of this fine bounty. I have never had these strange fruits before. Tell me, Lady Fraygar, what are they and where do they come from?"

Milly managed to not flinch. She lowered her fork and wiped her mouth clean. "They are a hybrid berry that we have developed on my planet. We call it the Centi-berry because it's spliced from the genes of over one hundred different berries. I ordered them specifically to be brought here to the Citadel."

Loga nodded as if deeply interested. "Was it at the governor's request? Special treatment might be considered a contributing factor to his corruption. Is it not our job as fellows to help hold each other accountable for our actions?"

There was a threat there. Uthraith wasn't sure what it

was, but he could sense the dangerous ground she was walking on.

Lord Deculhut smiled faintly down at his plate, enjoying Milly's distress. Despite all this, Milly simply smiled and shook her head. "Not at all, it was for the benefit of the Empire," she said with soft confidence.

Loga's eyes seemed to narrow. Though no lids could be seen, they felt the intensity of his gaze. "How exactly would it benefit the Empire?"

Milly plucked a berry from her plate. "These were not grown on my home world, sir. They were grown here. In fact, we negotiated with the Citadel to have access to several of the atriums. They allow us to try growing our seeds in controlled environments. It gives us a chance to see if the seeds will root in other soil. If they take, then we can offer those seeds to other worlds for growing and harvesting. This gives those worlds the ability to improve their own agriculture. Feeding this food to the diplomats lets them see for themselves if the food is worth the price and effort to grow."

Lord Deculhut was now glaring at his food.

Loga leaned back, a bit surprised. "I didn't know the Fraygar were willing to share their seeds and knowledge."

Milly looked down at her plate. "There is much we try to share, though we do have our special methods that we keep to ourselves. After all, it is what helps keep my people safe."

Loga nodded and considered her for a moment before he smiled. His posture was relaxed and informal as he leaned on his elbows. He gave a little smile, putting a hand up to share some private tidbits. He acted as if the rest of the diplomats were not between them. "I have a question to ask you, Lady Fraygar."

Milly nodded and leaned forward to play along. Uthraith tensed, his fist tightening around the handle of his blade. He sensed their presence before the icy tip touched his neck.

One of the female robed figures had taken position behind him. One finger sheathed in a razor-sharp metal claw rested against his neck. In a whisper he could barely hear, she sighed like a lover, "This is the only warning you get."

Uthraith considered doing it anyway, but he remained still. His eyes never left the deadly dance happening at the other end of the table.

"You say it is your duty to feed the people of the Empire . . . even those that betray the Empire?" he asked. His body was relaxed and open. There was a tone in his voice that hinted at the danger beneath.

Milly blinked, and her carefully crafted smile faltered slightly, and fear crept in on her face. She took her time to consider the best way to answer.

In the heartbeat of hesitation, Lord Deculhut pounced. "If they are traitors, are they even of the Empire any longer? They are no longer deserving of the Empire's bounties," he said smugly as he looked at Milly.

Uthraith felt the prick of the metal against his neck as he instinctively shifted forward. He suppressed his snarl as best he could. *Yes . . . you will live a long time, little pest.*

Fear left Milly's face, as did her practiced smile—it melted into a stubborn, hard line. Her eyes narrowed as she looked at Lord Deculhut. She sat up straighter and her shoulders squared. Uthraith smiled and relaxed. *Ahh, there she is. Anger overcomes fear every time.*

"Our duty is to feed the people. All the people. We feed not just those born to the Empire but its allies as well. We feed those in the prisons and re-education camps. So yes, we feed those that have betrayed the Empire; we even feed those that actively try to harm our people. During the field wars, we fed all the armies, those that protected us, and those that attacked. Everyone deserves to eat."

She looked at Loga and waited. He watched her for a

moment. His face had grown somber as he considered that and nodded.

"Interesting. Lord Deculhut was really hoping that you would answer just the way you did. See, he thinks that will make you look like you conspired with the governor and weaken your position. He even sent rumors out about your people using dark magics and demonic rituals. He wants to use me and my people like a weapon against you. He is actively trying to have you arrested and have his allies take over your clan's control of the food supply trade."

Lord Deculhut paled and looked between Loga and Milly. His back straightened and confusion played across his face. Milly just continued to look at the robed man.

Loga watched her intently. "What should you do about it?"

Milly looked back at Lord Deculhut, and they stared at each other for a moment before she rose slowly from her seat. Moving deliberately, she walked around the long table. The room seemed to hold its breath.

When someone moved to stop her, the Faithful raised a hand, and they moved out of her way. Lord Deculhut glared at her. He waited for a blow to come. Uthraith grinned, hoping it would be brutal.

Milly stood in front of him, and with slow, steady hands, she took up a pitcher and carefully refilled his wine glass. She then put a small roll from the breadbasket on his plate.

"I will do my duty," she whispered softly before she returned to her seat.

Lord Deculhut grimaced and under the heavy scrutiny of the arbiter, Deculhut took a sip of his wine.

Loga smiled at everyone and sat back. "Fantastic! I am glad we are beginning to understand each other. So often people think that you can just whisper dark magic and the Faithful will come running. We serve the Emperor, but we aren't a mindless horde. False accusations are just as dangerous as actual traitors." He took a deep drink of his wine and gave another flick of his hand.

One of the men in robes stepped forward and with one brutal gesture stabbed a spike through the table into Lord Deculhut's hand. He let out a sharp startled cry before biting it off and closing his mouth. His face turned pale and sweaty as he tried to control the pain.

"Let's all be clear; I will root out all those disloyal to the Empire. But I serve no one but the Emperor. Anyone seeking to use the God-king's divine weapon for personal use will be considered a corruptor and persecuted accordingly." He rose from his seat and dusted his fingers.

With an exaggerated sigh, he looked around the table with a big smile. "This was fun. I look forward to the next one. Lady Fraygar, the Faithful thank you for your service, but I think it would be better if you were no longer responsible for resourcing the food provided here. Lord Deculhut will be responsible from now on. Dismissed," he said as he turned and strode from the room. The rest of the Faithful followed behind him like a flock of dark birds.

People rose and fled the table quickly in a mass exodus. Only a few lingered. Lord Deculhut was still nailed to the table, and Uthraith was waiting for Milly.

Milly sat watching Deculhut. His companions from before were nowhere to be found. Uthraith waited to see what she would do. If she were like the women from his world, Deculhut would not survive the next few minutes. *But Milly is nothing like the women from my home.*

Milly slowly moved over to stand next to Deculhut. He glared as he clutched at his bleeding hand, shaking, and sweating with effort.

"You must be enjoying this." He snapped towards her, his eyes flashing. "What are you going to do now?"

Milly just looked at him with a hard expression. And with a hard, sharp thrust of her hand, she yanked his hand upward. This forced the nail to pass the rest of the way through and unattached him from the table. He let out a shout of pain and surprise before he gripped his now free hand. Milly pulled a cloth napkin from the table and handed it to him. He wrapped it up quickly, looking at her with both surprise and resentment.

Milly sighed; she seemed very tired. "I will send the instructions you will need to provide dinner for everyone. There are many different meal requirements, and it's no small task to make sure everyone has what they need." She moved past him to stand next to Uthraith.

Uthraith watched with a slight smile. *Behold, this is duty.*

"I am ready to go if you are," she said with a soft smile.

Uthraith nodded and rose; his eyes narrowed at Deculhut. His coiled muscles rippled with taut, restrained power. His eyes narrowed in anger, growling low in his throat, as he moved towards the wounded man. His eyes never left the smaller male, and he spoke in a deep guttural timber.

"The food at the table does look delicious."

The lord paled. Everyone knew the cannibalistic rituals of Uthraith's tribe. Just as he stood towering over Deculhut, Uthraith gave a snarling cough and cleared his throat. He leaned over the quivering man. Deculhut had to sink down low into his seat to avoid touching Uthraith's torso as Uthraith reached past Deculhut to snatch up his goblet.

Uthraith downed the wine and smiled. "Ahh . . . better. Clears the throat."

With a small, satisfied smile, he turned and caught up with Milly, holding out his arm as he escorted her from the dining hall. She gave him a side-glance, and he felt her little fingers grip his forearm. There was a tiny tremor that traveled from her fingers into his skin. It caused a strange sensation to fill him. The urge to turn and murder that human-shape pile of Krugg refuse made his skull itch. He didn't speak for a long time as they moved through the halls and out the door of the great hall. He walked with her all the way to her designated suite inside the Citadel. Once they reached the door, he paused, his mind still turning over what he saw. She didn't speak on it. She smiled up at him.

"Thank you, Uthraith," she whispered softly and opened her door.

He watched her expression change as the door shut. Her eyes were unhappy, tears were forming in the corners. Confusion filled him.

She should be proud; she acted honorably and did well tonight.

He frowned at the closed door, staring at it for a long moment before he turned away. *I do not understand Fraygarian women.* He turned and walked back towards his own quarters and tried to put the expression on her face out of his mind. But even as he tried to contemplate the more important business of getting a drink, the thoughts of her expression lingered.

MILLIANYA TOOK a moment to collect herself once inside her dimly lit chambers. She walked to her bed and sat down slowly, trying to stop the shakes that had formed in her hands.

Millianya Fraygar understood the danger she found herself in. Her assigned bodyguard had gone missing, which of course meant he was dead. The governor that owed favors to her clan was executed for treason. She was alone and far from home.

She would have to be very careful. She would have to make sure she was everything a Princess of the Clan Fraygar should be dutiful, respectful, and loyal to the Empire. Kindness was weakness, generosity was wasteful, forgiveness was foolish, these were the lessons the nobility was to learn. The lessons she had always failed. Even then, as her enemy was pinned to the table, she hated his suffering.

She wanted to go home. But she knew, if she wanted to keep the cruelty of the Empire away from her people, she had to remain here.

"I need to find a new bodyguard," she whispered to the dark room. She moved to set up her private communicator so that she could send a message home.

NOT CHAPTER 11: ILLEGAL BIOMASS EXPORTATION IS PUNISHABLE BY LOSS OF CITIZENSHIP

"With no major imperial rights violations, we're ready to take a look at conduct," a male voice echoed from the panel chairs. "I think the needless assault on the station guards is a great place to start."

"The topical approach," Fallrick answered. "Very well. For the record, I am unaware of any needless killings. A team from the N.E.B. or the U.L.A. would be allowed to defend themselves when attacked or directly endangered."

"Defending themselves is a different matter. Initiating combat is subject to certain limitations, especially when people empowered by the social body are involved. And don't even start on the pursuant-to-mission nonsense: their actions were completely outside of the assigned investigation."

Fallrick nodded and turned his eyes to Raza. With a smile, she answered. "It's a shame that the guardsmen were involved in illegal activities. This would have been much easier if the people at the warehouse where the children were being smuggled had been independent civilians. As it stands, our minor secondary investigation has identified that the social body was likely uninvolved in this crime, but it could use a follow-up. Our team's psychic was following Ether anomalies and had specifically focused on fear and suffering. Our investigation brought us there."

"A psychic with a non-psychic handler," the female voice on the panel stated. "And these anomalies would be human in origin, not starting in the Ether. I don't see where this ties into your assignment. Scythia? Can you explain how and why you followed the path to the children?"

Scythia remained silent in her seat, her hands clasped and a gentle smile on her face. Even when Fallrick and Raza turned to her, she didn't speak.

Djaem gave a soft chuckle. "You told her not to speak without approval," he said to Fallrick before leaning in to face her. "It's alright now. Tell them. Be truthful and honest. Don't hide anything."

Scythia nodded, her face brightening up. "It was very bad. The entire place, the hive, it was so loud. But then I heard the crying. I could feel the fear and the pain. You know, you can feed a demon that way. I mean, by making people suffer. When I looked closer, it was like I could see them. And then I could see what happened before. This wasn't the first time. Nobody should take children from their mothers."

"She felt a human-to-Ether release," Djaem clarified, "that was similar to the ones that we had seen warp demons attempting to create. She used her powers to learn more and realized it was a human smuggling operation."

"Human smuggling isn't exactly a crime," the female voice answered. "It is illegal to sell humans between social bodies without the knowledgeable consent of all involved. Did you know there was no such consent?"

Djaem gave a frustrated sigh, shaking his head. "You missed the crime that was being committed. I'm not surprised . . . most would. Growing up in the Balial system, it's a law I'm all too familiar with." He paused, taking a few breaths to recenter himself.

"The transport, even the unwilling, of humans within a social body is completely permissible. As a part of our investigation, I had glanced at the station's manifest when we transferred our compound rights. I had noted, to my surprise, that the system had an impressive level of self-sufficiency. Their organic imports were minimal, with algal nutriments being exported as biomass exchange." He paused again. "Pull the records if you must, but that nutriment is their only biomass export. The metals and ores they export are inorganic."

"Does this argument come to a point?" the female voice asked.

"Well," Djaem said uncomfortably, "if these children were being transported out of social body, they were being excluded from the logs. If they were being transported within it, the station and transport ships would be teeming with children. As it stood, there were no children on the station, not even family of the crew. Human or not, this was illegal biomass exportation. That is a violation of the Universal Law Authority's Planetary Protection Act. Without balancing water and biomass, worlds like Balial can be made, where a self-sustaining biosphere is next to impossible. With the U.L.A. classifying this as planetary destruction, that puts it into the purview of disloyalty. Every person participating in it lost their right to citizenship within the Empire and all protections as such . . . including the one Uthraith . . . ate."

Fallrick nodded and turned to face the panel again.

"Still," the female voice responded, "this crime falls outside of your investigation. It should have been reported to the U.L.A."

"True on the first part," Fallrick said so quickly he must

have known those words were coming, "but an N.E.B. enforcer is never allowed to ignore situations of disloyalty, and a U.L.A. inspector is never allowed to turn a blind eye to a violation of universal law. It was outside their investigation, but to leave it would have been a crime in any imperial circle."

11

SELF-CARE IS THE BEST CARE

THE TEAM common room was quiet without Uthraith or Scythia filling it with noise. Djaem finally came out from the bedroom and found Raza enjoying the brief peace. Scythia had fallen asleep, tired after the long day.

He almost didn't recognize Raza. She had her hair up in a towel. She was in a fluffy bathrobe and lounging on the couch, her feet draped off the armrest. Her toes were held apart by pieces of colored foam. Raza's perfectly manicured toenails were painted in bright green with a golden shimmer. She had a bright-orange-and-green speckled mud slathered all over her face. She had a large bowl resting on her stomach. It was filled with brightly colored kernels of corn that had been heated until they expanded and hardened. Djaem had never seen corn, much less popped corn. However, he did understand that it was a snack, and this was a pampering and relaxing session.

He sighed and looked around for Uthraith, but he had not returned from whatever duty he was being forced to complete.

"So where does Scythia go to train?" he asked calmly as

he tried not to show his worry over this new development. Even when she was out of sight and resting peacefully, he found himself thinking of her.

Right now, he understood completely that their fates were entwined, and her success was his survival.

Raza waved a hand. "I will take you to drop her off tomorrow. She will get to know the mentors. Don't worry, I know them. They will look after her. They like little lost ones like her. Misfits and outcasts are their specialty."

Djaem nodded and tried to relax but found himself pacing around the room, and finally, he stopped and looked at the bowl. Raza grinned and shifted her position to an upright one.

"Bet you have never tried this, hiver," she said in a superior tone.

Djaem understood that it wasn't malicious. Barbs and insults were how she spoke. He nodded and raised an eyebrow. "Why is it brightly colored?"

Raza grinned a little. "I guess they think it's festive. It's considered cheap food here, the kind that they eat for fun."

Djaem made an annoyed face as he tried to stem the surge of anger and resentment. "Eat for fun? Food is a pastime here?" He managed to keep his tone even, but Raza recognized the secret venom in his voice. She knew it because she had it too.

"Yeah, the fucking shitbags. They have so much food that they can eat for fun. Whole worlds kept on the brink of starvation, and here, they can make different things to eat just because it's fun to eat them." Raza looked down into the bowl again and lifted a bright-blue dyed piece of popcorn.

"This one kind of reminds me of Scythia." She smirked a bit as she held it up to Djaem.

He took it between his fingers and looked at it for a long time. Anger was replaced by curiosity. "Is it fun to eat?"

Raza grinned mischievously. "It sure the fuck is. Eating and doing nothing are my two favorite pastimes." She shifted over on the couch. "Come on, hiver, let me show you what the elitist cunt nuggets have been keeping from you."

Djaem placed the piece of popcorn in his mouth carefully. His eyes widened in surprise as he tasted the salts, and fats exploded in his mouth. His stomach clenched in instant hunger and appreciation. He moved next to Raza, and she handed him the bowl so he could carefully pluck different colors. The tastes varied slightly but this satisfying crunch in his teeth and the saltiness was always there, with either sweet or savory overtones. Raza provided the perfect drink, a simple-flavored sugary syrup with added carbonation to make it fizzy. The liquid tickled and danced across his tongue, the sudden flood of sweetness making him feel light and bubbly. *She was right. It is fun to eat this. Scythia will really like this. I can see why so many rich are afraid of losing their wealth. If this is just snack food, what are the other things like? Do they bathe for fun as well?*

It wasn't long before Djaem was relaxing with pleasant-smelling mud slathered on his face, a warm towel on his head, and cooling packets over his eyes. His feet were in the soft warmth of cushioned slippers as Raza played some interactive game on the data screen.

He was too comfortable to move when he heard the door chime open. Raza's voice was a little curious but for the most part unconcerned when she addressed the arrival.

"You're back early."

Djaem jumped as Uthraith's deep grunt came from just off to his right. Fuck! *How the hell does someone so large move so quietly.* He snatched the packets off his eyes. It was far more frightening not being able to see Uthraith. At least, that's what he thought until he saw the dark look on the Murder Mountain's face.

Djaem reached out a hand and shook Raza's shoulder to get her attention off the game. She snapped at him with an angry look until she looked at Uthraith. She frowned and paled slightly.

"Back early and sober. What happened?"

Uthraith's gaze was firmly fixed out the window, his fist clenching and unclenching as his mind wandered in dark, violent thoughts.

Raza shut down the game and stood up, moving towards him. Uthraith grunted, only one word escaping his mouth. "Work."

Djaem didn't need to look at Raza to know the annoyance on her face.

Her voice was tight as she tried to keep her frustration to a minimum. "We both know you only do two things at those diplomatic events: drink and get laid. Now your monosyllabic answers aren't gonna cut it. What happened?"

Djaem watched with interest at their exchange. He was still too relaxed with his feet up. He was slowly putting more brightly colored popcorn in his mouth. His eyes darted between the two as Uthraith visibly struggled to find the words he was looking for.

"Danthmaw women don't cry!" he said in frustration.

Raza's frown deepened. "You made a woman cry? What did you do?"

Uthraith growled in frustration.

Djaem's mind spun into action, instantly connecting dots and processing the information. He gasped in excitement. "Oh, I got it! A female person of his acquaintance that he feels is under his protection is weeping. It makes him feel like he should go do some freelance work. To go do what he is best at and remove the head of whoever caused this woman distress . . . urk—"

Panic seized Djaem's voice, cutting it off. Uthraith's

massive hand grasped Djaem's skull and slowly started lifting him upward. Djaem's spine and neck gave a satisfying pop as he was stretched until he was lifted from the cushions of the couch. He didn't dare speak as he dangled from Uthraith's clutch. Though the pressure was uncomfortable, it wasn't yet painful.

Uthraith lifted Djaem till their eyes met. Djaem had never noticed the exact shade of Uthraith's eye shift. They were golden brown that shifted into a yellow-green towards the center. He also realized that his pupils were not circular but ovals that could open very wide. His voice was a low, angry snarl. "I could easily close my hand, Stickman."

There was more than just anger in Uthraith's posture.

"My apologies . . . Didn't mean to offend." Djaem's voice squeaked out in a rush.

Raza snapped. "The old ones take you! Did you forget we are on the same team? Or what Little Blue did the last time someone hurt her Gem?"

Uthraith seemed to pull himself out of the bloodlust and lowered Djaem gently, petting and ruffling his fluffy hair. "Sorry, Stickman . . ."

He took a big step over the back of the couch and sat next to a wary Djaem. He reached out and picked up a delicate handful of popcorn. Djaem watched him morosely eat the brightly colored kernels and slouch. *Fuck-n-ell, he is sulking . . . how can a man that large pout?*

His shoulders were slumped and curled. His face was drawn down into a frown, and he seemed tired.

Raza brought him an open can of beer and sat down in front of him. "Ok, what's her name?"

The question sounded calm and rational. Djaem looked at her closely. Surprise filled his mind as he considered her body language. *This is not a jealous woman, but she does seem upset.*

Djaem had expected her to be a little possessive, and he wasn't sure how she was able to keep calm about this.

It took another long moment before Uthraith finally answered. "Millianya Fraygar."

Raza's mouth fell open as her eyes went wide. "The Pink Princess Creampuff? *That* Fraygar? She has you all in a twist? Were you trying to bed her?"

If it were possible, his face became even more irritated. His expression darkened again as he chugged his beer. "No . . . protection detail. Her escort went missing."

Djaem frowned as he considered the implications. *If her bodyguard is missing, he is probably dead. I wonder if the security force will even bother looking. Back home they wouldn't investigate anything without a body.*

Uthraith continued to ponder out loud. "Maybe I bed her. Then she let me eviscerate Lord Deculhut."

Raza looked like she had swallowed something sour. "Why do we want to murder the diplomat to the clan that supplies the Empire with all their elite soldiers?"

Uthraith didn't seem concerned by this fact as he took another bite of Djaem's popcorn. "He sent the Faithful after Milly. He is threat."

Raza looked even more surprised. "The Faithful were at the diplomat dinner?"

Uthraith nodded and sighed. "I sent word to Fallrick. The Faithful executed governor. Took his wife. And his seat."

Djaem and Raza sat in stunned silence as they joined him in serious contemplation. They were lost in their own dark thoughts of the implications when Uthraith reached for the large jar of facial mud. Raza looked at Djaem, and they both watched as Uthraith sniffed the mud once, made a little nodding expression, and began slathering it on his own face.

Ten minutes later, all the three of them sat on the couch, faces covered in matching mud. They wore monogrammed fluffy robes, head towels, and the special cushioned slippers that warmed the special cream on their callused feet, eating their snacks and watching one of the many programs on the data screen.

Uthraith's robe was custom made to be large enough to fit him. The embroidery was more than just his initials. Down his back marched neat little rows of cute little insects and fluffy creatures. They were in a riot of colors and all in adorable, childish styles. Djaem was too cautious to ask.

None of them were sure what to do about the grim turn of events. There would almost certainly be trouble tomorrow. But tonight, was their night off.

FALLRICK MOVED EASILY through the poorly lit pathways of the under city. Far from the inner workings of the Citadel, the walls were grimy and ill kept. The pollution and filth of human cities had begun to wear at the edges. Those that lacked ranking, and position were regulated to the less protected edges. Little nodes of power generators kept the air flowing and lights on. But the nodes couldn't compete with the inky blackness at the outermost edges. Fallrick was traveling inward, towards the center. His plans had been disrupted twice tonight, and both times by the Faithful. Word had come over the interlink that the governor had been found guilty of corruption and treason. His wife was in custody, and he had already been taken to the death speakers.

Fallrick felt the shiver of fear spider-walking under his skin. With the governor in custody, the Faithful were wasting no time in taking control of the Citadel. He would have to be very careful until the new governor was announced. The Faithful were forbidden from holding seats of power. They could only be loyal to the emperor, and that loyalty could not be tempted by positions of title or wealth. They could hold no other office; they could only help hold the peace until a suitable replacement had been found.

Whatever Loga was planning, he would set it into motion quickly. They had started their clock. Fallrick considered his options. He was deep in thought as he rounded the corner to his private residence. He froze as he noticed the figure leaning on the wall next to his door. The tall figure was hooded in the Faithful robes, their sigils glittering slightly in the light.

He forced himself to move forward, his face a carefully blank expression. The figure didn't move as Fallrick stepped past him and went to open his door. His hand was almost to the panel when the door opened from within. He snatched his hand back quickly. The figure next to him didn't move.

From within his quarters, he heard, "You're certainly out late."

Fallrick tightened his fist as he slowly stepped into his room. He removed his cloak and moved towards the small group of Faithful that had taken a seat at his table.

"I am sorry. If I had known I was having company, I would have been here sooner," Fallrick said calmly. "Would you like some tea?" He headed towards his kitchen.

Loga shook his head. "No, unfortunately, I can't stay. I just wanted to make sure I gave you the news personally since you were friends with the governor."

Fallrick smiled softly. "I knew him for a long time; that doesn't mean we're friends."

Loga studied him for a moment. "Well, as we get older, it is important to keep ties with those that knew us when we were young." He gave a deep sigh that almost sounded regretful.

"I am sorry for your loss either way." He patted Fallrick

on the shoulder as he moved towards the door. "I just wanted to check up on you. I know the shock of finding out your friend betrayed the very Emperor you fought for can be hard. If you need anything, don't hesitate to ask. I will be keeping my eye on you and your team."

Fallrick gave a nod and respectful bow. "Yes, thank you. It is appreciated."

Loga moved easily out of the room, his back to Fallrick as he went. Fallrick sighed as the Faithful left, then slowly sank onto his chair. *This is so much worse than we had imagined.*

NOT CHAPTER 12: HONESTLY, IT WAS JUST A LITTLE RIOT . . . WE DIDN'T KILL EVERYBODY!

"As to the riot this team incited," the female panelist said, "there was substantial property damage, multiple injuries to both officials and civilians alike, and it appears to have been triggered intentionally and with the purpose of disrupting the social body."

"If we wanted to disrupt," Uthraith mused, "the explosives from the mines would have done very nicely."

Fallrick cast a harsh glare, then looked at Raza.

"Intentional, yes, and with the result of disrupting the social body, also yes," Raza answered. She waited for the grumblings about the panel to fade before she continued. "An N.E.B. team is empowered to conscript assistance from the social body when needed. When unavailable, that power extends to conscripting civilians. We had identified the presence of a fully bound demon. We had hypothesized the involvement of an N.E.B. official's involvement in its presence. It was clear that the local social body and the imperial soldiers were all taking orders from the questionable official. We couldn't turn to either for support, so we turned to civilians."

"You didn't recruit them to your cause," a voice called from one of the large oval chairs. "You incited a riot that was beyond your own ability to contain or control."

Raza grinned and narrowed her eyes. In a voice filled with enough malice to make a demon jealous, she hissed, "Given my way, this would have gone down very differently and with a much higher body count. Riots lead to damaged property and injuries. That's nothing that time won't heal or a repair crew can't fix. I was ready to just cut Uthraith and myself loose. We could have handled the garrison."

"If you did that," Djaem jumped in argumentatively, "Artos would have been gone before we could question him!"

Fallrick's glare was joined by a flash from the psychic suppression lanterns that filled the overhead. Djaem's face pulled tight, showing his anger, but he fell silent.

"Are you really trying to pose inciting a riot as an act of moderation and mercy?" The voice from the panelist sounded genuinely curious, not sarcastic.

"It saved many lives," Uthraith noted. He barely had a chance to start chuckling when the surprised groan was pushed from him. Rubbing his side, he gave Raza a look of bratty defiance.

"Swift, efficient, and only hurts the guilty," Raza said. "It was Djaem who thought this would work out better. He insisted that most of the guards and soldiers had no idea about what their boss may have been up to. We didn't know for sure yet, either, so we couldn't accuse him. It saved time, it avoided his escape, it got the job done. And, yes, it was a conscription. They weren't coerced. Just because they didn't know what they were actually fighting for is irrelevant. Now that the corruption is gone, they're all better off . . . even those the weakling spared."

"Death doesn't cost money," the female voice from the panel said. "The damages of the riots were clearly the option of the team. Medical care for those injured will be held against the social body, but the property damage is staying with you."

"Will the panel consider partial assignment? There are mitigating circumstances."

Fallrick flipped through papers, quickly scanning them. Because Djaem thought it was a nervous motion, he was surprised when Fallrick's expression showed that he found what he was looking for. He made a mental note that Fallrick was an amazing speed reader.

The five gathered in the small booth in the middle of the room watched as the lights turned yellow then green. The panel voted quickly. They would allow the damages to be mitigated.

"Reports from the guardsmen and the locals account none of the damage directly to the team. My records show that one rock was thrown, nothing more. The situation of the mining hive was already tense. One man worked them into this riot with only a few minutes of time. I find it hard to believe that this is actually their fault." Fallrick put the paper back in the stack. "They were being abused, neglected, exploited. My team changed the timetable, but they didn't create the violent environment."

Scythia nodded and flashed Djaem a look of urgency. He nodded and she immediately blurted out, "I could feel it!" She waited a moment before she explained further. "They were calm. Mainly happy. They flowed almost like water, acting on each other. Once the guards or the soldiers came around, there was disruption and anger. Djaem didn't make them fight. He made them brave enough is all."

"This is the same Djaem, rated T4 for manipulation?" The female voice sounded less than impressed with the position. "People distrust authority. That's the way of life throughout the Empire. People don't generally rise up against armed guardsmen and imperial soldiers. Unless you have something substantial, each member of the panel will assign a portion of the damage this team will be responsible for. I remind the panel that the citizens caused the damage with their own hands, so more than half is unreasonable. The average of the assessments will be the rate of assignment."

12

CUE SCYTHIA'S TRAINING MONTAGE

RAZA WALKED Scythia into a large open area within the Citadel. It was far from the main entrance and several levels down from the sleeping area. It wasn't complicated to find. The honeycombed area was attached to a major artery of the under city. Even though it was clearly marked, Raza made sure Scythia would be able to find her way both out and back in if needed.

The training hall was divided into different sections. There were areas for physical training and hand-to-hand [combat, and firearms training was in the far back, down a long gun range. There were separate sections for specialized training. Raza didn't bother with group training or the trainers for the typical guards. She knew Scythia would need someone specific. Someone who could tailor a regimen that would fit her.

Finding a psychic to train Scythia had not been easy. The list of those even capable of the task was short, and the team had rejected half a dozen immediately. Then out of the small number that remained, the answer was simple and glaringly obvious. The insane should be the one to train the insane.

She went to the hall and headed down a narrow corridor. There, just before the end of this hall, was a small forgotten room. Raza motioned to Scythia to keep up, and she stepped through the door. The room was large but mostly unlit. There were pieces of equipment that looked broken and had gone unused and unreplaced long enough they had dust coating them.

Scythia walked in and looked around.

Raza smiled and called out, "Keeva, are you here?" She looked around and sighed, turning on a light. There was a groan from somewhere behind a group of mats. A man who looked like he had been busy day-drinking lifted his head up and looked around.

"What do you want, Raza?" he grumbled.

"I am looking for Keeva. Where are they, Dolaki?"

From somewhere in a back room, Keeva appeared. "I am here. What have you brought with you?"

Keeva was tall and slender. They had rejected the long flowing robes of most of the psychics. Instead, they wore the black leather of the warriors. Their hair was cut into a sharp, flat, and angular bob around their high cheekbones. Their strong jawline framed out the rest of the face under the dark hair, and full lips rested in a perpetual downturn. They wore no extra adornment, or physical decoration.

Keeva was a very powerful psychic, once a well-respected arbiter in the Capital. Once they fell from favor, however, they were sent here. The Citadel was where those with power sent those they wished to forget. As Keeva grew in strength with the Ether, the physical world held less and less significance. Prestige, money, power, physical wealth, lust; Keeva considered those things all but irrelevant. Now there was only the Ether and that which lay beyond

The demotion was something Keeva both resented and appreciated. They had adjusted quickly. Training the misfits that were dumped into the Citadel was both rewarding and soothing for the outcasted psychic.

It was Keeva's lack of interest in the physical world, lust, and its corrupting wealth, that allowed Raza to trust them. It seemed unlikely that they would try to trick or use Scythia.

"This is Scythia. She must be in a training program by the end of the day. I couldn't think of anyone else I would trust with her but you."

Keeva stepped forward and Scythia gazed at them curiously. Dolaki pulled himself up off the floor and moved to a chair not too far away. He too was looking at Scythia through red swollen eyes. He yawned as if bored.

"Dolaki, what does this person look like?" Keeva asked quietly.

Raza smiled reassuringly at Scythia's worried expression. Scythia didn't know if she should be offended. Raza held up a hand, signaling her to be patient.

Dolaki looked Scythia over. "She is an adult psychic. Close to twenty cycles, looks like she has had the complete mind wipe, but they forgot to put anything back in. Never seen that before. The damage to her mind is recent, also weird. Basically, a big open door. How she avoided having a demon rip her in half is a miracle. There is a lot of power there but no precautions. It would be possible to train if she has any talent."

Keeva began to circle Scythia, considering her thoughtfully. "I can feel your energy. It is like standing on the beach next to the ocean."

Keeva finally stopped in front of Scythia. "Tell me, Scythia, are you the ocean or the sand?"

Scythia blinked and considered this question. Raza

silently waited and Dolaki no longer looked bored. Everyone seemed to lean forward in interest.

Scythia smiled softly as she looked up at Keeva. *They have no eyes at all.* In the place where their eyes should have been, sat black reflective shells. "I am neither. I am the mermaid on the rocks singing to the moon."

Dolaki barked out a laugh and almost toppled over. Keeva managed to look annoyed and shocked at the same time. Raza grinned a little. Scythia looked confused and looked at Raza.

"Did I get it wrong?"

Raza smiled and shook her head. "No, you did just fine."

Keeva huffed, motioning a hand, annoyed, to Raza. "Bring her in." They grumbled under their breath, "Mermaid nonsense."

Scythia nodded and followed them in. Dolaki waved to Raza as she turned to leave.

"Someone will pick you up later, Scythia. Stay here and listen to your teachers."

Scythia nodded as she followed Keeva farther in.

RAZA LED DJAEM DOWN the long hallways, past the other groups training. He was careful to pay attention to the route so he could find his own way back. They walked in a companionable silence. Djaem had learned a great deal last night. His face had never felt so clean or soft. The strange muds once again had wonderful rejuvenating effects on the skin. His hair was clean and soft as well. He decided not to paint his fingernails but had picked a lovely pink shade for his toes. It reminded him of petals of flowers. He wanted to make sure he didn't have any identifying features for people to remember. But since he wore closed-toe shoes, he had opted to decorate his toes.

The vid-dramas they had watched were very entertaining even if they were painfully predictable. It had been a delightful way to pass time. For a while he had managed to relax and not think about his many plans. He had finally heard back from the contacts he had reached out to.

They passed the many different rooms, going so far that Djaem began to wonder if they were leaving the training halls altogether. They were in the back of the Citadel, far away from the standard soldiers. He sent a questioning glance to Raza, who waved him off and walked through a heavy bulkhead door. It looked more like the entrance to a storage area.

He followed her in, shutting the door behind himself. The area looked as if no one had maintained it in years. There was broken training equipment and dust layering different sections. Raza continued on, past the forgotten and obsolete items.

Once past the obstacles, the area widened out into a well-designed and compact space. Scythia currently stood in the center. Her face and form were a picture of concentration. Another figure paced slowly around her. Tall and lean, the figure was covered in leather armor, with rows of buckles that created an indecipherable pattern.

"Hold the gate. Do not let a drop get through," the figure spoke. Their voice had changed, becoming multiple vocalizations layered together speaking at once. Human and not blending together in that strangeness of the Ether. *That must be Keeva.*

Scythia groaned under the strain of an invisible weight pressing down on her.

"Keep your walls up. It will wash you away if you don't

keep yourself together. It doesn't matter how much Ether you can move if you can't control it."

Djaem felt his body tense and a frown take over his face. Djaem was surprised to find Raza's hand holding him back. He hadn't realized he had stepped forward. Regaining his sense, he nodded and moved back to lean against a broken piece of equipment. *Get a hold of yourself. Scythia needs training. Protecting her from this is a detriment to her and us.*

"The smallest drop of Ether can power ships, end lives, and destroy enemies. It is delicate and precious. It should be handled with care, like a dancer with smoke. You slop it around yourself like an infant in a mud puddle."

A cry escaped Scythia's clenched teeth as she was pushed to one knee. Djaem shifted uncomfortably and gripped the metal edge of the equipment. He forced his face to remain blank.

"It is not about willpower; it is not about how hot you can make the flame." Keeva continued to circle, never slowing, never stopping. Djaem felt the pressure of the air become heavy and thick. "What good is it to turn yourself into a sun? What will your strength get you if you crush those you are meant to protect?"

Tears of blood flowed from Scythia's eyes as she panted.

"Hold the gate, Scythia! Not one drop. Show me you can hold it, and I will teach you to use it. I will show you how to alter the very fabric of the universe if you prove you can hold your own power." Keeva's layered voices whispered in a strange reverberation, the murmurs overlapping and growing over themselves. The reverse echo started soft and became a shout.

Djaem's heartbeat hard against his ribcage as he willed her on. *Come on, Scythia, you can do it. I know you can.*

As if she heard him, her shoulders hunched as she pushed herself against the invisible force. Djaem felt the air shift this time, swirling upward, a fog forming around them as the temperature difference collided. He forced himself to remain still, hoping Raza was right about this instructor.

The instructor's stance changed. There was a feeling of excitement even though their speed and gait never changed.

"Our first enemy we must defeat is always ourselves. The Ether is a continuation of this world, one feeding and growing the other. They are inseparable and forever entwined. Never touching, always together. We are the bridge. We are the gate. You must hold your gate. Control your flow, and you will control the universe."

Ice had started to form around Scythia's feet. Her orange hair was floating as if underwater, the strands dancing like flickers of flame around her.

"That is enough, Keeva. She has passed your test. She has been pushed enough." A stern voice broke through the thrumming echo of murmurs. A Noxambri strode in from a different room. Her scaled skin gleamed in the light, and her relaxed posture belied her well-worn battle armor. As she moved closer to the training circle, she towered over Keeva and the straining Scythia.

Keeva gave an irritated look. "She has years of training to make up for. She needs to be pushed."

The Noxambri reached out and took a hold of Keeva gently, brushing a clawed hand across their face. "You saw what they did to her mind. She has been pushed enough. She needs someone to repair her, not break her."

The thrum died down and they seemed to focus on the Noxambri.

Keeva shook off the effects of their trance and let out a startled gasp. "By the stars." They waved a hand and Scythia gasped, wobbling as the sudden pressure was lifted off her. She fell the rest of the way to her knees, slumping forward as she tried to catch her breath.

"I am so sorry. I got lost in the training. I shouldn't have pushed so hard." Keeva hurried to help Scythia to her feet. Scythia rose and looked up between them with a tired smile. "I held the gate!"

Keeva blinked in surprise at Scythia's response. There was no resentment or anger. No blame or judgment, just pride at her accomplishment.

Scythia didn't notice the instructor's surprise. Her entire focus was on Djaem. Smiling, she waved and rushed on wobbly legs over to him. He hurriedly caught her before she tripped.

"Did you see? I did it! I held the gate!"

He held her up and showered her with praise.

KEEVA WATCHED Scythia beaming at Djaem. They could see the brilliant kaleidoscope of colors pulsing with intelligence and power inside his mind. It was what Scythia had described and more. They understood why Scythia was pulled towards that light.

The difference was that Scythia hadn't seen what Keeva saw: the way the light had changed. Djaem's light had been diamond sharp, cold, calculating, and unforgiving, before it had shifted, taking on warmth and heat. It was reflecting her heat, refracting and building it within his own light.

Scythia was more than just a gateway. She was something different altogether. Keeva had never seen a psychic like this before. Scythia had to learn control before anyone came to take it from her. Keeva was certain there would be many that would try.

Keeva looked at their beloved, leaning in towards them. "She will need all the protection she can find."

Their beloved nodded without needing an explanation. "Those who find themselves tangled in fate often do."

Keeva gave a skeptical scoff. "You know I don't believe in fate." They ignored the feeling of gravity pulling them. Keeva straightened and cleared their throat.

"She needs to be here every day. She will work here till I say she is done. She gets one day a quarter cycle for rest. And, of course, whatever time she needs for the review."

Djaem nodded but kept his thoughts from reaching his face. He pulled out a cloth and carefully wiped the blood off her cheeks. She was beaming with pride as she sat on the bench in front of him. He didn't want to take anything away from her accomplishments today.

"I am hungry. Is it time to eat?" Scythia asked eagerly.

Djaem smiled back at her as he took her hand. "Yes. I know the way to the cafeteria."

She grabbed his hands and got to her feet. Within minutes, they had departed with Scythia waving goodbye at the door. Djaem was eager to leave; he didn't like the way they all stared at him.

A half-drunk voice came from the corner. "Well, that was fucking adorable. I give them half a rotation before the young lovers are both dead and–or reclaimed," Dolaki said from where he was propped up with his bottle. Keeva frowned but found it hard to argue the point.

Lehmay sighed as she shook her scaled head, her spikes rattled slightly. "You should not underestimate the power that such a thing can give you. They give each other strength and courage. They will need both. It is how we survived, after all." She said the last to Keeva.

Dolaki huffed with indignation. "You survived because I kept saving you dumb lovebirds."

Keeva smiled at both companions. Lehmay made a rattling hiss sound that was her laugh. "True, but who said fate didn't send you to do so. Maybe that means it is our job now to pay it forward to those coming after us." She made a motion towards the door with a clawed hand.

Dolaki groaned and took a long pull from his bottle. "Things are going to get rowdy with those two around." Keeva nodded but gave a faint smile. "Such are the laws of entropy: chaos is inevitable."

Dolaki smirked and nodded. "Well at least it should be a fun ride."

NOT CHAPTER 13: NEVER TRUST PASTRIES FROM THE AUTHORITIES

"The slain guardsmen are simply being counted as casualties of the investigation?" a voice from the panel grumbled.

"Be glad they aren't considered accomplices," Fallrick said, back in a mild tone. "That could get the entire social body under investigation."

After a brief pause, the female voice redirected the discussion. "Perhaps we should break. Let your team take a short rest and give certain members of the panel time to cool off. As a reminder, we are only here to find justice and to ensure fair treatment. We are never supposed to seek punishment for the team, personal vengeance, or personal gain. Thirty minutes, I think? Get some drinks, a bite to eat. We can all come back more focused."

Scythia was the first to rise to her feet. Uthraith moved with his unnatural swiftness and grabbed her calf and forearm. As the arc field discharged into her, Scythia let out a yelp, and the suppression lanterns blazed brightly again. Most of the current, however, channeled through Uthraith. He chuckled at the tingling it spread across him.

As Scythia dropped back into her chair, Raza said in a

"

rare, apologetic tone, "Yeah, breaks aren't like the close of a day. We have to wait until the nanobots show us the way out. Sorry, Blue."

All the lights on the board turned red. The observational psychic's voice hummed across the room. "I would like to speak with her during the break. That was . . . no discipline I'm familiar with. Non-Offensive. Everyone's safe. I'd register this as accidental and reactionary."

The blue glow separated from Scythia's chair and formed a path for her to walk. It led deeper into the dark portions of the room.

Djaem shifted uneasily as she disappeared into the shadow. Only the click-click sound of her shoes told of her movements after a few brief seconds. His chest tightened and he could hear and feel the gritting of his teeth. *What's wrong with me*, he questioned. *It's not like she can't handle herself, is it?*

The annoyed buzz of the nanobot swarm snapped him out of his focus on her. Glancing down, the floor had become red around him as the path had started moving off without him. Hustling to catch up, he realized the rest of his team had already moved ahead, barely visible on the path to the door. The protocol monitor stationed by the door was a tall, slender woman, likely Star-born like Scythia. The woman watched Uthraith pass with worry in her eyes, but she gave a very mild smile at Djaem's approach.

"Don't worry," he said to her. "The big guy probably doesn't even remember it anymore. He's more reaction than action."

The woman nodded. "Hostility to the facility is unacceptable. Your assurances are appreciated." Her voice was so level, evenly paced, and devoid of inflection, it sounded more like a synthesized voice than ones that were actually digitally produced.

"As is your service," Djaem said, giving a pleasant smile.

When she looked up and made eye contact, he let his worries go. It was a simple success on an insignificant task, but it reassured him that he still had control over something.

Abruptly snapped out of his distraction, Djaem yelped as Raza yanked him the rest of the way out of the room.

"Ain't time for flirting."

She dragged him the rest of the way to the tiny waiting room. Fallrick and Uthraith sat waiting for them.

"Djaem," Fallrick said, not even waiting for the two to settle in, "I need your insight. The other panelists . . . What can you tell me about the woman? Is she friendly towards us?"

Djaem smiled. "Absolutely not. She's a Drop Marine. I would guess captain or above, but I can't narrow in on it specifically. She served in at least one live dive operation. Seeing an N.E.B. team burn would be more satisfying to her than anything else."

Fallrick nodded. "I was suspicious of her disposition, but I couldn't figure it out. A Marine. That explains it. And if she knows who I am—"

"She does," Djaem interrupted. "Both you and Raza, but she seems to have more spite for you than for her. I don't know what you two did to her specifically . . . but I don't want to know, either."

"That's the opposite of good," Raza said. "I'll get rid of her."

"No!" Fallrick shouted reflexively. Raza's playful snicker followed. "There are ears everywhere. You can't joke like that right now!"

"The new person is attached to the colonial morale at one of the social bodies, no idea which one." Djaem moved on, denying the two a chance to bicker. "I haven't been able to identify the N.E.B. or the U.L.A. sit-ins. Should be one of each and one of either for this one."

Fallrick shook his head, a growing smile on his face. The door towards the exit opened, and a man stepped in with a tray of tea and donuts, but even the unexpected arrival didn't break Fallrick's moment.

"What a fantastic talent I've found," he muttered.

"What from the Ether is this?" Raza picked a cup off the tray, rising to her feet. Uthraith gently touched her arm.

"The facility sent it for you," the man replied. "Organic, too. Very unusual."

Raza looked at Uthraith and relaxed her expression. With a nod, she put the cup back on the tray and sat down. Without another word, the man tapped the wall and set the tray on the shelf that extended, not even waiting for it to stop moving. Before Djaem even got out, "Thank you," the man was at the door. He didn't slow down to even respond.

13

AND THAT MY FRIEND IS CALLED 'STALKING' AND 'MURDER.'

"OF COURSE, I COMPLETELY UNDERSTAND." Milly smiled and gave a respectful nod as the door to the private conference room opened. The ambassador of the Nakruim system stepped out of the room ahead of her and left swiftly down the hall. She kept her smile in place until the last of his entourage disappeared. Then a worried frown wrinkled her brow. Her fist clenched as she took a long moment trying to pull her emotions into line.

Someone is sabotaging me. I thought it was bad luck, but for this many things to go wrong all at once—no . . . someone is actively working to make me look bad. She had been dealing with one emergency after another. First, it was the entire shipment of cracais fruit spoiled in a malfunctioning cargo freighter. Then, there was some glitch in the system that caused an entire shipment to be rerouted, along with manifests mistyping, and raiders stealing cargo; and now there was someone else undercutting the price of planting seeds.

The U.L.A. and Citadel security still haven't been able to figure out what happened to Pexiale. *It's been two days. Would Lord Deculhut be this bold?*

She let out a slow breath and headed down the hall toward her room. She had to go untangle that rerouted mess. She paused only once to look over her shoulder. She still couldn't shake the feeling that someone was watching her. The hallway behind her remained empty. She shivered as the hairs on the back of her neck stood on end, and her instincts screamed for her to flee. She put a hand on her hidden weapon and slowly moved down the hall. She saw nothing out of place, but she knew something dangerous was near, just out of sight.

SHE WAS CORRECT, of course. Uthraith watched her move past him, close enough he could have touched her. *Her instincts are good. Raza is right: she is well trained.*

A predatory smile curved his lips as he waited to move, continuing to follow her as he had since she left her room early this morning. He moved in silence, avoiding the detection of not just his prey, but the surveillance cameras. He had watched her deal with one problem after another. And though her face was always smiling, he could see the tension in her movements. He could smell the chemical reactions of her anger and frustration. He was glad she was returning to her room. He had already been inside and made sure it was secure. He had removed the secret monitoring devices he had found. Once he knew she was secure for the evening, he would find out who had put them there.

Uthraith listened to her door close and put his sensor above her door. It would alert him if she left again. He had slipped one onto her person earlier today, but this would allow him to know if anyone else tried to enter her room. Her quarters were safe enough for now. He would do his best to make sure her routine wasn't disrupted. Her job was very important, but he had places he could hide her if it became necessary.

Satisfied that his self-appointed charge was secure, he headed out in silence, looking for the unfortunate soul that had put the monitor in Milly's room.

HIS PREY MOVED with the confidence of a seasoned warrior, passing quietly beneath his hidden perch in the dark walkway between the buildings. Their den was at the end of this path. They had thought it a safe location because it only had one entryway. Silly creature. What it really meant was that they had no means of escape. The man smelt pungently of alcohol, women, and food. He was alone now and sober. Uthraith could smell the chemicals of his weapons. He was armed and had the natural caution of a hunter. Uthraith grinned as he waited. Maybe this would be fun after all.

Uthraith shifted slowly, lowering his legs till they touched the ground beneath him. The man reached the entrance of his small den. Uthraith felt his muscles straining, eager to be in motion. His blood rushed heavily in his veins, he could smell everything, and his vision was sharp in the near darkness. Uthraith knew the exact moment his prey became aware of the danger. The instinct that told prey a predator was near finally surfaced.

It didn't matter; it was far too late.

Uthraith was impressed at how quickly the man responded by pulling a weapon. He even managed to pull the trigger before Uthraith had him. It was completely ineffective, but he was still impressed. He dragged his prey into their own den to do his bloody work. He didn't want to be disturbed.

DJAEM WALKED ALONG BESIDE RAZA, and they returned to their personal quarters.

"Thank you for your assistance," he said as he carried the large packages through the door.

Raza shrugged and gave him an annoyed expression. "I don't understand why you couldn't just take her with you." She stalked into the main room as the door shut behind them. *Can't even admit you enjoyed shopping.*

"We both know if I let her pick her own clothes, they would be brightly colored, sparkling monstrosities. It's much better for now if someone else picks her outfits. I don't have the knowledge or the eye for women's fashion, and you have a keen understanding of the fashions and know how powerful the right outfit can be." He gave her the praise required to mollify her.

It worked, and Raza nodded. "Well, that's true. Tomorrow, I will show her how to do her hair. We can't keep letting Uthraith do it."

Uthraith's voice called out from the kitchen area. "What's wrong with how I do her hair? She looks like firebird with her hair like that."

Djaem set down his burdens and looked in. "Yes, but we are trying to make her look less fierce, not more. We need to appeal to the board. If they think she is wild and dangerous, it will make it that much harder too—"

Djaem stopped mid lecture as he looked at Uthraith and Scythia in the kitchen. Scythia was helping scrub pieces of Uthraith's armor. The sink was filled with bits of red-smeared gear.

"What are you doing?" Djaem's voice was deceptively calm.

Raza appeared next to him and angrily shouted, "Who was that? It had better not have been that ambassador from last night!"

Uthraith held up stained hands, palms up. "No, no, I won't be giving him such a quick death." He turned back to Scythia. "It is important to make sure you get little bits out of crevices. Or smell will remain. This can be useful at times to throw off some predators but can attract others. It also will damage gear over time."

Scythia nodded seriously as she watched his hand motions and mimicked them.

Djaem squeezed the bridge of his nose as he tried to ease the pressure building in his head. "We are in the middle of a review, and you are eviscerating random people?"

Uthraith's face took on an offended, almost hurt look.

Scythia piped up. "Not random. The man put monitoring devices in Princess Milly's private quarters. Uthraith had to find out who was behind it."

Uthraith's face brightened into a smile, and he patted Scythia's head. Neither of them noticed the bloody handprint he left there. "Thank you, Little Blue."

Djaem took a deep breath to calm himself. "And that couldn't be accomplished without the evisceration?"

Raza just held up a hand. "Don't bother, Uthraith does what Uthraith wants, because he can. Besides, he has immunity to the review." She rubbed her temple, seeking patience. "Well, Uthraith . . . did you find out who was behind it?"

Uthraith shrugged. "I find clue." He pointed to a data pad on the counter.

Raza sighed and walked over, taking up a rag to wipe off the blood and viscus from the screen. "Fuck's sake, Uthraith. Why are you always so messy?"

He just shrugged and went back to cleaning. Djaem

curbed his irritation and put the packages in Scythia's room. He returned quickly to try and extricate Scythia from the whole exchange.

Uthraith laughed and shrugged. "He was bleeder. You find clue on next dead man."

Raza made a growling noise of displeasure in her throat as she broke the security encryption on the data pad. Djaem made a mental note to get better security measures on his own data pad.

"So, you're saying that this man put monitors in Princess Creampuff's quarters," she said as she quickly searched through the electronic contents.

Uthraith nodded as he finished rinsing his hands. "Yes."

Raza looked almost smug. "Well, you're an idiot. Because according to what I have here, this guy was working for Lord Hessamir. That's Princess Creampuff's betrothed. He probably hired him to make sure Little Pinkie wasn't having sex before they tie the noose." She huffed and continued looking through. "See, they want to know where she is going and with whom. It looks like they have been watching her for a while now."

Djaem frowned as his brain started to roll with that information. "Can I have a look?"

Raza nodded and handed over the data pad. "See, you just made a mess for no reason."

Djaem scanned the messages, the crease in his brow deepening with every swipe. "Well, maybe not without reason." He sighed with irritation. "This is what I get for not minding my own business." He held out the data pad to Raza. "Did you read the messages? It seems they are working with Lord Deculhut. They kidnapped her escort."

Raza snatched the data pad with a frustrated sigh. Uthraith just looked smug as he cleaned off the last of the blood.

Raza let out a string of profanities. "They can't really be stupid enough to believe this nonsense."

Scythia looked over her shoulder curiously. "What?" Raza let her read it and Scythia snickered. "They think she can summon and control demons?" She grinned as she considered that. "Hey, do you think I could summon and control demons?"

Raza snatched back the data pad and pointed a finger at Scythia. "Don't even joke about that! Djaem!" She looked at him with a frantic look.

Djaem smiled and shook his head. "Scythia, darling, don't tease Raza. It's not nice. That would get us into a great deal of trouble if you summoned anything. We would be executed for treason."

Scythia nodded and smiled, though she looked mischievously at Raza and wiggled her fingers. Raza sighed and shook her head. "You are a brat, Blue."

Scythia giggled and went to get a snack out of the cupboard.

Uthraith looked at the data pad. "I kill those two and fix."

"No!" Both Raza and Djaem shouted in unison.

Raza threw her hands up. "For one thing, that guy is her fiancé. He is to be her husband. The other thing is that he's a high-ranking official that comes from a powerful, noble family." She looked at Uthraith's face. His expression didn't change. And after a moment, she let out her breath, looking defeated. "Ok, ok! I will help you. But we don't just go around killing high-ranking nobility. That is how we all get executed or reclaimed."

Djaem sighed and nodded. "Fine. I will see what I can find out about these two. Maybe there is a way to get out of this without getting reclaimed."

Scythia grinned and put a cookie in her mouth. "Yay! See, Uthraith, I told you they would help! We are a team!"

Raza and Djaem shared an exasperated look.

NOT CHAPTER 14: DON'T EVER LET THEM KNOW THAT YOU KNOW . . . YA KNOW?

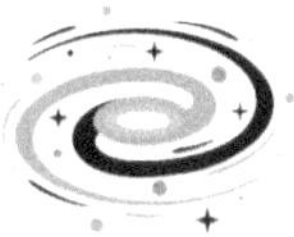

"We have to be clear about something," Fallrick said, grabbing one of the donuts. "The Faithful are not our friends, but they put a lot of pressure on the panel. I think their involvement benefits us."

"But it could also kill us," Raza added nonchalantly.

Djaem nodded. "How do we use that?"

Fallrick drew a heavy breath and let out a long sigh. "I'm not sure. I was hoping you could come up with that."

Djaem nodded, smiling. "Listen, I don't really know anything about the Faithful. I've never been off my planet before. Even there, I was nobody. If you could fill me in, maybe I could come up with something."

"Hah!" Raza blurted. "Nobody? Djaem, we did our research. We know who, or rather, what you were. Don't play innocent over there, Mister Familia."

Djaem gave her a puzzled look, then turned it to Fallrick. Rolling his eyes, Fallrick explained: "It's an old term used by some of the organized crime figures. You're not even twenty years old, but you had a full criminal network established:

fences, strong arms, extortionists, hit men, purchased police, thieves. All sorts, really, we know." He smiled again and leaned closer. "We know why your competition was so afraid of stopping you and had to turn to the N.E.B. We also know you've been working at setting it back up."

Djaem's eyes darted to the door. Slowly, they pivoted back to Raza. "On the Citadel, there's so many people, so many different regions, I could just fade from existence. You'd never find me here. Nobody would."

"Ha! Blue would." Raza chuckled. "Time to settle a bet. I put five lux against Uthraith that you let us find you. Were you trying to get out, trying to expand, or just messed up?"

Djaem laughed. "You all overestimate me. The real bosses back on Balial were no joke. I was honestly nothing more than a negotiator, working the gaps between the different families." He let out a sigh. "I think they were all afraid I was going to pick a favorite, and that would make them the winner. Better they all get rid of me than risk being one of the losers, right? I knew it was coming . . . I just couldn't stop it."

Fallrick nodded. "Truly amazing. It's almost enough to get me to push aside the facts that I know to be true. You really sound like you believe that." He looked to Uthraith with a nod. "You won. She owes you five."

"But he was lying," Raza protested, giving Djaem a friendly glare.

"The Faithful," Djaem said with an air of impatience. "What can you tell me?"

Fallrick grabbed a replacement for his missing donut and leaned back against the wall. "They're imperial. They don't answer to any law you or I know. If they kill you, it proves your disloyalty, as does you hurting one of them. They answer to the Voice of the Emperor and the Eyes of the Emperor.

"You almost never see them," he continued. "If they are visible in a location, it means something big is happening. If they were here for us, the review would already be over. Most people at the higher ranks seem to believe they take an interest in the review panelists. They make sure that the Will of the People stays in line with the Will of the Emperor."

Djaem nodded as he listened to Fallrick finish speaking. Djaem closed his eyes in thought, forehead creasing with his concentration.

"Two of the panelists got quiet after it was known the Faithful were here." Eyebrows scrunched together more as Djaem tilted his head. "Our Marine girl isn't worried about them, not at all." He pursed his lips for a moment and then started silently mouthing words. "The guy with the commerce fleet is worried"—Djaem's eyes snapped open and he looked full into Fallrick's—"about the Empire's current involvement in a major military operation."

Raza's mouth dropped agape. "What the hell was all that?" She gave a scoff. "And as far as I know, the Empire is only involved in the usual conflicts in the Reaches. A couple uprisings from some of the inner hives."

"Why do you say that?" Fallrick followed.

"Just . . . just the way things are lining up. So, if they're nervous, we have to put the pressure on them. Challenge their competence, loyalty, and reasons at every turn. Ask them questions, Fallrick. Act like they're the ones on trial."

Fallrick nodded and pushed the last of the donut into his mouth. "Normally that'd be high risk, but if you say it's what should work, I'll try. Just let me know if you see the signs changing. Oh, and Raza? Don't hit him like that." She looked at Djaem and then to her hand. She turned a puzzled face to Fallrick as he continued. "You can get away with it with Uthraith, but he's damn near bulletproof. That little jab you gave him; I don't want to see that again."

Realization lit up her face and she snickered. "Don't worry, Boss. You won't 'see' it again."

14

CUE DJAEM MONTAGE

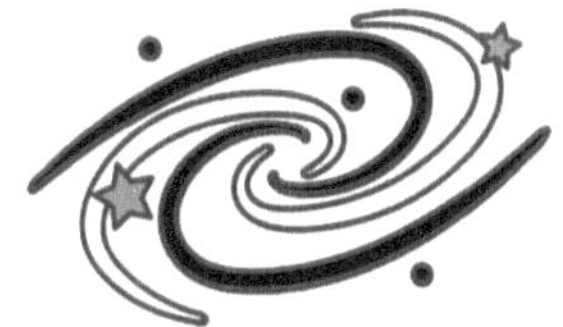

DJAEM GLARED AT HIS TARGET. Every nerve in his neck and arms grated and burned. His frustration churned and curled in his chest. Again and again, he tried squeezing the trigger. His target remained unfazed at the end of his line. His hits were getting closer but never touching the infernal circles. Over and over, his shots went wide. He tried breathing out, breathing in, squeezing the trigger gently, yanking on it hard. He tried one hand then the other, then both. He could see the scorch marks all around that human-shaped outline. Djaem ground his teeth. He didn't know what he was doing wrong. He was following the instructions. As his frustration grew, so did the distance between his shots and the outline.

Scythia had fired all her bullets and was currently getting a lesson on how to reload.

"This is ridiculous. I am fine with blades," he spat out. Djaem knew he was being petulant, the embarrassment at his own ineptitude growing.

Scythia came over and patted him on the shoulder. "You are already doing much better. You can do it."

Uthraith bent down to look Djaem in the eye. "If you hit Artos with gun, no need for knife."

Djaem winced as the memory of pain flashed across his bones as he recalled that moment. He grumbled and turned back to the target. He squeezed the trigger again, breathing out as he did so. A scorch mark appeared just outside the outline of the figure, closer than any of his previous shots.

"You are overthinking." Raza's tone lacked her usual biting condescension. She took up a position to his left. "Scythia, go with Uthraith and learn some hand-to-hand." Scythia followed Uthraith to the other side of the training facilities where mats had been set up.

Djaem turned his focus back to Raza. "Overthinking?"

Raza nodded slightly and took up a position behind him. She lifted her arms on either side of him, invading his personal space. Her instructional tone was at odds with her physical position.

"Yes, your mind is on the target, the weapon, the breathing, the aiming. It's even on the wide-open distance between you and the target."

Her breath tickled his ear a little as he kept his eyes on the target. Her body was pressed along his back and hip. The tightness in his shoulders relaxed as he felt the closeness of another body.

"Clear all of that out. Focus on the target. Nothing else matters. Relax your body. Now, imagine something you hate."

"Like this training exercise?" He kept his tone even and low. He was able to roll his neck and shoulders. Raza's proximity helped him block out the empty space surrounding him. He rolled his neck and shoulders again, forcing the muscles to loosen and relax.

Tread carefully, Djaem. It's another strand of her web.

Raza smirked even as her voice carried a heavy seriousness. "Imagine someone you wish was dead. See them instead of the target."

Djaem pictured Artos standing there in his uniform. Djaem's mouth curled into a cruel and confident smile. *There it is . . .* Under the fear, the helplessness, he found it, the hate and rage. *That man had called me a flea, broke my bones like toothpicks.*

The source of his nightmares, the face that haunted his dreams. Djaem's heart picked up speed. Artos flashed in his mind, a set of twin sunrises burning out his eyes. Djaem's hand clenched and something buzzed, vibrating his fingers.

He blinked and the flashback disappeared. His vision cleared and he saw the scorch marks had finally made their way into the lines. It was still a scattered mess, but within the lines.

Raza nodded her approval. "Well, it's a start. If you don't let go of the trigger, you will damage the gun." Her tone was low and surprisingly soft.

Djaem realized the continued buzzing was from the firing mechanism on the energy pistol. When he overfired, its safety protocols had locked the trigger. This kept it from overheating. He forced his finger off the trigger and set it down. "I see."

Raza didn't look at him as she set up a different pistol. Lifting it, she fired rapidly and in a pattern. "You should alternate your rapid fire with single shots. This will allow the relays to cool and recharge so you can continually fire. There is also the option of overcharging. It isn't good for the relays, but they won't burn out right away. You half pull the trigger, so it warms up, and when you depress the trigger, you get a bigger blast."

"Yes, I see that." Djaem knew she was overexplaining to give him a moment to collect himself. He didn't waste it and shook off the trauma response.

Raza pressed the button to reset the targets. "It will get easier. That battle was brutal. And the way he died would have shaken anyone. Even Uthraith was taken aback." She fired a full load at the new target before she finished her thought. "I don't blame you for being freaked out. I keep dreaming that she is dancing while she burns the world around me in blue fire."

Djaem watched Raza as she spoke and pulled the trigger. *She thinks I am afraid of Scythia . . . because she is afraid of Scythia.* He looked at the new target and considered it for a moment. *I should be afraid of Scythia; she is the one that could destroy us all.*

He reset his target as he masked his inner confusion. *I am not afraid of Scythia . . . not even a little bit. Maybe I have gone mad.* He listened to Raza's instructions and took up the stance with the rifle. He did better this time, not taking as long to start hitting the edges of the target.

Raza and Djaem both froze as Scythia's squeal of laughter filled the air.

Uthraith had her lifted over his head and was swinging her around. He spun and did a rather impressive maneuver where Scythia landed on her back on the mat. However, Uthraith had made sure to put his arm in the way to make sure she wasn't hurt. Raza's face turned angry as she put her pistol down hard and started towards the training mats.

"That isn't training, that's playing. If someone attacks her, you think they are going to treat her gently?" Annoyance made her voice sharp and hard.

Unfazed, Uthraith shifted his weight, a predatory gleam filling his eyes.

Raza froze, her eyes narrowed.

"No . . . No!" She snapped her mouth shut with a click. Uthraith was already moving.

He moved forward, low, and fast. Raza seemed to blur as

she jerked and flipped over his charge, landing in a dancer-like motion back on her feet.

Scythia watched in wide-eyed amazement. She had made it up onto her elbows on the mat. Djaem moved himself quickly out of the way. He moved in a wide circle and pulled Scythia to her feet and off the mat. They assumed positions on the sidelines.

The two professional predators circled each other until the amateurs were clear. They both were smiling. The air took on a tension that Djaem could feel.

The all-out melee began between one blink and the next. There was a whisper of clothes and the thud of a powerful hit on the mat. No other sound could be heard, not grunts or heavy breathing, just a silent dance of death.

She used his size to his disadvantage, slipping through the gaps in his personal space. He compensated with his speed, closing those gaps as fast as she could make them. Djaem realized he was tracking her moves, learning the pattern so he could anticipate her next move. Djaem realized this about two heart beats before Raza did.

For her, it was too late. Uthraith grasped her leg as she slid past. His massive hand pulled her towards him, trying to entangle her. She bent in an impossible angle, using the tension his grasp provided to lift her into position. She rapid-fire jabbed his face and then his underarm. His grip loosened and she freed herself, darting out of reach again.

Uthraith grinned as he crouched. Raza grinned back and gave him a wink.

Djaem watched the silent communication between the two combatants: the daring taunts and counterthreats. *They aren't trying to kill each other, but they are putting their all into this fight . . . What happens if their instincts take over?*

Djaem wasn't certain when they had gotten weapons. It was nearly impossible to follow all their movements as they traded blows. Djaem's mind spun, filling in the possible actions and reactions. He watched with rapt attention, predicting and calculating. He had completely forgotten about Scythia.

Raza gave a startled scream as Uthraith roared. They jerked violently; their graceful movements turned into a spastic spasm before collapsing to the mat.

Scythia rushed forward and put a foot on Uthraith's back with her arms raised in the air. "I win!" The massive stunner was still in her hand as she cheered. Uthraith was the first to recover and laugh.

"Yes, Little Blue, you win. I shouldn't have taken my eyes off my opponent."

Raza groaned but smirked as she got to her feet. "Ok, fair. You win. Come on, it's time for lunch."

Djaem smiled at Scythia's beaming expression.

"Lunch!" She quickly helped pick up and put away the weapons. After she was done helping, she grabbed Djaem's arm. "Gem! It's time for lunch!"

He nodded and patted her hand. "Alright." He followed along behind Raza and Uthraith.

No, I don't fear her, not even a little. Perhaps that is the most dangerous thing about her.

As he walked with her, he considered what he could do about it. After a few steps, he shifted his focus. *Since I cannot fix that, how can I use this to my advantage?* He did his best to ignore the little voice that whispered back, *Do you really want to?*

NOT CHAPTER 15: NOBODY PUTS LITTLE BLUE IN A CORNER

The four returned to the review chamber with all the pomp and ceremony they had shown before. While approaching the booth under the lights, Djaem slowed, his eyes scanning the room. A distressed crease appeared on his forehead and the confident smile melted off his face. Even under the lights that made it impossible to see out, he continued to scan.

"Something wrong?" Fallrick asked. "We need to focus, and besides, they really don't like it when you try to overcome the security measures."

Djaem simply lifted his hand, middle and index finger in an almost straight position that was clearly supposed to convey some message.

"Ma es'gah rhea'ipu, Uthraith?" The alien words had barely left Raza's mouth when the snicker that followed them came. The unfamiliar communication grabbed Djaem's attention, and he snapped an annoyed glare at her.

"Easy, lover-boy," Uthraith chuckled. "Blue is with good people. She is safe. You stop your worry."

"One of our team is missing, the review session is about to start, and you two are full of jokes?" He intensified the displeased look at Raza. "And it's not like flower-wine. Did you forget I'm responsible for her?"

The laughter quickly faded as Uthraith and Raza traded shocked looks.

"He speaks Tokaweran?" Her voice sounded genuinely distressed.

"Both of you, stop!" Fallrick barked. "No. No, he doesn't. He figured out what you said. And if you think about it, he got it wrong. Can we focus here?" He turned to look Djaem in the eyes. "She was pulled aside by someone trusted enough to be security at an N.E.B. hearing. Whatever paranoia you have spinning around in that head of yours, stow it! They can't address anything she is involved in until she returns."

"Be still," a dismissive voice ordered from within the darkness. "Your panel now returns."

All four turned their eyes to where they remembered the chairs being. When they began to move and the back light came on, the vote panel flared up with all lights red. One by one, they turned green.

"We are prepared to dismiss one of your members," one of the voices stated. "It seems the charges he was named in only call for additional education."

Fallrick's smile grew, and he croaked out, "This is good. If one goes, all charges are weak." Djaem noted that his lips parted but didn't move. Even his throat barely shifted while he formed the words.

"Uthraith," the female panelist took over, "you are to be trained on bodily consent. We are not monsters here. It is understood that you thought he was participating, but to violate the rights of the body is unacceptable. The body and the mind are the possessions of the individual citizen, even if they are enslaved. The thought of losing that is one no imperial would ever stomach or tolerate. Fortunately, the family was understanding."

"So," Uthraith called out, "this charge has been cleared?"

"No," she answered. "Not entirely. While the family has accepted this as an accident, we would be derelict to let it go without taking steps to avoid any future accidents. Your mandatory education profile has been updated. With that, however, you may go."

Uthraith nodded and leaned back in his chair. He swung his massive arm across the back of Raza's shoulders. The blue glow formed on his chair and started to create a path towards the doorway. As it moved, Raza leaned forward to break direct contact with the giant.

As the buzzing started, one of the panelists spoke, "You have been dismissed, Ambassador. You are free to go."

With the first of the arcs shooting up into his legs, Uthraith nodded. "I think I stay. This is my team. I do not leave my team, especially when there is danger."

The nanobot swarm that formed the glowing path quickly rushed back to Uthraith, stopping the arc cannon from reaching a more powerful discharge.

"You were not asked, you were dismissed," the female voice called from the panel. "This hearing is without an observer and without a witness. No persons, regardless of station, are to be admitted."

"Then do not admit me," Uthraith chuckled back. "I am to be stopped from entering. I understand."

A burst of words came from Djaem as the flashes from the electrical arcs lit up the area around the booth. The words, not intended to be spoken, and barely formed, were "There she is." It was enough to get Raza to look, spotting some of the blue features as the momentary lights reached Scythia.

"Once admitted," Fallrick addressed the panel, "a diplomat can only be dismissed for cause. That would present an entire hearing all in itself and would risk harming our alliance with his world. I see no reason he can't stay."

A heavily synthesized male voice from the panel answered, "He's absolutely right. He knows his universal law. Since this panel is governed by both sets of rules, we have to let the ambassador stay."

15

SO DOES THIS MEAN WE ARE FRIENDS NOW?

FALLRICK LET OUT a grumble as he rubbed his chin. He took a moment to contemplate the report in front of him. His network of spies had been hard at work. The one-page report was disheartening. If anyone knew what the Faithful's purpose was here at the Citadel, they weren't letting on. *Looks like I will just have to wait and see.*

He sighed as he looked at the steam rising from his mug of tea.

"I don't know," he said finally to the man sitting on the other side of his desk.

Lucias arched a brow as he took a sip of his own tea. "You don't think it will work?"

Fallrick picked up his mug and shrugged. "Oh, it's an excellent plan. However, the problem is I don't trust anyone."

Lucias smiled and nodded a little. "Yes, that is the wisest course of action. I don't trust anyone either. However, you can trust my ambition. I have been trapped in the post for too long. If I don't make a move, I will live and die in mediocrity. I have already sacrificed too much to end up here; I need to make my moves while I am still young."

He took another sip, and a sneer marred his handsome face as he spoke. "The youngest child of the higher ranks must be sent to the Conclave while the older child goes into the military. My sister has become a sentinel and is rising through the ranks. Here I am, buried alive in logistic nightmares and bureaucratic bullshit."

Fallrick considered his words. *Most don't get assigned here unless they come from token houses or have offended someone. So, what did you do, Lucias?* It was pointless to wonder. Lucias would never tell.

Lucias' mask of contempt never wavered. Fallrick knew he played the arrogant noble because it was what people expected to see.

They had been competing for long enough to know. Lucias was far more than he appeared. In this place, a rival was the closest thing you could find to a friend.

"How is the training for your new weapon going? I hear she is working with Keeva. Excellent choice. They are the most experienced combat psychics in the sector." Lucias' tone was nonchalant. Fallrick knew a probing question when he heard one.

"Raza made an excellent choice." he matched Lucias' energy.

A comfortable silence filled the space between them as the pleasant scent of their tea drifted upward. Lucias smiled faintly into his cup. "Did you ever dig up any dirt on me?"

Fallrick shrugged. "Even if I had, I certainly would never speak about it. That is just bad manners."

Lucias let out a chuckle and looked around the room. "You still have that thing?"

Fallrick gave a curious look and opened his desk drawer. He reached in and pressed a button, activating a special device. It was designed to create a small bubble of interference. It meant that all the listening and watching devices couldn't hear them.

Lucias closed his eyes and concentrated. Fallrick knew he was using his psychic abilities to create a pocket of protection. It would keep those that could listen in the Ether from spying. It was as close as they would ever be able to come to having a safe place to speak.

"It has been a while since we did this." Fallrick said in a low whisper as he relaxed in his chair.

Lucias sighed and leaned back. His whole demeanor changed. His arrogance slid off his shoulders like a heavy blanket. His face lost its practiced blankness. He sighed and leaned against the table and looked like anyone else with a world of responsibilities.

"Over the years, you and I have scratched and fought each other many times. Sometimes I win, sometimes you win, but there has always been respect. I do not want to have to deal with someone new." His face was serious and more than a little tired.

Fallrick nodded as he pulled a small bottle of alcohol from his bottom drawer and poured a little into both their cups. Lucias smiled and picked up his mug. After a click of their mugs and a long pull, he sucked in a breath through his teeth.

"I heard what happened on hive colony IX47326. More importantly, I heard about Artos. I met him once a long time ago. He was a middling psychic from a small house. He didn't have much power to speak of."

Fallrick had never seen Lucias like this before. *If this is a ruse for something, it is a totally new approach.* He wasn't sure at all what to make of this development. He nodded and motioned for him to continue.

"Artos must have been in league with someone. He didn't have the resources or the backing to set this all up on his own. Either he had very powerful friends inside the Empire, or he was getting help from outside the Empire," Lucias said as he leaned forward. His voice was very low as if even in this bubble, he still felt he might be overheard.

Fallrick looked down at his spiked tea. *I might need something stronger.*

"He managed to hide the presence of a Tyrling nest. Even summoned a full one into being. He seemed powerful enough on his own." Fallrick managed to maintain his calm whisper.

"That is my point. Artos did not have that kind of power. With time and training, any psychic may learn finesse and control over their power. They can learn to manipulate it to serve any purpose. But there is no way to increase their raw power, no matter how long they train, a rank 5 cannot train their way to a rank 1." Lucias shook his head and gave Fallrick a pointed look. "You know that better than most. Even if Artos used crystals to have the power needed for summoning, the monster would have consumed him long before it was able to be bound."

"So, one of two things happened; he discovered a means of increasing his raw power or someone else summoned the demon for him," Fallrick responded with slow consideration.

"It would seem more likely that a more powerful psychic was using him to gain a foothold as well as a foolish patsy." Lucias leaned back slightly, relaxing a little.

Fallrick frowned and took a long pull from his cup. *There is no point in arguing. Lucias knows more about psychics than me. I should focus on the physical world.*

"Inside or outside, whoever they are must have a long reach. Where did they take the children? Where did the supplies go? How did he get so many of those crystals?" Fallrick found himself also leaning in to continue the whispered conspiratorial conversation.

Lucias shook his head. "I don't know. The materials, including the children, are likely sold off in the black markets by now. But the crystals and the power are something we can track."

Fallrick nodded. "Even if all that is true, and he had a trainer, and they were using him, it doesn't matter. This is way beyond our jurisdiction."

Lucias nodded and looked eager. "That is true, but your new team was able to uncover his actions and put a stop to it. Right now, you are in the shit. If I help you, I can get your team out of this mess."

Fallrick frowned, leaning over his mug, and feeling the heat rise up around his face. "Why would you want to do that? I thought you would still be angry about Scythia putting you on the floor."

Lucias snorted and shrugged. "Oh, I had wanted nothing more than to return the humiliation. However, when I heard about her battle with Artos, I realized she might just be powerful enough to help me reach my goal. If I help you, you help me. We both get out of this star-forsaken pit. We can go back to one-upping each other later."

Fallrick scoffed and nodded. "Oh, she is powerful enough, but why should I let you play with my new weapons?"

Lucias smirked and leaned back. "Because without me, you might not get to keep your weapon very long. Even if she agrees to wear the suppressors, there are whispers that someone higher ranking is looking to take control of her training."

Fallrick stiffened. "If that is the case, how would your help change anything? If the higher ranks want to take her, there isn't much we could do about it."

Lucias nodded. "Maybe, but if we get those reassignments, they must go through the chancellor. And that requires a review by the Oracles. Those take a long time, and that would put whoever was trying to take control under a great deal of scrutiny. If they are trying to use back channels to get her, they wouldn't want that kind of attention."

Fallrick considered that. "If we get them on a special joint division, then they would be protected from reassignment as well as the review panel. That still leaves the question of how to get them into a special joint division."

Lucias' face broke out into a smile. "I have managed to get an assignment to investigate what Artos was up to, where he got the crystals, and how he managed to summon a thrice-bound demon. I am allowed to organize my own team."

Fallrick blinked in surprise. "How did you manage that?"

Lucias grimaced at the unpleasant memory. "You don't want to know that. And it's irrelevant. Are you in?"

Fallrick frowned as he considered that. "How do I know I can trust you? Why would you be willing to do this?"

Lucias sighed and looked frustrated as he considered what to say before looking Fallrick dead in the eyes. Anger flashed across his face as he said quietly, "I had a son. When he was five, he was taken for testing. He didn't survive the training."

Fallrick gaped, almost spilling his tea. "I didn't know you were married. I thought being from a noble house helped."

Lucias sighed. "I am not married, and even if I was, my children would still be tested. They are supposed to go to specific training. Noble children aren't supposed to die during their training. It was a 'fluke,' an accident."

Lucias' hand gripped his cup hard as his whole body clenched. "I know that isn't true. I will find out what happened to my son. But to do that I have to keep moving up in the U.L.A. This is a way to fast-track that option. We will always be rivals, but this isn't about that. This is about getting closer to the person responsible for my son's death. I will do whatever I have to."

Realization dawned on Fallrick as he thought over their years together. So much of his behavior made much more sense now.

"Alright then, Lucias. Let us form our alliance and move us forward."

Lucias smiled and relaxed, nodding. "Excellent." He snapped his fingers. His arrogance returned as he stood up. Fallrick took a deep breath and pressed the button, turning off the sound suppression system.

He smiled as he sipped his tea. He put in a message to summon Djaem to his office. Leaning back, he contemplated his options. "Yes . . . this just might work. Now we are getting somewhere."

DJAEM SAT in the chair that Lucias had occupied and considered the development that Fallrick was discussing.

"Do you think he will keep his end of it?"

Fallrick nodded. "I do. He has much he is trying to achieve. I don't know what he did that got him assigned here, but I am sure it had something to do with his son being taken."

Djaem nodded and smiled. "That is very useful information. I will make sure that Scythia is secured until we can get this moving."

Fallrick nodded. "I want you to see what you can learn about who is trying to get their hands on her. How's your network going?"

Djaem smiled. "Not a problem, sir."

RAZA FROWNED as she looked at her empty container of cosmetics. It was a liquid that she used as the base coat of her makeup. It was almost completely empty. She sighed as she knew immediately who was responsible. After all, it wasn't like Uthraith was worried about his complexion. She left her bathroom and headed into Scythia's room.

Raza understood that Scythia was in a state of sensory discovery. Without being able to see in the Ether, she was forced to learn about the physical world. Raza had been helping Scythia with relearning the many aspects of being a woman in the physical world.

Djaem could teach her many things, but there were just things men didn't understand. Scythia was curious by nature and asked endless questions. Raza admired Djaem's patience and seemingly endless knowledge.

She didn't bother knocking and just stepped in. Scythia was sitting on the floor, her whole face slathered in the beige liquid. It was uneven and blotchy, but she had layered it on heavily to cover her robin-blue skin. Without any color correction, it came out looking sallow and unhealthy. But she was staring at herself in the little mirror with an intensity Raza had rarely seen.

"What are you doing, Blue?" she asked, confusion replacing the anger she had felt. Raza had learned to redirect Scythia's questions by asking her own.

Scythia gave a guilty smile. "I just wanted to see." She tried again to smooth the blotchy makeup.

Raza shook her head and moved to sit down next to her. "You know that you are beautiful. What are you trying to see?" Raza winced, picked up one of the makeup-remover cloths, and started wiping the mess off Scythia's face.

Scythia frowned a little, looking down. "Djaem and Uthraith said I can't help because I don't blend in. I stand out too much. If I wasn't blue, maybe I could go with them and help Princess Pink puff."

Raza laughed. "Don't call her that, ok? Only I get to call her that." She considered the issue and then nodded. "I can see why you would think this could help. It might be useful to figure out how to hide your coloring. But even if we dyed your hair black and covered your blue skin, it wouldn't matter."

Scythia frowned and held still while Raza wiped her face. "Why?"

Raza smiled a little. "Because you are almost as tall as Uthraith and are covered in sparkling jewels. You are unique, and there is nothing wrong with that. There is power in standing out."

Scythia started to help clean her own face as she listened to Raza. "There is?"

Raza nodded and looked at the other stolen makeup. "Of course. Just as it can be useful to blend in and disappear in a crowd, being able to command the attention of everyone in a room is useful too. It means that you can help those trying to blend in. It means you have power over others. People will listen, respond, and give respect."

There a few minutes of silence as Raza helped prep Scythia's face. Once cleaned and primed she pulled out shades that would work to enhance rather than conceal.

Raza smiled as she started Scythia's makeup. "There are few things more powerful in the universe than a woman that can command the attention of those around her. A woman who understands her own power and knows her worth is a force to be reckoned with."

Scythia held still as Raza applied something to her eyelids. "Like you?"

Raza smirked. "Yes, like me. What makes you strong isn't

just your psychic abilities. Just like me. It's not my knives or guns. It's knowing yourself. Your will, your confidence."

She finished accenting the shape and color of Scythia's eyes with liner, adding a touch of color on her lids that joined the contrast of orange and blue. Raza left a bit of sparkle on the edges. Then, putting just a touch of gloss on Scythia's lip, Raza smiled.

"You will never blend in. No matter how you try. You will never be like any other Star-born, or anyone else. Don't shy away from that. Own it, flaunt it. Let everyone that sees you know that there is no one else like you. They will be in awe and fear. That will give you an edge like no other."

Scythia smiled and sat up straighter. "Someday, I will be as powerful as you."

Raza had to look away from the admiration she saw shining in Scythia's face. She did her best to ignore the growing warmth in her chest. There was a painful ache in her heart as the voice of her long-dead sister echoed those words from a distant memory, the faces and moments over-lapping inside her mind.

Ah, Fuck . . . No. No. No. She is a weapon, not my little sister. Get a grip, Raza. Don't get attached.

"Raza, will you show me how to do those braids like before? We have to go to the next review meeting. I want to show them, so they will stop trying to bully everyone." She looked at her with those big eyes.

Scythia was far too clever and learned at a frightening pace. *Let men think she is weak and needs protection. I will make sure that she understands how much power she has in just a smile.*

Raza paused as she realized how proud she was of Scythia's progress. She groaned and rubbed her forehead in frustration.

Raza clenched her fists as she realized it was already too

late. *Fuck it, then. I guess I have a new little sister. I suppose we are all doomed now. Well, at least she is hard to kill.*

She gave a little smile. "Sure. I will show you how. Let's knock their socks off."

Scythia considered that for a moment. "Won't we have to knock their shoes off first?"

Raza laughed and nodded. "Yeah, those too."

NOT CHAPTER 16: NOTHING IS AS IT SEEMS

"Eren-et'hi Dja'ehm ki-ki'a mo lienivenne?"

Djaem barely shifted as the voice from the panel spoke in a strange alien language.

"Ee. I'enden rielle va—" It had taken him several seconds to realize what had happened. The great trickster had been tricked. "I . . . am ready," Djaem abridged in the common galactic trade-tongue.

"I was afraid of that," the panelist hissed. "Even more reason he can't be trusted. And he's the one responsible for the greatest amount of damage!"

"We will be calm," the female panelist said in a mildly scolding tone. "For those who don't understand the language of the demon-tainted Ether Life Forms, the question from the panel was 'Are you ready to face your own actions, Djaem?' His response was 'Yes. I own every,' with the rest of the sentence being untranslatable due to the multiple tiers of conjugation." The area around her egg-shaped seat shimmered for a moment. "Djaem, this is a rare language to speak and even more rare to have your name be in it! How can this panel trust that you aren't an E.L.F. spy?"

Djaem looked to Fallrick, who was staring back at him in shock. Closing his eyes and shaking his head, Djaem explained, "Balial wasn't always such a wonderful place to be." The thick sarcasm filled his voice as he made one of the most retched non-correctional hives in the Empire sound like paradise. "When the Svarda occupied it, they kept the humans intact. One of my ancestors was Dja'ehm, or disobedient slave, due to his incessant attempts to spark an insurrection. My family has worn the name as a badge of honor ever since. As to why we keep the language, if you review the civilizations list, you'll see. Our value to the Empire is less than most uninhabited worlds. Everything of any worth was stripped away long ago, and now we only remain because the Empire insists we be allowed to survive as long as we are independently able. Just like before, when my home world gets in trouble, the Empire won't even bat an eye. When the Svarda or the Lafui return, we'll know what they're saying."

"Phah. And we're supposed to just believe that?"

The look of rage at the panelist's words hadn't even fully finished twisting Djaem's face when an unfamiliar voice chimed in from the right of the egg-shaped chairs. "There is no deception in his mind. I pick up anger, conviction, disgust, and pride. Based on what I'm sensing in him, I have doubts as to his commitment to the Empire, but his hatred of the few enemies that we have is much more intense." There was a brief pause before the voice resumed. "The psychic Scythia is unable to exert the same control over her abilities as most psychics. She developed most of her talents instinctively. She is only now learning to shape them and limit their flow. She is capable of manifesting in ways outside standard imperial doctrine. For these reasons, the Eyes of the Emperor will not permit the charges of excessive use be held against her. These words are backed by the detachment of Faithful here on the Citadel."

The groans from several panelists rose above the suppressors. There was an awkward pause lasting more than a minute. Fallrick assumed they were discussing amongst themselves. He took the opportunity to give Djaem one of his own observations. "The Faithful aren't on our side, but the panel has more to fear from them than we do. Their presence has gotten noisy recently. Use this."

Djaem nodded but didn't talk as he saw the shift in the chairs that had always come moments before the female panelist spoke.

"She has been enrolled in training and is being assigned an ongoing personal coach," she said plainly. "This panel is satisfied with the proactive work done in arranging this. She is to remain under constant suppression when in populated spaces and is subject to imperial recall."

The voice from the right gave a mild objection. "Under suppression, she is building up . . . it's like pressure. When she leaves a suppressed state, there may be unintentional manifestations."

The panel fell silent for a short time and the voting lights came on. Quickly, they changed to showing green. A very hasty vote found them all in agreement without need for more discussion.

"The risks are understood. We will leave it to the handler and the coach to help minimize the risk. With that, we are closed on this matter."

"To be clear," a male voice sounded from the chairs, "that is for her part. We haven't finished with Djaem."

16

THE CANNIBAL AND THE CREAMPUFF

MILLY MOVED through the halls with a quick, deliberate step. She felt it again. The sense of someone watching her. She rested a hand casually on the edge of her hidden weapon. The blade was small, well honed, and would cut through almost any armor. Years of training helped her stay alert and take many precautions. Many assumed that her plump figure meant a life of idleness and decadence. They didn't understand that under her lush curves were muscles that came from years of hard work and dedication. *I may not be able to see you, but you will regret any move you make on me.*

She turned another corner, leading her would-be stalkers toward her ambush point. She was careful with her speed to not alert them, casually greeting those she passed. Milly smiled, keeping her pace purposeful but not panicked. She led them along a carefully thought-out path, waiting till she could loop to a new direction. Before stepping off the path, she waited for her stalker to follow. Milly kept herself hidden in the deep shadow of a stack of crates against a corner wall. She coiled tight like a snake. As the figures passed her opening, she flashed a strike. The low heel of her fancy shoes made contact with the back of the largest one's knee. She hit her mark, sinking her heel into the tender tendon just behind the knee.

It brought the giant man to his knees. Milly wasted no time shoulder checking the thinner man into the wall as she spun out and stabbed her blade into the soft spot just under the ribs for the larger man, angling up towards the diaphragm. She felt the hit but heard a strange sound as a huge hand slapped her wrist. Her fingers instantly went numb, and the blade glittered as it skittered away down the hall. She brought her other hand up for a strike at the massive man's throat. It was caught a hair's breadth from its target.

"Milly!" Uthraith's pained voice came from the face hidden in shadow.

Realization dawned and horror filled her. "Uthraith!" she gasped, all the fight leaving her. *I've killed him . . . Oh god, I killed him!* A kind of panic took over. "By the stars! Uthraith! I've stabbed you. Oh no! Oh shit—hang on . . . I will help you." Panic took over her movements.

Uthraith bent over at the waist, holding his side over the wound.

DJAEM PICKED himself up off the ground, his shoulder throbbing in protest. It still ached from when it had broken from the last time he had shoulder checked a pillar. He certainly hadn't expected the princess to fight like a street brawler. He looked over to where the pink-haired royalty was frantically fussing over his companion.

Djaem looked over at the blade that had come to rest next to him. *What kind of blade would be able to hurt our Murder Mountain? He was shot in the chest by a sniper rifle.*

He picked it up carefully, studying the blade. It was shiny and had a small chip at the piercing tip. *There is no blood. Good. I was worried he would have to 'honor' the princess . . .* Djaem shivered in revulsion.

Djaem stopped and examined the blade again, considering its shiny surface. His gaze shifted to Uthraith's bent form still holding his side. Uthraith's face was twisted in pain as he rested on one knee with Milly trying to examine his injury. She settled for helping him to his feet. He leaned heavily on her much shorter frame. She pulled off her shawl and handed it to him so he could push it against the wound. He took it gratefully as she 'helped' him to sit on one of the crates.

Djaem fought the smirk off his face. *Clever dog.* He moved over to where the two were arguing in low voices.

"What were you thinking? I could have killed you!" She scolded him as she looked at his knee that she had kicked. Djaem looked over her head to Uthraith.

"See, I told you this was a bad idea, Uthraith." He smirked as he held out the blade handle first. "My lady," he said with a deep bow.

She quickly took the blade, and it disappeared in the folds of her clothes. She gave him a tight smile and looked Djaem over. "Are you alright?"

Djaem gave a nod and rubbed his aching shoulder. "It's nothing more than I deserve for causing you any worry, Princess Fraygar. Please accept my deepest apologies." Still bent low at the waist, he waited.

She sighed, still irritated but mollified. "Well, as long as you realize that I don't appreciate being followed around without my consent. You both scared the life out of me."

Uthraith grumbled. "Obviously not all the life." He gave a pained expression. Djaem raised an eyebrow as he righted himself.

"Oh, yes. How is your wound? Should I fetch a surgeon?" Djaem asked with a little smirk.

With Milly's back towards him, he gave Djaem a warning gesture before returning to the wounded bear facade as she turned around.

"I can't believe you followed me. I told you I was fine." She scolded Uthraith again.

Uthraith shook his head. "No, you aren't. You are target, you need protection."

Milly sighed in apparent frustration. "You can't be my bodyguard. There are rules. You are an appointed ambassador. There are all kinds of implications if people think I am playing favorites."

Uthraith made a face. "I don't care."

Milly groaned and rubbed her face. "Well, that is obvious, but I do care. There are many people counting on me here. I can't just decide to ignore protocol because I feel like it."

Uthraith growled low in his throat.

Djaem stepped forward. "My lady, let me get him to a doctor. It wouldn't do for you to be seen involved with this. An ambassador attacking another ambassador could be seen as an act of war."

Milly gasped and put a hand over her mouth as she realized the gravity of what she had just done. "Damn it all, Uthraith."

He smiled faintly. "It's alright, Milly. I won't report it. My friend Djaem here will make sure I get patched up, and no one will ever know."

Djaem smirked. "It will be like it never happened," he assured her. "But you should get going."

Milly nodded and sighed, giving Uthraith's free hand a squeeze. "I am so sorry. Please make sure he sees the best doctors." She looked back once or twice as she disappeared around a corridor.

Djaem stood there as Uthraith rose and dropped his hand away from the small nick in his heavy armor. The piece of blade that had broken off in the attack glittered in the side of the armor. Djaem smirked and noted that there was no blood, but there was a gash in his armor. If that knife had penetrated, it would have killed almost anyone.

Uthraith noticed his gaze and looked down. He looked almost surprised to see the hole in his armor. He smirked a little to himself.

Djaem laughed as Uthraith pulled the broken piece out. "Well, I see she made contact. I suppose it's a good thing that your hide is the toughest around."

He nodded and smirked a bit. "Yes. It is good."

Djaem shook his head. "I feel bad for whoever does attack her. That was no light hit."

Uthraith smiled. "Yes. She is strong. And fast. I like it."

Djaem nodded. "She did a good job of luring us in."

Uthraith fingered the hole in his armor. "A well-placed attack." He smiled and gave a little sigh.

Djaem shrugged. "Wouldn't it have made more sense to stab the neck or an artery?"

Uthraith shrugged. "If your intention is to kill. This wound is to cause most pain. Victim barely breathes. Ruins ability to move, designed to incapacitate without death. Perfect for interrogation."

Djaem looked at Uthraith's face with growing concern. He had an almost wistful look. "Did you want her to stab you?"

Uthraith laughed and gave him a wink before he started following her again. "She already did."

Djaem sighed and followed along. *Is this what it looks like when a Murder Mountain falls in love?*

UTHRAITH FOLLOWED Milly from a greater distance. Her pink hair was easy to follow through the crowds, and he watched her move with new appreciation as the people around her responded to her smiles and words. They didn't cower or grovel and moved towards her instead of away. No one flinched away from her.

The predators of the streets moved away and past her. Younglings followed behind her as if she was a herd mother. Milly moved from the ship dock, out of the safety of the Citadel, and past the main market area. Her destination was the outer reaches of the city where those with little lived. It was dirtier, wilder, and more dangerous.

Milly headed to the center square of the slums. Her royal emblems were on full display, though her expensive clothes were more than enough to declare her status. She moved with confidence and grace as if she knew her way by heart. Once she reached the small open square of the district, she waited. After a few minutes, a small curious crowd had formed. Uthraith remained on the outskirts to keep from causing a disruption to her plans.

She pulled out a data pad and a hover skiff drone approached. With the precision of an AI assistant, the drone lowered a large crate into the square. She used smaller helper drones to open and sort the crates. She pulled out a table and other logistic equipment. By this time, a much larger crowd had formed. The whispers had turned into a thrum.

A stranger appeared at Uthraith's elbow and spoke with Djaem's voice. "Shall I go find out what is happening?"

Uthraith just gave a nod.

A few minutes later, a different man arrived at his other elbow. "She is distributing the food that was going to go bad because of routing delays. She had been trying to sell it, but the buyers fell through. She refuses to let things go to waste, so she is giving it away for free to the poor."

Uthraith looked surprised, considered the information, and nodded. He approached the crowd and passed them. Women, children, old men, and sick people had already begun to crowd around as she was setting up.

Milly looked up at him, sweat on her brow as she worked to get the items ready.

"Tell me," he said simply.

She smiled and started instructing him on what to do. He helped unload heavy crates and put together bundles so that it was more evenly distributed. Djaem arrived to assist, recruiting people from the crowd.

Uthraith knew these were men of violence and crime, but for today they followed instructions and helped give out food bundles.

Uthraith watched as a strange sort of magic took place. Children played and laughed in the filthy square. Women gossiped together, smiling and relaxed. Men helped each other carry food away. There was a sense of comradery that didn't exist before.

He thought of his home. When the hunters brought meat back to the village, everyone gathered as they butchered the beast together. Some were eaten then, and the rest split among the Danthmaw. Everyone shared in the joy and food provided.

Milly wasn't just distributing food; she was speaking with the people. She treated them like they were members of her tribe. She did not just give them food but also gave them hope. Uthraith began to understand everyone's reaction to her. She was a beacon for these people. The symbol of her house was not just another crest, it was the symbol of food. Food was life. Food was hope. She was the representative of those ideas.

Uthraith looked around at the strange gathering of people and considered what his tribe might have thought of this.

Those who bring food back to the village are considered second only to those that protect the younglings. If she is the food bringer to all tribes, what does that make her?

DJAEM WATCHED WITH BITTERSWEET DISBELIEF. He hadn't put it together until he had seen the symbol on the food crates. That symbol was on food crates all over the Empire. It was on the crates that had been shipped to his world. The Empire supplied the nutriment to sustain the population. They had come from many different sources. But of all the suppliers, there was none better than Fraygar.

Djaem helped silently pass out the packets to the people in the square as his mind wandered through his childhood memories. Packets like these were stolen and sold all over his hive. Entire riots had started and ended over crates of these. In his youth, he had learned to steal these before anything else. Food was the highest commodity on the hive.

Clan Fraygar not only brought the food, but they had also set up the growing pods, the small bio-domes that lined the edge of the hives. These pods grew several different plants that helped provide sustenance for the population. Their protein bars and vitae-paste were known to have the most nutritional value.

Djaem looked down at the packet he held in his hands, and his stomach growled in response. His mouth watered in anticipation. He had stolen enough of these over the years to know when it was the genuine article or not. He remembered his youthful excitement when the shipments would come in.

Djaem looked over at the pink-haired princess crouched

low to speak with a group of dirty-faced children. The children here were much cleaner and bigger than the children of his hive. His mind spun and whirled as it studied her behavior. *She can't be real. This is fake. It's a lie somehow.* He watched intently, looking for some telltale sign that she was faking it. That it was all an act. He found none. She was genuinely happy to interact with these children. She wanted to help them. The only deception he read was her hiding her sadness at not being able to do more. *People like this don't exist.*

In his hive, this symbol was not just about some royal family. It was sacred. It was worshiped. Djaem had never seen a home without one. A small shrine was built where the nest mothers gave thanks to the benevolent angels that ensured full bellies. He remembered bowing his head with all the other children in the nest, closing his eyes and earnestly praying that Clan Fraygar would come and bring more food.

To the elders, Clan Fraygar was not just a noble house. They were special beings that spread benevolence to all. A dream of those giving food to all. *I thought it was all propaganda. A lie told to give them just enough hope to keep us in line. To make us believe in the good of the Empire. But there she is . . . doing just as promised. How much have I stolen from her family over the years?*

He had become an expert at stealing from Clan Fraygar, rerouting shipments, and collecting them to distribute to his people. One of the most lucrative illegal enterprises he had ever run was distribution of additional rations. An unfamiliar weight settled on him, and it took him a few minutes to identify it. He watched as she opened packets with the little ones and talked about her favorite parts to eat. Memories flooded back from his youth with the nest mothers singing as they opened the packets, and they all shared the food within.

Djaem dropped his eyes down to the symbol in his hands. *Someone is targeting her.* The weight of guilt shifted to a cold, calculated anger. His thoughts cleared. *They will regret that.*

He went back to helping pass out the food and speaking to the many people surrounding her. They may not have been hive-born, but they were a crowd of humanity. And now he understood they all had something in common. They were all hungry, and someone was threatening the hand that feeds them.

NOT CHAPTER 17: REVIEW PANEL . . . 0/10, WOULD NOT RECOMMEND

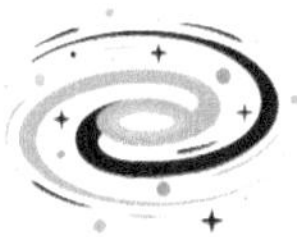

"While the panel must accept that Djaem isn't a spy," the female panelist said in a slow and even pace, "he has been named in a large number of transgressions. To start, many of those he engaged in combat with survived with horrible shallow slashing wounds. Can you explain?"

Djaem stared blankly in the direction of the chairs. His mind raced over the charges, trying to figure out what the issue was. Raza used knives as well, so it wasn't the choice of weapons. She had taken down more people than he had, so it wasn't the use of violence. He couldn't figure out why this was directed specifically at him.

"He's new and he's soft," Raza said, rescuing him from his inexperience. "When encouraged to just let people die, he seems more inclined to find a way for them to live. It's his way. It won't last. I've been helping him understand that death is preferable."

"Wait, what?" Djaem shouted, eyes going wide. "You mean that's actually a rule?"

"Any who would stand in the way of your investigation," one of the panelists said, "is showing disloyalty. As such, they have already voluntarily given up their lives. Those you left wounded would now be a costly expense. Fortunately, your team helped mitigate that."

Fallrick chuckled. "They'd have to get patched up, and you know how costly blood is on a hive. They'd have to be fed and tended to while they recover. They'd have to be given a trial. Most would have to be relocated to a prison world or re-education facility."

Djaem looked to the others on the team, scanning one face and then the next. "So, we just kill anyone who gets in our way?"

Raza leaned back in her chair, folding her arms behind her head. "Yep. That is, unless we need to ask them questions. It's in the rule book."

Djaem tried to regain control of the flow of the discussion. "But . . . this is all in 'would have.' The team took care of it. That means the team did what it was supposed to, right?"

"The team, yes. You were personally derelict in your obligations." The female panelist sounded very pleased with herself. "Impersonation of officials has already been addressed. Next, unauthorized access to protected navigational systems."

Djaem smiled, suppressing the laugh that started to grow inside him. "Weighed risk. That was a major violation of universal law with some imperial overlap, but the consequences of failure need to be considered and offset. Failure to take that action would have permitted a trained psychic rogue to escape with a large number of illegally harvested psi-crystals. It had already been determined that this rogue agent was connected with the demonic presence. Did the momentary disruption cause more harm than the escape would've? If not, what is the next charge?"

"The resulting crash," the female panelist followed, "set

fire to the entire spaceport. While we have no records of unlawful loss of life, the property damage was extensive. The dock was no longer in an operational state."

"Yes," Djaem replied with a mocking level of patronization in his voice. "The ship fuel damaged the endurium plating. If that's the case, there's no way of knowing how much damage was already there! There was equipment damage, three ships downgraded, two destroyed. I'm well aware of where I put that drone fueler down. Again, are a few pieces of equipment remotely comparable to the escape of a demon-summoner?"

"The damage to the plates was extensive. An entire section was stripped to the anchoring stone. The metal was found granulated across the entire length of the dock."

"I'm sure it was," Djaem replied. "This would be from when Scythia vaporized it. In a perfect stoichiometry and pressurized to the point of liquifying the oxygen used in burning it, the fuel in that ship couldn't melt endurium, let alone vaporize it." He paused for an additional moment. "The rogue psychic that was stopped had a long service history. He likely still had friends throughout the Empire, ones who are not disloyal, but might have their perceptions skewed by their history."

One of the other voices joined in from the panel. "It wasn't just equipment on site. The atmospheric shield was overloaded. It damaged power systems throughout the hive."

"You need to learn the proper weapon for the proper time, and this is only one example." The female voice took over again. "This was excessive and led to widespread damage. I still can't wrap my head around this last one." She paused for several seconds. "If I didn't have the video, I would assume it was a lie. Did you try to bodily engage with a telekinetic knight?"

"Well," Djaem said, stammering. His eyes turned to

Scythia. "There was no time. There was nothing I could do. I had to try."

"What kind of idiot handler puts his own life in danger to protect his monster?"

Her words hit Djaem's ears like a bombshell. The last time he heard that, it was in his own thoughts, about a different idiot handler. That one didn't recover from his mistake. He lowered his head, knowing he had no reason and no excuse. He had panicked. He had forgotten what was going on.

"I briefed Djaem on Scythia's unpredictable power," Fallrick said, finally stepping in. "She knew how to lash out, but not how to defensively shield herself. If she were struck, there is a chance the damage would have been much more severe. He simply followed the instructions in that briefing and was willing to sacrifice himself for all the souls on that rock."

Djaem barely even heard the words. He didn't have the mental reserve to weave the lie into a more thorough story. *Why did I do something that stupid*, he asked himself over and over.

The panel fell silent for quite some time. The voting lights turned on and went through several passes. When the chairs pivoted to face the tiny booth in the middle of the room, there was only one thing left for them to do.

The woman by the door called to them in her nearly-robotic voice. "You're all dismissed. Within the next two days, you will receive a summons to hear your outcome and sentencing."

Even as the others rose to leave, Djaem remained unmoving, captive to his own thoughts. Uthraith gently lifted him and carried him on a shoulder. The giant cast Raza a glance and gave a short questioning grunt. She looked up at him, shook her head, and passed him another coin.

NAH AH! I DON'T HAVE FEELINGS . . . YOU HAVE FEELINGS

RAZA RELAXED, almost dozing, on the overstuff cushions in the quiet of the living quarters. Scythia wouldn't need to be picked up from her daily training for a few more hours.

Raza heard the team returning before the door even opened. Djaem entered first, his focus on the data pad in his right hand. He set down the crate he was hefting in his left hand onto the kitchen counter.

Raza felt her pleasant mood evaporate immediately.

Princess Millianya entered, with Uthraith maneuvering through the doorway after her. Every nerve in Raza's body came alive. Raza tried to maneuver off the couch to make a dash for her door, but it was too late.

"Raza!" Milly's voice was high with surprise and delight. Raza froze in place a second before she was engulfed in soft, lightly perfumed warmth. The squeezing hug was stronger than Raza remembered. Milly lifted her clear off the ground as she gave a happy cry and twirled around.

Raza grimaced as she endured the ritual without resorting to stabbing objects. She refused to return the hug or acknowledge the pleasant warmth that seeped into her.

"Hello, Princess," she grumbled as she was set back down.

"Oh. My. Goodness. Look at you! I haven't seen you in ages. You look amazing. I am so glad you healed ok. I sent letters; you must not have gotten them. I was so worried about you." Milly was rapid-fire talking as Uthraith and Djaem stared at the interaction.

Raza tried to keep patience in her voice. "What are you doing here?"

Milly blinked, wide eyed, and smiled. "Ambassador Uthraith invited me. We just finished distributing some food packs that weren't going to make it to their normal destination. I offered to buy them lunch, and Uthraith insisted we come here and have it."

Raza snapped an angry gaze over at the Murder Mountain that was suddenly very interested in putting his gear away and avoiding eye contact.

"I had no idea you would be here. Are you working as his guard?" Milly smiled brightly.

Raza winced inwardly as the innocent question opened the door to a long line of painful stories. Raza slammed those mental doors shut as quickly as possible.

"No. We are on a N.E.B. enforcement team together," Raza finally said. Her voice managed to be level and even.

Milly's brow curved inwardly in confusion with a hint of concern. "Why would either of you be assigned to one of those?" Everyone knew these teams were designed to be disposable.

Because, you little happy idiot, that is where they send those they want to dispose of.

Raza almost growled out, "It's none of your business."

Milly's smile dimmed. Raza tried to ignore the twisting feeling in her gut. A courtlier, guarded smile took its place. Raza hated that one more.

"Of course. My mistake. I was just so excited to see you again. It will be so nice to have drinks and catch up."

Old hurts bubbled to the surface, making Raza mean. "Oh, I think it's way more important that Uthraith tell you what he found in your room."

Uthraith finally returned a glare at Raza, his mouth forming a flat line.

Milly's smile disappeared as her demeanor turned suspicious. "In my room? Why were you in my room, Uthraith?"

Djaem watched the drama unfold from the spectators' seats at the counter in the kitchen.

Uthraith gave a shrug. "Making sure you were safe. I found listening devices."

Raza didn't remove her gaze from Uthraith's still angry one as she continued hammering away. "Oh, yes. He has been so concerned for your safety he has been following you for two days."

Milly looked between Raza and Uthraith, anger flashing across her face briefly before she put on a blank expression.

"I see. Thank you for informing me. Don't die, Sister Raza." Her voice was smooth and sweet. The only hint at the anger underneath was her apple cheeks turning a bright shade of pink. "I will let Kotex know you still live. I am sure he will be pleased." She gave the formal bow and turned towards the door.

Raza flinched inwardly as Milly said the name of their shared mentor. His voice played in Raza's head as if he stood behind her. *Petty. Spiteful. We have no need to be this way. Pettiness and spite are for those too weak to control themselves.*

Raza turned away and sat back down on the couch.

Milly passed Uthraith on the way to the door. "We talk . . . now." Uthraith gave Raza a departing glare as he followed Milly out the door again.

Raza gritted her teeth. *Way to go, Raza . . . Way to show how calm and collected you are. You are a child throwing a tantrum,* she berated herself silently.

Djaem was the first to crack the brooding silence. He looked up from the data pad he was studying.

"I had no idea you two even knew each other," he commented in an upbeat, neutral tone.

Raza's resolve popped, and she couldn't keep all the anger from her voice. "What the hell are the two of you thinking? You know very well we can't get involved here. We are under review."

Djaem gave an unconcerned shrug and nodded. "So we will have to be careful. Besides, helping her will be a huge boon to use later. Everyone loves Clan Fraygar."

Raza cursed under her breath and fought the urge to punch Djaem in the face. He was giving her that look . . . The one he had when he was dissecting people with his mind. It set her teeth on edge and made her skin crawl when he looked at her like that.

"I have to say I am surprised. I didn't expect you to be so . . . upset." Djaem's voice was still in that neutral tone. It did little to settle Raza's nerves. She knew what he was doing. She had done it enough times herself.

"Oh, cut the bullshit. I am not in the mood to dance with you," she grumped and went to fetch a drink from the cold storage. It was a twisted, spiraling container that kept the two fluids separate before they were pulled into the top. Glowing blue alcohol shimmered against the bright yellow juice. Mixed, they became a glowing iridescent green. Raza took a deep pull and sighed.

"What is really bothering you? I know it's more than just worrying about the review. Princess Milly seems to have you in quite the twist."

Raza looked over at the little enigma of a man and shook her head. "You like her too. I thought you would be smart enough to avoid it. But she is like a sickness. She gets under the skin and makes people weak."

Raza came back to sit across from Djaem, watching the colors swirl and mix in the glass.

Djaem went back to his data pad. "This is a personal dispute?" he responded evenly.

Raza made a frustrated noise. "It's not a dispute, exactly. We spent some time together when we were younger. Rosic is a Belacist; he has been her families' personal security since she was a toddler. I was sent to train with him for a short time. So, we ended up training together."

Djaem leaned forward, interested. "Was she cruel? Spoiled? Arrogant?"

Raza made a disgusted noise in her throat. "It would've been better if she was. If she was just a rich selfish bitch, hating her would be simple. If she was spoiled and whiny, I could pity her and ignore her. But no, she was so much worse."

Djaem finally prompted her to continue. "How so?"

Raza heaved a sigh. "She wasn't strong or fast. She neither had the physical conditioning of the Belacist nor the breeding and genetics. She didn't have the instincts of a killer, or the awareness. She shouldn't have been training with Rosic. She is too soft. Instead of making her go do something more suitable for a Princess of Fraygar, he doted on her, indulged her."

She tried to suppress the old resentment, but it bubbled to the surface. "Belacists have no room for softness. We are ruthless and brutal. She made him weak. In a fight or a deadly encounter, she becomes a liability. All her cute smiles and eager, fumbling attempts . . . It's like when someone sees a baby or a puppy. They all just want to pinch her cheeks and keep her safe.

"People feel like they must protect her. And now Uthraith

has fallen for the same damn trap. I thought you would be smart enough to avoid it. But here you are, risking yourself to protect her. She is a liability that weakens the people around her."

Djaem's face was the very picture of contemplation as if he were trying to solve some great philosophical debate.

"It seems to me that someone who is soft and weak would need to seek out strong protectors to keep them safe. So really isn't she doing exactly what would be appropriate? Trying to fight her enemies the way you do would be much more foolish. Which would imply that the reason you are so upset isn't that she is getting help, but that she is getting it from Uthra—" Djaem's words cut off when Raza's fist found his cheek.

Raza slowed her breathing as she stared down at Djaem. He held his jaw. She didn't miss the knowing look in his eye. *Fucking bastard knew I was going to hit him. And he just stood there and took it.*

"What game are you playing?" Her voice had a grinding hiss quality as she forced it out from her clenched teeth.

"Just returning the favor you did me. I am too attached to my monster, and you are too attached to yours," he said as he regained his feet, rubbing the bruise on his jaw.

"Oh, fuck you . . . At least I am not in love with mine." She spat the words at him.

Djaem flushed, and in a rare flash of anger, his mouth ran away with his thoughts. "That's right, you aren't! So where is all this jealousy coming from?" Raza could almost watch his mind putting the pieces together in real time. His words coming out almost too fast as his brain expelled its reasoning. "You aren't worried that Uthraith might get hurt protecting Milly. You are just mad that he is the one doing it . . . because you want it to be you." Djaem's eyes went wide as the realization dawned. His hands came up again a second too late to block Raza's left hook. He slumped to the ground.

Raza stepped over his form and stormed out the door. She missed the smug smile that curled on Djaem's swollen lips.

UTHRAITH FOLLOWED behind Milly as she walked them to just outside the housing unit. She tried to put her thoughts in order as she considered what to say to the giant man. *I am glad it wasn't someone out to hurt me, but for fuck's sake.* She took a deep breath and turned to face him, shoulders squared.

He was smirking at her. He seemed entertained more than anything. It made her want to kick him, but she knew for a fact it would only hurt her own foot. She took a deep breath and tried not to lose her temper.

"Anger looks good on you," he said with a less-than-respectful leer.

Milly flushed and tried to hang onto her anger. It was hard when he flashed that dimple her way. *How dare someone so dangerous have an adorable dimple!* She glared in frustration.

"You are making this very difficult," she said in exasperation. "You have no right to be so forward. I realize that things might be very different where you come from, but I am a Princess of Fraygar. There are rules I must follow."

Uthraith considered her seriously and nodded. "What rules?"

Milly was stunned silent for a moment. She had mistakenly assumed that any official ambassador would have had at least some training in decorum or at least a sense of respectability. But he genuinely had no idea what she was talking about. She fumbled for a way to explain it so that it would be very clear where the boundaries were.

Uthraith moved forward and bent slightly over so they were closer to eye level. "What rules?"

He is teasing me. Milly could see the faint twinkle in his eye, and that dimple was making another appearance. Milly forced herself to stand up straight and not back up. She slid her left hand behind her back and pressed against the wall for support.

"Rules about who is allowed in my chambers and to escort me places. Rules about who may see to my security and who I may consort with," she said, trying to find the best terms to use.

A large hand reached out and took a hold of a thick strand of her pink hair that had come free from its bindings. Milly watched him swirl it around his index finger. The thick callus caught the silky strands, preventing it from falling away. The pale pink was a stark contrast to his darkened skin. She noticed that his fingernails were a dark, greenish color. His natural mottling looked like little dots on the back of his hands.

He watched her face as he twirled his finger around the curl again. His voice was in a low, soft whisper. "Who can do these things?"

Milly watched his finger swirl around and around. "Well, I may choose my guards, but the rest is close family and my future husband, of course."

Uthraith tilted his head. "Future husband?"

The way he shaped the word sounded strange to Milly's ear, but she nodded. "Yes, you see how this could reflect poorly on me."

Uthraith smiled and nodded, standing up straight. "I understand. I fix."

He turned abruptly, stepping away. His sudden absence

made Milly's head swim. She leaned against the wall, her heart racing and her cheeks flushed. She was still trying to catch her breath when her vision filled with Raza's face.

"Milly . . . Milly, are you ok?" Raza's voice sounded stressed. Milly felt like her head was fuzzy and shook herself. "Raza? What's wrong?"

Raza was frowning and reached up to touch Milly's cheeks. "Are you ok? Where is Uthraith?"

Milly blinked in confusion. "He was right here." She looked at the empty hallway.

RAZA LOOKED at Milly's flushed cheeks and slightly dazed expression. She knew what this was. She had seen it a time or two before. She sighed in frustration. She dug through her pockets and pulled out a small tablet.

"Here, dissolve this in your mouth. You will be fine. You just aren't used to his pheromones." She made a noise with her teeth.

Milly nodded and sighed after a moment, looking up at Raza with an apologetic smile. "I am sorry, Raza; I didn't know he was on your team. I didn't mean to bother you."

Raza looked away, focusing down the hall and trying her best to show how much she wasn't bothered by anything. "It doesn't matter. Just try not to get the team pulled into your mess. We are under review."

Milly straightened and her face became serious. "True, and with the Faithful taking over the governor's seat, things have become very dangerous. I am not sure why they have come, but when they arrived, the whispers were going nonstop with speculation. After the leader killed the governor and took his seat, there has been nothing but silence from the gossips. Everyone is trying to keep their head down. I imagine that was part of the point. I suspect that is why they are making their move now. They knew the Faithful were coming."

Milly rolled the problem over in her head as she considered what to do next.

"I will have to make some drastic counter moves. I have managed to minimize the damage to the shipments. However, if I don't make some visible retaliation, it will make the Fraygar look weak." Milly let out a sigh as she turned and started moving down the hallway. "I can't kill him, but by the time I am done, he will wish I had." Milly's voice was filled with icy conviction.

Raza glared angrily as she followed Milly. *this . . . This is supposed to be my free time. I should be relaxing with my feet up. Not Following Princess Pink puff to confront her stupid pig fiancé.*

"Hey, hiver, come on!" Raza shouted down the hall. She waited only long enough to ensure that Djaem was following before she moved to catch up to Milly.

Fallrick is going to be so pissed.

18

STRANGER DANGER!

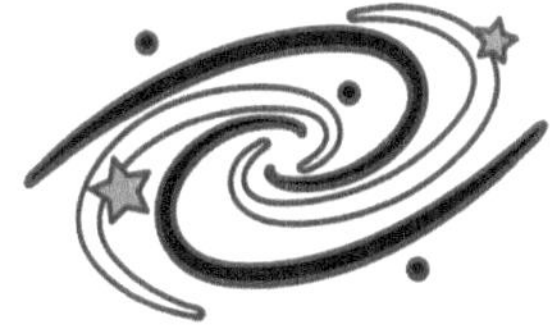

SCYTHIA TAPPED her heel against the floor as she waited in the empty training room. A gurgling and rumbling accompanied the protesting clench of her empty stomach.

Where are they? I am hungry . . . Raza said Djaem would come to get me. But he has been so busy lately. Always talking to people on the communicator, running off to meet someone. I bet he is in a meeting.

A frown creased her angular blue brow. A look of determination spread across Scythia's face. *I don't know why I need to wait. I know the way.*

Scythia sighed in frustration. "We are inside the Citadel. How dangerous could it be?"

After five more minutes had passed, Scythia rose from her seat and headed out the door. The halls were empty and the training hall was quiet.

To help her ignore the echoing silence of the world, Scythia tapped and clicked her metallic heels and toes as she went on her way. Her humming filled the surrounding silence. The sparkling blurred figure reflected back at her, dancing down the dark halls, bending and stretching with the contours of the walls. Scythia's delighted laughter was alien in the gloomy space. The joy of it bounced and echoed lightly down into dark, quiet spaces. It took root there, waiting for light to grow and spread.

"It has been a long time since I heard such laughter," a deep, even baritone said from behind Scythia. She slowed and looked towards the man she had seen at the atrium.

He still wore his robes but his hood was down and was leaning against the wall. Scythia realized the reason she didn't notice him was that his robes matched the dark gray of the walls and floor.

Scythia considered what he said and offered this solution: "Then you should be funny or laugh yourself."

Loga smiled and nodded. "I see, that would make the most sense." He unfolded his arms and gently pushed off the wall to glide over to stand beside her. Scythia could barely make out his reflection as he moved.

His feet seemed to whisper as they walked. Scythia decided to keep moving down the hall closer to the living quarters and her friends. He easily kept pace with her, moving to walk beside her on the right.

"You have made quite the impact since your arrival. I hope you are settling in well. I hear you are working hard in your training. How is it going?" Loga's tone was pleasant and relaxed. Scythia stole a glance at Loga's face as she continued to walk.

"I am doing well. I enjoy it." She said in a soft voice. She wasn't sure what she was supposed to say. Scythia swallowed as her mouth went dry. The hairs on the back of her neck stood on end. She felt her heart start to thump loudly in her ears. The skin on her palms was clammy and wet. *Am I sick? No . . . I know this. This is how Djaem felt before we went to space. I am afraid. But why?* Her eyes traveled back over to Loga, who was still speaking. She turned her attention back to what he was saying.

". . . It's important that the review panel remains impartial, of course." He wasn't looking at her while they walked.

"Of course," she said noncommittally. *Why am I afraid of him? What is he doing that I am so scared of?* They turned with the hall, passing by the opening toward the cafeteria. Scythia didn't even think about her decision to avoid going that way. She pushed herself past the smells of delicious food and continued towards the living quarters.

"Come, Scythia I wish to discuss this with you further. I am sure you are famished, let me treat you. I have heard you enjoy sweets. There is a delicacy from the inner worlds I want to show you. It practically melts in your mouth," Loga said pleasantly. It was not a question, just a soft order.

Scythia felt herself recoil inwardly as she shook her head. She couldn't figure out why she was afraid of him, but she wasn't going to ignore the voice inside herself.

"No. I have to return to my team." Her voice came out softer, less confident than Scythia had wanted. It was like something was squeezing her voice, making it hard to speak. Her heart had turned into a rapid tapping inside her chest. A cold sweat was trickling down her back.

"It's good that you are making friends, Scythia." Loga smiled and took a step closer to her. "Friends make all the difference. They protect you, and I know you want to protect them. The best way for you to do that is to do as you're told." Another step closer. "As long as you remain obedient, they will remain protected. Obedience equals safety."

Scythia couldn't tell what changed, but his face had shifted. Loga's pleasant smile had become a mask to hide the rage beneath. His eye replacements made the mask unreadable. Fear roiled beneath Scythia's skin.

"They won't even notice. Afterwards, I will make sure you are delivered to your team." His voice had become a candy-coated razor, sweet and sharp.

Scythia stepped back from Loga. "No, I really can't. Thank you . . ." Her voice was pinched and higher now. She forced a smile on her face as she turned to leave.

Loga's smile flattened and his voice shifted to a hard tone. "I must insist."

Scythia gasped as he snatched her wrist in a viselike grip. He immediately started to drag her in the direction of a side hall. A rainbow of light flashed around them as Scythia's crystals scintillated in color from suppressing her instinctual attack.

He froze as he watched the swirl of glowing colors trail around her. Scythia leaned away, pulling against his hand with all her might. He didn't budge. *How can he be this strong?*

Loga's tone was deadly. "Do you know the punishment for attacking a Faithful?"

Scythia opened her mouth to speak when a hand came over her mouth. A hand pulled her head back and to the side, blocking her view of anything but a well-made silk jacket.

Forced off balance and tilted back, her height made the position awkward. Scythia twisted a little and bent to let her head be held against a man's chest. *Whoever this is, they are too tall and muscular to be Djaem but far too short to be Uthraith.*

Scythia ended the motion stretched taut between the two men. Her wrist was pulled tight by Loga, and she was in a bent twist, face planted into someone's shoulder.

"Then I suppose it's a good thing that she didn't attack you, Arbiter Loga." Lucias's voice came from just above where her head was secured. He sounded bored and uninterested. Scythia's heart slowed down and her breathing came easier. The raw ends of her nerves settled. She relaxed into his grip and didn't fight the strange, awkward embrace. Lucias was familiar. *He won't hurt me.*

"I am terribly sorry if I startled you, Arbiter. I was

attempting to contact Scythia's mind. I was late to pick her up, and I was attempting to locate her." There was a forced politeness in Lucias' voice as he spoke. Scythia couldn't see; her face was still firmly held in the crook of his shoulder. He was gentle, and the pressure was firm as he pulled her away from Loga. This strangely unacknowledged tug-of-war continued as they spoke politely with each other.

"No harm done. Please do be more careful in the future. Can't have people thinking that psychics are running around doing as they please." The friendly and upbeat tone in Loga's voice sent a shiver through Scythia.

How can he sound so pleasant while he is squeezing my wrist so tight? Scythia reached her free hand around to hold onto Lucias.

The release of her wrist tipped her heavily into Lucias. He managed to not sway under her loss of balance. Scythia was finally able to straighten and shifted around behind Lucias. She watched Loga wearily from over Lucias' head.

"It was lovely to speak with you, Scythia. We will do it again soon. Have a pleasant evening." Loga smiled at them both before turning and moving silently away. He seemed to float across the floor, his robes barely brushing it as he turned down the hall towards the cafeteria.

Scythia blinked against the prickling of tears as they formed. Her body sagged a little, and she leaned against the wall as relief washed over her.

Lucias was silent as he pulled her to her feet and started walking her briskly down the hall. His face was an angry glare, and Scythia bit her lip.

"I am sorry," she whispered as her shoes clicked rapidly to keep up with his pace.

Scythia banged into his back as he stopped moving forward. He spun on his heel and pulled her down so her face was very close to his. Scythia blinked as she stared into his eyes. They were a funny color, somewhere between blue and green.

His eyes narrowed as he whispered, "That man is very dangerous. Far more than you will ever realize. Did you really try to attack him?"

Scythia looked defensive and leaned back. "I didn't try . . . The suppressors stopped me."

Lucias gave Scythia's shoulders a hard shake. "You must never do that again. Ever. If you had succeeded in attacking him, everyone who was responsible for you would have been executed after you were. May the old gods forbid it if you should have killed him."

He took a steadying breath. "If you had managed to kill him . . . well, let's just say they would have to find a new crew for the ship that discovered you beyond the rim."

Scythia gave Lucias a confused look. "Why would they need a new crew?"

Lucias straightened his coat and smoothed his hair. "Because the repercussions of killing one of the Faithful, especially a leader of a fist, is death to everyone who has ever had any contact with the traitor. This ensures that the infection of treason does not have the chance to corrupt anyone else. And, yes, that means all those people in the hive."

Scythia blanched as she realized what he was saying. "Why?"

Lucias sighed and gave Scythia a sympathetic look. "Because fear and brutality are necessary to maintain obedience and control. It is how the Empire works. Fallrick does you no favors by keeping you naive." He turned and gently took Scythia's arm. "Come on, let's get you back before anything else happens."

****

Fallrick was more than a little annoyed by the time Scythia and Lucias got in the door.

Scythia walked in and gave him a bright smile. "Hi, Fallrick. What are you doing here?"

Fallrick had to take a breath to calm down. Yelling at Scythia would not get him anywhere good. "I am looking for the rest of the team . . . Do you know where they are?"

Scythia frowned and shook her head before looking at Lucias.

Lucias sighed and moved over to check the state of the tea kettle. The water was still hot. "I found the Little Blue here wandering the halls about to be snatched up by the Faithful. I figured you had worked so hard to get her, you would like her returned."

Scythia pouted and went to sit down at the table. "I wasn't lost. I know the way home. I was told that I was supposed to listen to people of a higher rank than me. He said he wanted to walk with me."

Lucias smirked as he poured himself a cup of tea. "Why is the only one who actually follows instructions the one everyone thought would be the troublemaker, the one everyone is so interested in watching?"

Scythia grinned and sat up very tall in her chair. "Because I am the bait. I stand in the light where everyone can see so they can move in the dark."

Fallrick let out a frustrated groan and rubbed his temples. He was going to have to have a talk with Djaem.

Lucias frowned over the rim of his mug. His eyes were serious as he shook his head. "No, Scythia . . . you are not the bait. You are the goal. You don't stand in the light . . . You are the flame. Don't ever forget that." He put down his mug.

"Come on, Fallrick. Send out the communication and summon your team. We don't have time for all this nonsense."

19

YOU HAD ONE JOB! . . . ONE!

"I DON'T THINK this is a good idea," Raza whispered as she followed close behind Milly. "Don't you need to call your folks? Like, aren't these things arranged?" She was careful to keep her voice low so that it didn't echo through the curved halls. Uthraith and Djaem followed along, bringing up the rear and making sure no one was following them.

Milly smirked slightly. "Oh yes, I probably should, but I am not going to. I opposed this arrangement from the start. I disliked Chadwick Hessamir from the moment I met him, but Father wanted Chadwick's allegiance for protection and freighting rights. If he is actively working against our interests, that is enough of an excuse."

Milly led them to one of the alcoves in the diplomatic grand hall. She took a moment to fix her hair and make sure her makeup was perfect. "If I don't make any kind of public show, it will seem like I don't care about what they have done. Sometimes that can be useful. To show them that they don't have the power they think they do. But it can also come off as I don't have the ability to react." Milly gave Raza a conspiratorial smile. "And this way I get out of this ridiculous arranged marriage. So, it's perfect."

Raza frowned and shook her head. "You should think this through. You are being rash. What if he retaliates? What if your father gets upset? What if . . ."

Milly put a hand on Raza's shoulder. "You worry too much. These things happen all the time. I will go out there, make a little scene, tell him I know what he was doing, and declare the engagement is off. The gossips will hear me break the agreement with the Nakruim ambassador and see me storm off in a huff. They will think it's me being emotional and young, so my father and mother can smooth over whatever ruffled feathers come from it." She grinned. "Trust me . . . it will be fine."

Raza frowned as Milly turned and headed out of the alcove, and Uthraith followed behind. Djaem looked at Raza as he moved to follow.

"I have a bad feeling about this," he whispered. Raza nodded as she trailed behind the group. *So, do I.*

UTHRAITH HAD AVOIDED THE EVENING 'SOIREES' as much as possible. The translators said it was dinner, but the food and drink weren't that good. Although, it was easier to get the ladies to come spend private time in alcoves at these gatherings. The clothes weren't as intricate. Or maybe it was the bubbly wine. Uthraith didn't care for it, but it seemed to make the ladies happy.

The gathering was already well underway. The light music brightly playing on one of the stages, the din of people talking, and glasses clinking irritated Uthraith's ears, but he ignored it.

It was easy to follow Milly's hair in the crowd. The pink

color made it easier, even if she was shorter than most of those present. He moved along easily in the crowd as they parted for him. He knew why they did, and he smiled a little. They came to a stop in front of two men. Uthraith didn't know them.

One was an older man. He wore the badge of an ambassador. Uthraith didn't know or care where from. The slightly younger man claimed his attention. He was tall but lanky. His hair was a dark brown and combed back with a slight wave. He wore a well-tailored uniform. Uthraith looked at his boring face. He had to resist the urge to break his very straight nose.

Uthraith was so focused on resisting the urge to commit violence on the man he almost missed it.

Millianya's hand landing on Lord Hessamir's cheek made a loud crack that broke the noise of the room and silence fell around them.

Lord Hessamir was slowly picking himself up off the floor. Milly stood as tall as her frame would allow.

"Lord Hessamir, I would like to formally inform you that any arrangements that may have been agreed to are, as of this moment, dissolved," Milly said with polite contempt before she turned to the ambassador. "Ambassador, I regret to inform you that due to the new arrangements you have made with my former fiancé, I will no longer be able to guarantee the shipments that were arranged. I am sure you understand. But since you are already in negotiations with Deculhut, I am sure it won't be a problem for you."

Milly held up a hand to the ambassador when he tried to speak. He had the good grace to close his mouth and nod. He was stiff as he turned and walked away. Lord Hessamir was obviously not as wise. His face was red with anger and embarrassment as he tried to speak. His voice came out pinched and through his gritted teeth.

"Millianya, what has gotten into you? Come, we will speak about this in private," he said, reaching out to try and take ahold of her arm.

Millianya stepped out of his reach. "We will not be speaking again."

Lord Hessamir lost all pretense of a smile as he stepped forward. "You are being emotional. Think about what you are doing. You don't have any protection. Our fathers are going to be very angry. If you miss any more shipments, people will start to lose confidence in Clan Fraygar. You need me. Don't be foolish." His voice was a low hiss, but Uthraith could see all the eager faces listening, waiting.

Milly tilted her chin up and smirked. "No, you need *me*. Over eighty-five percent of the cargo your family ships is Fraygar food supplies. Good luck filling your hauls. I have already made new shipping arrangements."

Lord Hessamir paled and frowned. "Bullshit, no one else can handle that much freight. Who?"

"That would be us." A stretched figure made his way out of the crowd. Uthraith recognized one of the Star-born he had seen at the Hubb. He wasn't as dark blue as Scythia, and his face was designed in elaborate scarification.

Lord Hessamir sneered. "What is the Constellation Confederation going to do with those floating junk piles?"

Milly smiled brightly as she dismissed Lord Hessamir. "That is no longer any of your concern. Clan Fraygar is eager to work with the Constellation Confederation for the betterment of all the people on the rim." She gave him a curtsy.

The Star-born smiled and gave a flourishing bow. "The Delegation is pleased to see that we are working with people of action and conviction. Enjoy your evening, Princess Fraygar."

Milly turned and with a flourish of her skirt, started to

leave the area. She was in the middle of her dramatic exit when Lord Hessamir shouted over the crowd.

"You stupid ugly bitch! How dare you disrespect me this way! You think you will survive without me? No one is going to protect you from me. This isn't over."

Raza moved up to a defensive position near Milly, and Uthraith moved in-between Milly and the pathetic little man.

Uthraith glared at the man who seemed to finally see him. The pathetic little worm paled and fell backwards slightly. His guards came forward. *They are braver than this piss-stain deserves.*

Uthraith didn't want these brave men to waste their deaths on such a pathetic toad, so he just puffed his chest wide.

"She has no need of you, fiancé. She has me. I am her man now. I will protect. I will be husband." His voice boomed over the crowd. There was a deep, rapid inhale from the crowd

All eyes turned on Uthraith, and he basked in it with pride. *Yes, I am fearsome. Look upon my might and know that none will harm those under my protection. I am the best husband.*

The Star-born smiled in response. "Even better. Don't you think so, Ambassador Blevak?"

The ambassador for the Pezsyk stepped forward in his strange suit. The visor of its little helmet of encapsulated water was closed, and only the strange, artificial eyes gave it a face. An artificial, childlike voice spoke. Uthraith suspected they did that to take advantage of their tiny stature.

"Yes, the Pezsyk is pleased to know that the fierce warriors of Kravanc 4 will be helping ensure our food shipments will arrive. This is great news. We must celebrate." The two delegates turned and melted away into the crowd.

Lord Hessamir had already used the moment to leave unnoticed from the room.

He turned and flinched back as he met Raza's death glare. He looked at Millianya's face and felt confusion. "What?"

The room was silent before Djaem said in a low voice. "I don't think you were supposed to announce that here . . . So sorry, folks, some people get so emotional in these moments." There was a nervous titter before the hum and din of noise returned.

Uthraith tried to ignore the creeping dread in his stomach. *It is never good when the females look at you like that.*

ONCE IN THE temporary privacy of the alcove, Milly turned on Uthraith like an angry cat.

Raza tried not to smirk at the picture the two of them made. Uthraith had to bend slightly if he was to stand in the small space. To be able to wag her finger in his face, Milly was arched backwards. She wasn't yelling, exactly. Her voice was elevated but hissed with angry ferocity. Uthraith looked confused, frustrated, and a little sad.

The big dope doesn't have a clue what he just did. Let's hope he doesn't try to kill his way out of this. That could get real messy real fast.

"You have no idea what you just did, do you?" Milly finally shouted in exasperation.

Raza was frustrated too and went to sit on the bench. "He doesn't. He never bothers to figure out anything beforehand. Because Uthraith does what Uthraith wants, no matter how it screws with his friends in the process."

"Translator said 'to husband' means to conserve, protect, cultivate. That is what husband does. Protect the flock. I am husband. I protect you, Raza, Djaem, and Little Blue."

"That is husband*ry*! That is not . . .," Milly spurted out

because she was so exasperated, and her mind just kept going. "Oh god, my father is going to hear about this . . . Oh no . . . Rosic is going to hear about this." She looked pale and sat down next to Raza.

Raza froze while Milly fell apart. Her mind shifted gears . . . Her eyes darted over to Djaem. They both realized the time at the exact same moment.

"Scythia!" They both sprung into motion as they took off running out of the alcove. Neither noticed if Milly or Uthraith followed.

Raza ducked around people in the pathways as they raced towards the Citadel. "It was your fucking turn to pick her up!"

Djaem didn't deny that but frowned. "Despite what people believe, I can't be in two places at once. You said I needed to be here to help with the crowd and make sure the tide stayed in Milly's favor. I was here doing this."

Raza glared and shook her head. *I always lose my brain when Milly is around.*

"Shut up and run!" she snapped. Their communicators went off in unison.

"Come to my office . . . Scythia is with me." Fallrick's voice was hard and icy. They stopped running. Panting in the hallway, they looked at each other.

Shit.

SCYTHIA SAT QUIETLY EATING the cold fluffy confectionery that Lucias had provided her. It was some lactose bi-product whipped with sugar and fruit flavor. It was a bright rainbow color that shimmered slightly. It was cold but light and dissolved on her tongue.

Scythia took a little peek at her teammates all standing in a rigid line along one wall.

Fallrick paced in front of them, his expression thunderous. Scythia worried her lower lip a moment before Lucias's voice interrupted her thoughts.

"Don't worry, he fought very hard to get this team together. He won't do anything to break it up now. But they need to have some penalty. If they had remembered to pick you up, Loga wouldn't have had a chance to corner you." His tone was gentle but serious. "Now eat your cloud before it melts." Finally, he smiled and took a bite of his own rainbow-colored treat.

Scythia nodded and went back to her treat.

Fallrick paced in front of the team as he read the report. The Princess of the Clan Fraygar had briefly explained what had happened and how his team had provided assistance.

Another report explained that there were some questions in regard to Uthraith's marital status and how that might pertain to his current position.

"I know I told you all to lay low. To stay out of trouble," Fallrick said in a soft voice as he set the file down. "I know I told all of you how imperative it was to keep out of trouble while under review. Especially with the Faithful in charge of the Citadel."

No one was fooled by his quiet tone. They remained in the attention position and waited.

"Would anyone like to explain to me how any of this was staying under the radar? The rumor mills are running full throttle about Uthraith's pending nuptials. The possibility that Raza may be responsible for the murder of Princess Fraygar's bodyguard . . . And the new black-market smuggler that has begun moving wares in the under city." His voice raised after every sentence till he was shouting the last word.

"The only one that did what she was supposed to was

Scythia! We should all count ourselves very lucky that Lucias came across her when he did. We don't know what the Faithful wanted with her, but it could have been disastrous," he said as he sank into a chair, looking very tired.

"Sorry, Fallrick. It won't happen again," Djaem said quietly, looking ashamed.

Uthraith nodded in agreement. "Sorry, Blue."

Fallrick waved a hand dismissively. "Either way, it doesn't matter now. You're neck deep in whatever intrigue is waiting for Milly here."

Raza looked at Lucias and frowned. "Is that a nebula cloud?" she said as she looked at the desserts they were eating. Lucias smirked slightly and took the bite a little slower.

"Indeed . . . Scythia has done such a marvelous job. She is working so hard and doing as she is told, so I figured she deserved a reward."

Raza scoffed and glared. "If you can even get one, they cost at least two months' salary. And she gets one just because she behaved?"

Lucias seemed to enjoy her attitude and took another slow, savoring bite. "Indeed."

Raza looked ready to throw hands when Djaem stepped up and interrupted.

"So, is that why you are here? To give Scythia a sweet treat."

Lucias shook his head and smiled. "Of course not." He held out a strange, wrapped envelope. Fallrick looked up and took it out of his hands quickly. "I was instructed to deliver the judgment from the review panel."

Raza and Fallrick sighed in relief. Djaem looked confused. "Why is that a good thing?"

Raza smirked. "Because it means they decided not to use any of the more serious penalties. They have so many smaller penalties, and they don't bother bringing you in for those judgments. You know you're in trouble when they want you to come in for judgment."

Fallrick relaxed and smiled at the team. "This is good news. We have fines and some restrictive duties. But all in all, nothing unexpected."

Lucias nodded as he finished his dessert and rose. "Yes. And you have already been given your next assignment."

Fallrick sighed and looked mildly annoyed. Raza glared at Lucias.

"What? We should have at least another week."

Lucias smirked and shrugged. "That's part of the penalty: they are cutting your recreation time to a quarter. And since it has been used up already for this review, you are back on rotation. Now my team needs to get up to speed, so you have twenty-four hours before we depart. I suggest you make the most of it."

The room was quiet as Lucias sauntered out of the room. His departing remarks trailed after him. "You will meet the team then. Have a pleasant evening."

Raza was silent for a long minute. Scythia got up and handed out spoons to everyone, including Fallrick.

"He said I wasn't supposed to share, but he can eat Kandaril shit and die." She smiled and held out the mostly full bowl.

Raza sighed and some of the tension left her body. "Thanks, Blue," she said as she took a spoonful. Her eyes widened in amazement and delight at the taste. "Wow."

Scythia nodded and beamed.

The team gathered around and took tiny bites until it was all gone.

Djaem sighed in satisfaction and looked at Fallrick. "So, do we have any information on what this assignment is supposed to be?"

"No!" Raza snapped. "No way, I refuse to do anything else on my day off. I have twenty-four hours to relax, and I am going to use every minute of it. So, no prep, no recon, no shop talk, none of it. I am going to have a full spa day, and that is the end of it."

Uthraith smiled brightly. "Oh, I like spa day."

Scythia frowned and looked curiously at Raza. "What's spa day?"

Fallrick nodded as he considered that. "Yes, I think a spa day is an excellent idea. And I believe Djaem can help make it even better."

Raza grumbled in her chair. "Who said anyone else was invited . . ."

20

THE POWER OF FRIENDSHIP . . .
MIMOSAS AND MANI-PEDIS

A FEW HOURS LATER, Princess Millianya Fraygar walked down the hall from the entrance of the living quarters area. It was late and she was worn out. It had taken hours to calm her father down. Rosic would be arriving in a few days. She trudged up to the door and sighed. *Should I just go back . . .?* She considered it for a moment and then rang the bell.

The door slid open and Fallrick stood there. His face was covered in a strange aqua-green paste. His hair was held back by a cloth headband. Milly looked at him in surprise as he smiled.

"Hello, Millianya. We weren't expecting you, please come in," he said and stepped aside. His slippered feet made almost no noise on the micro-carpeted floors. Milly stepped in and looked at the whole team. They all wore matching fluffy bathrobes. They matched in color, a deep rich green, with gold-accented piping. Each robe had initials of the wearer embroidered in gold thread.

"Milly is here," Fallrick said as he returned to the kitchen, where he was preparing snacks. As the team turned towards Milly, she realized they matched in more than just the robes. All the faces were coated in a variety of different colored pastes. Hair was tied up into buns or pushed back with headbands. Raza was in the middle of applying some thick cream to Scythia's hair.

Scythia was sitting very still, watching a wall-mounted screen that played a vid-drama.

Djaem was carefully painting his toes an iridescent pink color.

Uthraith smiled and stood up. Milly blinked as she saw that on the back of his robe was over a dozen little patches stitched to the back. There were bugs, butterflies, little fuzzy critters, all adorably portrayed in a childish fashion.

"Milly! You have come for spa day?" Uthraith said as he approached. "I get robe for you." He hurried past her before she could answer.

Milly frowned as she took a step in. "I didn't mean to intrude. Sorry, Raza."

Raza sighed and looked over her shoulder at Milly. "It's ok. Uthraith was moping because he thought you were still mad at him."

Uthraith scoffed. "I don't mope. Here, we get your mark put on later."

Milly looked down at the large fluffy green robe Uthraith was holding out. Milly smiled a little as she took it. "Yeah, why not."

Uthraith relaxed on the big couch. Scythia was diligently painting Milly's fingers a soft blue color that complimented her pink hair. Raza relaxed with her feet up on a cushioned stool, cooling packs rested on her eyes, and a warming towel over the rest of her face. Fallrick was in a matching position next to her.

Djaem sat next to Uthraith. He wore a strange device on his face. It was shaped like a mask and was coated in a strange gel that glowed yellow. It did however allow him to continue to put little tarts and treats in his mouth.

Uthraith enjoyed the heating mud on his neck and face. His feet were in a large foot-bath device that bubbled and churned with hot water. The pink powder he had added made his skin tingle pleasantly.

"Ok, I have to know. What is with all the cutesy patches?" Djaem finally asked. "Is it like how many missions you have been on?"

Uthraith laughed but didn't bother lifting his head. "No . . . Each was chosen by one of mine. They leave their mark so I think of them in happy moments."

"There are twenty-two patches there. You have twenty-two kids?" Djaem said in disbelief.

Uthraith lifted his head to look at Djaem. "No, my children, my wives, Fallrick, and Raza."

Djaem blinked in surprise. "Raza and Fallrick?"

Fallrick smirked but didn't move. "I picked a night predator bird with big eyes."

Raza scoffed and grinned. "It's an owl. He picked a cute owl with a book because he thinks he is smart." She also didn't move from her position.

Fallrick snorted and shifted a little as if settling more firmly into his cushions. "At least mine was an animal not a food."

Raza was completely unfazed. "Moon drops are my favorite."

Uthraith nodded and looked at Scythia. "Little Blue, you must pick what mark you leave on my robe. Milly and Djaem too."

Milly nodded and smiled. "I believe I am beginning to understand how you think, Uthraith."

Raza snorted. "Great, when you do figure that out, make sure to tell the rest of us."

Milly made a face at Raza, who didn't see it, and then went back to picking through the basket of self-care products. "Where did you guys get all this stuff? Most of this is only available in the inner core. This is Galo-ash cream; it would take me a month to get this shipped in."

Scythia beamed with pride. "My Gem got them for us. He is so clever at getting things we need."

Milly frowned and looked at Djaem, who shrugged. "Well, the black market moves much faster than the regular market. It just costs more."

Fallrick sighed. "If we could please refrain from confessing to dealing in contraband to a high-ranking clan official, that would be great."

Djaem gave a little salute. "Yes, sir," he intoned with grave seriousness. The room laughed and continued their lighthearted banter.

Uthraith watched his slowly developing clutch of companions relax and enjoy themselves.

We all know the dangers that surround us, the enemies that lurk. There will be many battles ahead, and many watches to keep. But tonight, we are safe; tonight, we are together. We have earned this.

Tomorrow will find its way here soon enough. I will worry about killing it then.

THE END.

ABOUT THE AUTHOR

Jesse M. Harvey debut book is 'Motherhood at the End of the World.' She writes many types of fiction, including science fiction, space fantasy, supernatural, thriller and mystery. She graduated from Syracuse University with a Bachelor's degree in history

Jesse currently lives in Syracuse NY. She is married with three school age children. Her family comes from a military background, and her husband is a veteran.

Through all her work, Jesse includes underlying themes of hope, compassion, courage and determination. She believes that fiction shapes the future. Jesse wants to help inspire a more diverse and inclusive world.

https://jessemharveybooks.wordpress.com/

ALSO BY JESSE M. HARVEY

Motherhood at the End of the World

The Dark Stellar Series:

Scythia Protostar: Book One

Uthraith Tauristar: Book Two

The Dead Detective Series:

The Barrel Full of Spirits